# About the Author

Laurie spent thirty years working in the Canadian criminal justice system. She currently lives in Ontario with her dog.

Fire

Laurie Reece

---

Fire

Vanguard Press

VANGUARD PAPERBACK

© Copyright 2024
**Laurie Reece**

A CIP catalogue record for this title is
available from the British Library.

ISBN 978 1 80016 987 6

*Vanguard Press is an imprint of*
*Pegasus Elliot Mackenzie Publishers Ltd.*
www.pegasuspublishers.com

First Published in 2024

**Vanguard Press**
**Sheraton House  Castle Park**
**Cambridge  England**

Printed & Bound in Great Britain

# Dedication

For My Aunt Mary

# Chapter One

Detective Sydney LaFleur wanted a cigarette. She'd stashed one on top of the doorframe inside the back door of the courthouse. She pulled into the lot across the street, hung her parking pass on the rear-view mirror, grabbed her binder for court from the front seat, and stepped out of the car. She had fifteen minutes before the trial started, plenty of time to sneak that smoke.

She didn't see where he'd come from. He was just there, in her face. A wiry guy, Brice Avery was a good three inches taller than her five-foot-five. She glanced down at his hands to ensure they were empty. He wore a tee-shirt, not bothering to cover the long burn scar on his left arm with long sleeves.

"I bet you're surprised to see me," he said.

She didn't step back from him, wasn't going to give him that. "Actually, I didn't see you at all."

Probably not smart. Her remark would make a guy like that feel like a zero. She glanced around. Other than his smirking friend standing five feet away, there was no one nearby.

"Don't you remember me?" he asked.

"I do."

"You put me in jail, bitch." He spat out the words, his face shiny with sweat.

"You put yourself in jail."

"Well now I'm out." He stared, as if expecting a reaction. He was acting much bolder than the last time she'd seen him. Probably a show for his friend.

"Good for you," she said. "I hope you have a good life and never have to see me again."

"You're going to burn."

"Not a good idea to threaten me."

"How is telling you you're going to burn in hell a threat?"

"You're an arsonist."

"Well it's not a threat; it's a curse. I curse you to burn."

He spat on the ground at her feet and walked away. She stood watching him until there was a decent distance between them. She ran her hands through her ash blonde hair. She suddenly felt a bit warm in her suit jacket despite the cool morning May air. Now she wanted that smoke even more and had less time for it.

She walked to the back door of the courthouse, a grey fire door not for public use. It was propped open as usual, contrary to the security rules. She stepped inside. Finally she would get her nicotine fix. She stood on her toes and reached up, feeling along the top of the doorframe for the cigarette. She heard footsteps coming down the back stairs.

"Syd, are you smoking?"

Detective Mark Lewis. She turned around.

"You promised the chief," he said.

"Well, the chief will have to be disappointed. Maybe when this trial is over," she said.

They could hear laughter coming from the police room which was only ten feet from the back door. She heard Pete from Forensics say something about "Liza's tits". She marched into the police room and stood in the doorway. Four uniforms and Pete had crammed themselves into the tiny room. The sergeant wasn't there.

"Why are we talking about Liza's tits?" Syd asked.

The uniforms looked at her sheepishly. Pete rolled his eyes.

"Sorry, Syd," one of the uniforms said.

Syd sat in the plastic chair beside the sergeant's desk and plopped her feet on top of the desk.

Mark leaned against the side of the doorway and said to the guy, "Apologize to yourself. You diminish yourself talking like that."

The red-faced uniform stared down at his polished shoes. Pete looked at Syd's shoes.

Pete shook his head. "Are you so broke you've got to wait for the clothing allowance before you buy a new pair of shoes?"

"Yes," she said.

Mark smiled. "Radar would eat the new pair anyway."

"Radar?" asked one of the young uniforms.

Pete grinned. "I've never seen such a smart dog fail police dog training so bad."

"Epic fail," Mark said, brown eyes smiling. "But an awesome dog."

"Ungovernable dog," Pete said. "I don't know why you took him instead of just letting him be adopted out."

"Because he's one of us," she said.

"Family," Mark said.

Pete put his feet on the desk. "Dysfunctional family."

Sergeant Wilkinson squeezed past Mark holding a sheet of paper. Syd pulled her feet from his desk to let him get to his chair.

"Hi, Syd," he said.

"Hey, Wilkie." She put her feet back on his desk.

Wilkinson looked at Pete and said, "Get your feet off my desk." To Syd he said, "Why are you back from vacation on a Wednesday? Who does that?"

Thinking this would be a good time to have her smoke, Syd stood up. "I got called in. I guess George wanted Mark and I both for the first day of the trial."

"George is not the Crown on it," Wilkinson said.

"Yes, he is. We worked for months preparing," Syd said.

Mark sat in a chair opposite her. "George had a heart attack last week."

"What?" She sat back down.

"You have some new guy," Wilkinson said. "Came down from Timmins."

Pete said, "Yeah, some hot shot. All the women are in courtroom 101 throwing themselves at him as we speak."

"Wait," she said. "How is George?"

"He'll be okay, but he's not coming back," Mark said.

"Well, they'll have to put the trial over then," she said.

Wilkinson shook his head. "You've got Judge Streng."

Syd looked at Mark, who grimaced, then at Pete who nodded solemnly.

"I definitely need that smoke," she said. She looked at Mark. "You coming?"

"No, I'm good."

She walked out and stood at the back door feeling for the cigarette.

Wilkinson called out, "I'm telling the chief."

"I don't care," she hollered back.

She couldn't find it. She ran her fingers along the whole length of the ledge. The P.A. blared out. "Detective LaFleur and Detective Lewis to courtroom 101. LaFleur and Lewis, 101". She met Mark in the hall. They walked together to the courtroom.

They walked into a half full courtroom. No judge or justice sat on the bench. No clerk or court reporter filled their respective seats. So many people present in the gallery was unusual during the time between assignment court and trial court. Women and men alike turned and stared as she and Mark walked to the front of the room. Tall and fit, but not muscle-bound, Mark looked good in anything, but particularly good in his suit. Handsome and with a strong command presence, people noticed Mark. Syd knew on an objective level that he was attractive but, to her, he was just Mark, her best friend and colleague.

Despite not sharing DNA he was the brother she never had, the best brother anyone could wish for.

Other than the two of them, the only other people present who worked there were the Crown, who was sitting at counsel table with his back to them, and a special constable for court security, who was leaning against the empty prisoner's dock, sometimes referred to as 'the box', with his eyes closed. The Crown swivelled in his chair to face them. Syd understood why there were so many spectators, particularly women, present. The hot-shot Crown from Timmins looked like he'd just walked off the pages of GQ magazine. Shiny black wavy hair framed his perfectly featured face. The most stunning thing was his eyes. Piercing green eyes with a thick rim of black around the irises looked at Syd and Mark. Those eyes were surreal, haunting, eyes belonging to a god or ghost. Uncharacteristically for her, Syd felt the need to inhale as her heart involuntarily sped up. She exhaled instead. She wasn't one to be enthralled by eye candy. He smiled at them, showing his perfect teeth, straight and brilliant white. *Nobody has teeth like that,* she thought. *Must be fake.*

He motioned for them to approach. She and Mark sat on the chairs reserved for waiting counsel. Syd recognized the trolley full of banker's boxes to her right, the reams of evidence for this trial.

"Detectives Lewis and LaFleur, yes?" the Crown asked.

"Yes," Mark answered. "I'm Lewis; this is LaFleur."

The Crown smiled. "I'm Branson Oleander. I stayed up all night reading the material, but that does not equal preparation. I'm going to need your help."

Mark nodded. "Syd is the one who knows the case best. I can stay, though. Maybe I can get out of my one-thirty press conference."

"Oh, are you on that case of the missing women?" Branson asked.

"I am."

Syd said, "Surely the judge will put it over. It seems unreasonable to expect a Crown to conduct such a trial without adequate time to prepare."

"The defence will argue 11b and win. I can't let a serial arsonist back out into the community without a fight," Branson said.

"If anyone can help you pull this off, it's Syd," Mark said.

Anxiety burbled in her gut. "Mark has too much confidence in me."

Branson looked at Mark. "You can get back for your press conference. Detective LaFleur can help me and we'll call you back when we need you."

Mark stood. Syd looked up at him and grinned, knowing what happens every time his face is in the news.

"I'll save you the chocolate ones," he said, resigned.

"Just a little. Give the rest to Records," she said.

Branson watched their exchange, a look of amusement on his face.

She explained, "Every time Mark is in the news there are women who send him baked goods trying to get his attention."

Branson smiled and nodded in understanding. "And you like chocolate."

Mark said, "She'll give it away. She makes sure the women in Records are taken care of."

Branson smiled at her.

She shrugged. "The police service wouldn't run without the people who work in Records."

"They bend over backwards for you," Mark said.

"Maybe because I appreciate them."

"I'm going to get back, then." To Syd, Mark said, "You coming to hockey tonight? Early game."

"Yes. I'm going to stop by home first to check on Radar."

Mark left.

She asked Branson, "Do you think I have five or ten minutes before we start?"

"Yes. Defence counsel isn't even here yet."

Leaving her binder on counsel table, she walked out, back down the corridor, eager for that cigarette. She stood on her toes and recommenced her methodical search along the top ledge of the doorframe, increasingly frustrated at her inability to find it.

"It's not there."

Startled, she turned. Branson smiled like a schoolboy.

"I smoked it," he said.

From his black suit jacket pocket he pulled out a pack of DuMauriers. He opened it and handed her one. She took it.

"What would make you look on top of a doorframe?" she asked.

"Habit. I've always hid mine on top of a door like that so I don't have to run back to my office. Sorry."

He handed her a pink lighter and pushed open the door for her. They stepped outside and lit their cigarettes. She took a long drag on hers, feeling the burn down her throat. She leaned against the grey brick wall and closed her eyes.

"Who is Radar?"

"My German Shepherd."

"Are you an animal lover or just a dog person?"

"I love them all. You?"

"I had cats, but not any more. I work too much. This new position will require a lot of my time. I have to get up to speed on everything and get to know everyone."

She nodded.

"Mark seems like a decent guy," he said.

"He's a great guy."

"We'd better get in there," he said. "Olympia awaits." He grinned.

She nodded, dropped her butt in the dirt with all the other butts and extinguished it with the ball of her foot. He flicked his out onto the road.

\*\*\*

Press Conference

"At this time it's still a missing person case," Mark said to the crowd of reporters in front of the police station.

"So why is Major Crime involved?" asked a reporter.

Before Mark could answer, another reporter shouted, "Is this related to the six other missing women?"

"We are not ruling anything out," Mark said.

Over the churr of cameras the first reporter said, "So it's possibly related."

Mark reiterated. "We are not ruling anything out."

"How did you determine it was related?"

"If anyone has any information, no matter how seemingly insignificant, about where Kaylee Anderson could be, call the number provided."

"Why did it take so long to link the cases?"

"Is there evidence that harm has come to Kaylee?"

"There is no reason why she would have disappeared on purpose. We will work tirelessly to find her. That's all for today. Thank you."

Click, click, click of the cameras. A cacophony of questions.

Mark, the Deputy Chief, and the media officer turned and filed into the station.

# Chapter Two

Syd sat at counsel table between Branson and the trolley of evidence. Liza, the platinum blonde, twenty-eight-year-old court reporter, had already taken her seat and was ready to start. When Liza looked over at Branson her pupils dilated like she was looking into a dark room. She smiled eagerly at him. Her cheeks flushed, almost matching the Popsicle pink nail polish of her perfect manicure. Syd glanced down at her own hands, her short nails unvarnished. She put her hands in her lap. Liza looked at Syd and smiled. Syd smiled back. She didn't know Liza outside of work but she liked her. For all of Liza's effervescent ebullience there was a sea of loneliness behind her deep blue eyes. The cat-clawed court clerks swiped at her when they weren't haughtily turning their backs on her and sticking up their noses in self-appointed superiority. Although salacious men flocked to her, their feigned interest was as hollow as they were shallow, treating her as a titillating object rather than a breathing woman with a heart and soul and life. Thus, Liza with all her sweetness and warmth was pushed out into the bitter and the cold created by the jealousy and lechery of others. Syd felt sorry for her.

Once the accused was brought from the cells and put into the box, Judge Streng addressed the Defence.

"Are you ready to proceed today, Mr. Riker?"

Riker stood, his grey suit with its cheap shine sagging at the shoulders. "Yes, Your Honour."

Streng said, "This trial has been delayed by the Crown four times. It would be reasonable for the Defence to argue 11b if the Crown seeks yet another delay."

Riker didn't bother to hide his smug smirk.

Branson stood. "The Crown is ready to proceed."

A look of surprise replaced Riker's smirk. That made Syd want to smile, but she didn't. Liza looked at Branson and smiled like a teenaged fan meeting her idol.

In a nasally squawk the court clerk stood and read the charges into the record, seven charges of arson. The judge alone trial was scheduled to last three weeks.

Branson stood and with his smooth voice full of confidence that didn't betray his concern about potentially losing this one, began presenting the Crown's case. He was thorough and articulate. It was impressive by anyone's standards, but more so considering he'd had so little time to prepare.

When court broke for lunch at the usual one o'clock, Branson and Syd walked to the back door for a smoke.

"Good job in there," she said, pushing the door open for him.

He smiled. "Did you see the look on Riker's face when he realized he has to actually do the trial?"

She grinned. "Yes."

They leaned against the grey brick wall together, smoking in comfortable silence, breathing in the gritty breeze and watching people wend through the parking lot across the street on their way to their cars. It was an okay silence and she thought it interesting how he chose to end it.

"I like that you say 'yes' instead of 'yeah' or 'yep'. People don't bother to speak properly these days." He offered her another cigarette.

"Thank you but I need to go buy a pack anyway and get some lunch."

"I have to get lunch, too, and bring it back to the office. I'm still unfamiliar with the city. Maybe we could go together?" he said.

"Sure."

They walked to his car, a new black Mercedes parked in the same lot as her unmarked car and the wending people. She looked around as they walked, wondering if Brice Avery was still in the area. She gave Branson directions to the deli. Although the drive was only seven minutes, he managed to pepper her with questions but smoothly, getting her to reveal something of herself.

"Sorry you had to cut your vacation short," he said. "I hope you didn't lose money on a hotel."

"I didn't go to a hotel. I went up north camping and canoeing for six weeks with my dog."

"I love canoeing. I haven't been for a few years, though."

"Oh? Where do you like to go?"

"Anywhere. There are lots of places in Timmins to canoe."

In the enclosed heat of the car, she could smell him. He smelled good, a cologne she'd never encountered before, clean smelling, not overpowering. She liked it. He parked and they walked into the deli together.

At the deli counter she said to him, "Go ahead."

"No, you order first. I need a second to decide."

"Salami on rye, everything on it except pickle and onion," she told the woman behind the counter.

Branson smiled at the woman. "I'll have the same."

They ate their sandwiches in his office, he in his well cushioned leather chair behind the grand mahogany desk that came with the office, and her sitting on the edge of the white upholstered wingtip chair across from him with her knees against his desk, not wanting to sit back in that chair lest she drop mustard onto it. A row of boxes sat neatly lined up against one wall, markers of a man who hadn't yet moved in but had intentions. Of course she wondered what was in the boxes. In between moments of discussing the case, Branson made jokes about Riker, and probed her for more personal tidbits. By the time they had their post-lunch smoke together and headed back to court, a new but cohesive team, she felt like she'd known him for ages and that he'd known her since the beginning of time. They clicked. That was unusual for Syd who had been given the moniker "Ice Queen".

\*\*\*

It was five-thirty by the time Syd walked into their office to find Mark hunched over his desk. The Major Crime office was a no-nonsense, just the necessaries, moderate room with a giant wall map of the city hanging beside a grey-smudged whiteboard. The beaten down grey filing cabinet stood beside a long narrow table that was often used for sorting papers and upon which lived the scratched up coffee maker for their sustenance, caustic black gold. Their matching clunky wooden desks sat pushed together, facing each other, perpendicular to the wall under the windows. The reason for their placement had nothing to do with anyone's idea of aesthetics, but was because that's where the phone and computer cables came out of the wall. They had a mini-fridge jammed in the corner, the one Mark bought with his own money, black because it wouldn't show messy fingerprints and no one had time to clean it. No personal items lived in the office. It was all business. No plants or any other non-functional thing resided there, unless you counted the old grey horizontal blinds that hadn't functioned for years. The year previous Syd, tired of never seeing the sun, climbed on top of her desk with a long length of yellow "police line do not cross" tape and used it to bind the blinds up, permanently open, thus hanging the one and only adornment in the place and giving them a grand view of the parking lot.

"Why are you still here?" she asked.

"Going over these missing person reports."

"You think they're really connected?"

"Kaylee and five of the other six had no reason to voluntarily disappear. But so far I don't see that they have much in common except for their age range, all young, between nineteen and twenty-five, and that they apparently all disappeared during the day."

"And the sixth?"

"History of domestic violence calls at her address. I think she disappeared on purpose."

"Or her partner disappeared her." Syd sat at her desk.

"His alibi checked out. I'll check it again, though."

"You want to re-interview everyone?"

"Yes."

"Are we getting a task force?"

"Tip line. The task force is you and me," he said.

"Let me guess, not in the budget."

He shrugged.

"And I won't be much help for the next three weeks."

"How did that go today? How is Branson in court?"

"He's quite good. Smooth."

Mark laughed. "Smooth, yeah, I got that impression."

She smiled. "That, too. Really, though, he's good. He doesn't need me like he says he does."

"You never know what detail he might need that you remember. There's too much paper on that case to expect one guy to remember with so little prep."

"True. Hand me some of those witness statements. Maybe we can get to hockey on time."

They spent the next hour in silence, going through statements and drinking bad coffee.

\*\*\*

Syd picked up the flyers from her cedar wood porch and opened the front door of the three storey Victorian house she'd inherited from her grandfather. Radar jumped on her, his big paws on her shoulders, his snout in her face. He was soaking wet.

"What happened to you?" she said as she closed the door behind her and kicked off her shoes.

She could hear water running upstairs. She walked up the carpeted curved staircase and halfway up felt water sop into her socks. She ran up the rest of the way, turned left, and ran along the flooded hall to the bathroom. Radar followed, wagging his tail. A waterfall spilled from the claw-foot tub into the lake on the floor. She turned off the faucet. A bath towel plugged the drain. As she pulled it up to give the water a better means of escape, Radar plunged into the tub wanting a game of tug with the towel.

"No. Drop it."

Radar complied, but then jumped out of the tub and, dripping wet, zoomed around the entire second floor. Syd wrung out the towel and set about cleaning up the water and assessing the damage. The job was more onerous than she expected. She worked away at it, the passage of time marked only by her increasing hunger and fatigue.

The doorbell rang.

Syd yelled, "Radar. Answer the door."

Radar bounded down the stairs, pawed at the front door knob until it turned and the door opened a crack. He stuck his snout in the crack and nosed the door open. Syd could hear Mark's voice talking to Radar.

"I'm up here," she yelled, dumping a full bucket of water into the tub for the umpteenth time.

When she looked up she saw Mark and Radar standing in the hallway at the top of the stairs.

"What happened here?" he asked.

"Radar thought it would be fun to turn on the tap and play in the tub while I was at work."

"Oh, boy." Mark went from room to room opening windows.

"Do you have a dehumidifier?" he asked.

"No."

"Me, either. I'll see if Mrs. Linton has one she could lend you. You have to get everything dried out."

"Mrs. Linton is too good to you."

"Best landlady ever. Like living above an adoptive grandma."

"I thought you were going to hockey," she said.

"I did. It's over."

"It's that late? No wonder I'm knackered."

"Have you eaten?" he asked.

"No."

He turned and disappeared down the stairs. Radar followed him. Syd stashed the bucket in the bathroom, then changed into her track pants and an old t-shirt. She tossed her wet, dirty clothes into the tub. She reached the living room just as Mark put away his cell phone.

"I ordered pizza," he said, walking toward the kitchen.

"Oh, good. With black olives?"

"Of course."

She flopped onto her black leather couch and put her feet on the worn antique coffee table.

"Guess who showed up at hockey," he hollered from the kitchen.

"Who?"

He returned holding two glasses of red wine. He handed her a glass.

"Thanks. Who?"

"Branson Oleander."

He sat beside her. She screwed up her face.

"Who invited him?"

"Pete."

"He knows Pete?"

"Apparently, he ran into him somewhere after work. They got to talking and Pete invited him."

She sipped her wine. "That's not like Pete."

"Smooth. See?"

"It's kind of weird."

He shrugged. "Guy in Branson's position has to win friends and influence people, I guess."

"I guess. Did Mrs. Linton feed you?"

He grinned. "Plate of lasagna wrapped in tin foil sitting in front of my door."

She shook her head. "You're spoiled."

He looked sideways at her and raised his wine glass. "I'd say you are, too."

She smiled. "Yes. You're right. And I thank you for it."

"Should we let Radar answer the door when the pizza guy comes?" Mark's eyes danced with mischief.

An image of a pizza delivery guy fleeing in fear popped into Syd's mind. She laughed.

"Oh, could you imagine? Probably not good to scare the poor pizza guy like that."

They laughed. They talked, played with Radar, ate, and laughed some more, as friends do, until it was time for Mark to go home. When Syd went to her room, eager for her soft bed, she found the sheets wet, covered in fur, and smelling like wet dog. She sighed, trundled downstairs, and slept on the couch, Radar on the floor beside her.

# Chapter Three

Syd walked into the office at 7a.m. to find Mark staring intently at his computer screen.

"Hey," she said.

"Hey."

"Bring me up to speed. I can help before and after court."

"Mrs. Linton lent you a dehumidifier. It's in my trunk."

"Tell Mrs. Linton she's a gem."

He nodded. "Seven young women disappear in the last six months, all during the day, all low risk except for the D.V. They don't know each other. So far, there's no common person they knew, no common place they went. The 'last seens' are all over the place."

"Phone pings?"

"Six cells, five different towers," he said.

"Who didn't have a cell?"

"Amelia Morrison, the domestic violence."

"Figures."

"Cells all turn off the same day they disappear," he said.

"Which two phones pinged off the same tower?"

"Williams and Green. Here." He handed her a print-out of a map showing the towers and the areas covered.

She looked at it. "Well that doesn't narrow it down much."

"Nope. Kaylee Anderson's mother is coming in for eight."

"I forgot to tell you, Brice Avery is out of jail. He approached me in the parking lot at court yesterday."

He looked at her, concern apparent on his face. "Oh?"

"Yes. He said I would burn, then he said he meant I would burn in hell and he was cursing me."

"Jerk."

"We'll see him again," she said as she stood.

She walked to the whiteboard beside the giant map of the city on the wall.

"Kaylee Anderson is the most recent," he said. "Nineteen years old, works as a barista on Vine, lives on Devon Ave. She left for work at ten after ten in the morning for her eleven o'clock shift."

"That's only six blocks away," she said. "Was she on foot?"

"No." He swivelled his chair so he could stretch his legs. "She took her mother's car."

"Did she always leave so early?"

"Good question," he said. "They already looked at the time after ten, but they didn't ask that one."

She wrote the times on the whiteboard. She was a fan of timelines and of putting them up where they could see them.

Mark continued. "They did a door to door between her house and work. Searched backyards, sheds, garages, found nothing."

"K9?"

"Yes."

"Boyfriend?"

"No. No known stalkers, no strangers around the house, no one new. I've already got everyone on a spreadsheet," he said. He gave her a look. "I very much want to find her alive."

She felt his pain. They both knew that if Kaylee had been abducted and managed to survive the first hour, her odds of survival would have dropped dramatically within the first twenty-four.

"We're going to do everything in our power," she said.

"Everything might not be enough." His statement was almost a whisper.

She stood still, feeling the weight.

He refocused. "I'm going to re-interview everyone she worked with. I'll ask if she ever showed up early."

They worked until Mark was called to meet Kaylee's mother. Syd stayed behind and worked on the timeline. At nine-fifteen she signed out a car and drove to court.

\*\*\*

Her addiction tugged her toward the back door of the courthouse where she'd stashed a cigarette. She retrieved

31

the cigarette, then stepped outside and smoked it. It didn't relieve the tug. She went back in and turned toward the back stairs. She saw the tops of Branson's feet on the stairs, unmistakably his with his Italian leather designer shoes. She waited and watched as he came entirely within view. He was looking down at his phone, oblivious to her presence. A dark-haired Apollo walking alone. She pushed away that thought.

"Hi," she said.

He looked up. He flashed that smile of his. "Hi. Smoke?"

"Sure." She smiled without wanting to, not like that, anyway.

He handed her a cigarette and offered his pink lighter.

"Have one," she said, holding up her black Bic.

"Do people steal lighters from you?" he asked.

"Sometimes. Why?"

"That's why I buy pink ones. The guys don't steal the pink ones."

She nodded as she lit her smoke and took a drag. It burned her throat. She realized the internal tug was gone. She didn't really need this cigarette.

"Are you going to show me a new place for lunch today?" he asked.

"I can give you directions. I was planning on going back to the station for lunch."

He faked a pout. It was cute.

"I want to put in some time helping Mark."

"How much can you really do? By the time you get there you'll have to turn around and come back."

She felt the tug of Mark and the case, but she knew Branson was right.

As they walked to the courtroom he said, "Can you get me a copy of Constable Tam's report on the second fire?"

"You have it."

He leaned into her and whispered, "I can't find it."

"Are the contents of those boxes still in the same order as George left them?"

"I think so."

"I can find it then," she said.

"I don't think there's time," he said as he took his seat at counsel table.

She stepped to the trolley full of boxes, opened the top banker's box, and found the file containing Tam's report. It took less than three seconds. Branson gave her an exaggerated look of surprise.

"Why didn't you tell me George had a system of organization?"

"He didn't have one. You should have seen his desk."

"Then how did you find that so quickly?"

She shrugged. "I remembered."

"But that was a fluke. You couldn't do it again."

"Maybe."

"All right." He leafed through his notes. "Is there a report in there dated June twenty-seventh of last year?"

"Several."

He stared at her.

"Oh, you want to see if I can find them?"

"Yes." He swivelled his chair to watch her at the trolley.

She pulled out the bottom banker's box and retrieved two separate files containing the reports.

Through squinting unbelieving eyes he asked, "Do any of the witnesses have criminal records?"

"Yes. Mr. Ford. Do you want me to find it?"

"No. Tell me what's on his record."

The court constable who was leaning against the wall beside the door to the cells smiled, knowing what Syd could do.

She rattled off Mr. Ford's record.

Branson smiled. "Do you ever play poker?"

"No. I don't know how."

"Somebody ought to teach you."

The court constable laughed at this.

The court clerk came in, glanced around the courtroom, and addressing no one in particular in her squawking tone that always sounded like a demand said, "Is Mr. Riker going to be on time today?"

Branson shrugged. "We don't have the reporter yet anyway."

"She'll be here in a minute," the clerk said. "She's fixing her make-up." She rolled her eyes.

*Catty,* Syd thought. Branson looked at Syd, one eyebrow raised, like they were sharing a secret.

Liza rushed in and sat down. "Hello Mr. Oleander, Detective LaFleur."

He smiled kindly at her. "You can call me Branson."

Liza beamed and sat up straighter.

Grey-faced Riker with his uncombed hair trudged in and dropped two thick, dog-eared and dirty yellow files on opposing counsel table. Court started. Branson continued his methodical presentation of the Crown's case. Riker sat back in his chair, not taking any notes, with that stupid smug smirk on his face.

During morning break when Syd and Branson were out for their smoke, she mentioned it.

"Riker has something up his sleeve," she said.

"You think so?" He leaned against the wall beside her, mirroring her position.

"He's not even taking notes."

"He does assert his guy has an alibi for every fire," he said.

She stepped away from the wall so she could face him. "Except one. He was seen in the area before the fire."

"But that was before the fire. His girlfriend states he was home at the time that fire started."

She shook her head. "The Fire Marshal's report says it was a slow burning fire. There's an elastic band around that report attaching my notes to it where I show that what time the fire was set coincides exactly with Mrs. Baker seeing him at the scene."

"Refresh my memory. And forgive me for not picking up on it," he said.

"It's a page of mathematics. If you know the composition of the combustible material and the amount of oxygen in the room, you can calculate the burn rate and how long it takes for the fire to become fully involved."

"Does the formula look like hieroglyphics?"

She smiled. "I suppose it could be described that way."

He nodded. "I do remember seeing something like that."

Sergeant Wilkinson poked his head out the back door. "Hey, you guys, you're being paged to courtroom 101."

Branson flicked his butt into the road and said, "Olympia awaits."

As Syd stepped through the door Branson said, "Wait."

She stopped. He stepped close to her. She felt electricity, heat, Icarus flying too close to the sun. She looked away, stared at the paint-chipped beige wall inside the back entrance, focussing on a tiny gouge in the wall. He picked something off of her shoulder.

"You had a thread," he said.

"Oh," was all she said. His gesture felt intimate.

The second half of the morning went the same way as the first. At lunch she took him to a Lebanese restaurant.

"This is my favourite restaurant," she said, choosing a table from where she could view the door. "And it's top secret."

He smiled, his eyes alight.

"The only person I bring here is Mark, and now you," she said.

"Then I'm honoured." He sat across from her, those eyes of his brighter than the sunny restaurant.

Her face felt hot. She wondered if she was blushing. The thought of that made her face feel hotter.

"I'm just showing the new guy around," she said, and regretted that as much as the blushing.

"I see."

She decided she should remain silent to keep from further embarrassing herself.

"Are you and Mark an item?"

"We're best friends."

"You two act like you're a married couple."

"People say that a lot."

"So maybe there's a chance for the two of you?"

"No. Think brother and sister. No chance of anything else."

He nodded.

"Plus I have a rule. I don't get involved with anyone from work," she said.

"That's disappointing." He paused, watching her. "For all the single hopefuls at work."

She laughed. "They have no problems finding dates and I am certain I'm not on any list of possibilities. They call me 'Ice Queen' behind my back."

"You? Ice Queen?" He laughed. "And that sounds so... so..."

"Fourteen-year -old boy with bad role models?"

"I was going to say puerile, but that works," he said.

She felt uncomfortable having so much of the focus on her. She shifted in her seat and checked her watch. He noticed.

"I have the same rule," he said, "so I understand. I don't know how it is among police officers, but in the courts there's a lot of gossip. I dislike being the subject."

She nodded. "You get it."

"I do," he said. "So, Detective LaFleur, I will *never* ask you out on a date." He grinned.

She smiled. She felt relieved, yet strangely disappointed.

At two o'clock Riker's assistant came into the courtroom to inform them he'd taken ill over the lunch break and needed a one day adjournment. Syd would have the afternoon free to help Mark on the Kaylee Anderson case. Branson asked her to smoke with him before she left. She agreed.

"You know, you could have been a lawyer. You're remarkably bright," he said.

She shrugged.

"Is it weird to say I'll miss having you around this afternoon?" he asked.

She smiled in mild amusement. "Maybe."

"It's just that it's nice to laugh with a colleague. I'm surrounded by stuffed shirts."

"Maybe you should have been a cop."

"Touche." He smiled at her.

"See you tomorrow, Branson."

As she walked away he hollered, "Don't go breaking any rules."

She shouted back, "I'm a law enforcement officer. I wouldn't do that." But she knew what he meant.

# Chapter Four

On her way back from court, Syd called Records. Lori answered.

"Hi, it's Syd. I'm going to that specialty coffee shop on Vine. Do any of you want anything from there?"

"Ooh, I'm sure we do. Hang on a sec."

Lori returned to the phone a minute later with their orders. Syd drove to the coffee shop where Kaylee Anderson worked. Maps were okay but a poor substitute for actually seeing a place. Vine Street was a treed strip lined with artisan shops plunked into the middle of an old residential neighbourhood. The houses were built before most people had cars, so few houses had driveways, and most of the houses had been converted into shops, so finding a parking spot was a routine challenge there. Syd parked the car a block away.

She took her time, looking in the windows of the shops as she walked. She took out her notebook and jotted down the name of each business. She would double check to make sure they'd all been canvassed at the time of Kaylee's disappearance and that all the security camera video had been secured. She stepped into the noisy shop, catching whiffs of vanilla, cinnamon, and chocolate along with the freshly ground coffee. Kaylee's face smiled out from a 'missing' poster taped beside the cash register. Lovely girl, with her whole life ahead of her, Syd thought. She stared at the poster.

The male barista asked, "Have you seen her?"

"No. Do you know her well?"

"No," he said. "I just started working here. Our boss wants us to ask every customer. Everyone here loved her."

Syd nodded. "You never know who might know something."

"What can I get for you?"

She rattled off the order. He prepared it, put it in cardboard trays, and gave her an extra box to carry the trays in.

Back at the station Syd put the box of coffee trays on the counter at Records. She realized she'd forgotten to get something for herself and Mark. They would drink the station sludge until they found Kaylee.

Mark was on the phone, a half-eaten cookie on top of a plate of cookies partially wrapped in cellophane beside him. Syd's desk looked like a table at a bake sale. She stacked some of the plates of goodies on top of each other and put two of them on top of the printer. She grabbed Mark's empty mug, walked to the coffee maker, and poured the dregs into his cup. She put it in front of him and sat down as he was hanging up the phone.

He looked at her. "Kaylee's mother said she always left early. Around ten o'clock every day. I just got off the phone with Kaylee's boss. She says Kaylee was never early for work and in fact often late."

"So where did she go for that hour?"

"Don't know yet," he said.

"There's gotta be a guy. But for no one to know about it is odd. Young women talk about these things."

"Maybe he's married, or older. Maybe he told her to keep it a secret," Mark said.

"Could be."

"Why are you back?"

"Defence counsel is sick. Adjourned to tomorrow."

"Good. I mean good for me because you can help me. Sorry for Riker."

"Don't feel sorry for Riker. Slimy little weasel."

He smiled.

"So what do you want to do first?" she asked.

"I've got her bank and phone records. We can have another look at those to see if anything was missed. Then we can talk to her female friends again. Maybe she mentioned something about a secret guy or let something slip to one of them."

"Was there a hint on her social media?"

"Nope." He took another bite of cookie. "Tech guys already went over her hard drive. Nothing. The last ping from her cellphone was off the tower in her own neighbourhood." He rifled through paper on his desk. "Here. Phone records for the last three months. I'll make some calls and set up some interviews."

"Let's get rid of this clutter," she said.

They loaded up their arms with the plates and headed toward the lunchroom.

"I wish we could take this stuff to the women's shelter or the homeless shelter," Mark said.

"Ecklund would get his knickers in a knot. Liability. He's afraid someone will send poisoned cookies," she said.

"Who would want to poison me?"

She laughed.

"What are *you* laughing about," he asked, following her down the stairs.

They walked into the gymnasium-sized lunch room, past the sea of small round tables, and into the attached kitchenette.

"Finally sharing the wealth," one of the guys said.

PC Mayfield said, "Yeah, but he doesn't share the phone numbers that come with the cookies."

Mark put the baked goods on the counter and said, "Because we don't take advantage."

Mayfield said, "They're just badge bunnies."

"Hey!" With fire in his eyes, Mark glared at him.

"What? Geeze. Between you and Ice Queen there nobody can have any fun."

"We're professionals. You should try it," Mark shot back.

Mayfield moped. "Why does he get the goodies?"

A young uniform hollered across the room, "Mayfield, you're being a dick. Just shut up."

Pete, who had walked in just in time to hear Mayfield's question said, "Mark gets the goodies because he looks like that movie star. You know the guy. What's his name?"

"Yeah, yeah," Syd said. "We all know who he is."

She and Mark left the guys to their bickering and banter and walked back to their office.

"That burns my ass," Mark said. "Some of those guys can't figure out how to be men without trashing women. Could you imagine being a victim of sexual assault and having to deal with that guy?" He shook his head. "No wonder the public hates us."

They spent the rest of the day chasing down their new line of inquiry on Kaylee. They got nowhere.

\*\*\*

As Syd approached her house, she noticed her front curtains were in tatters. Radar. She shook her head. She took him for a run. She did their three kilometre route that took them through Liza's neighbourhood and to the path through the woods nearby. She needed the run after sitting most of the day. Radar loved it.

When they returned home she showered, threw on her track pants and a tee, poured a glass of wine, and stood in front of her biggest bookshelf, the one that took up an entire wall of her living room. It wasn't organized in a manner that would make sense to anyone, with LeCarre wedged between Wilde and Tolstoy, and Stephen King nestled beside a text on wildflowers which sat beside the volumes of Proust. She found the textbook she wanted and pulled it down. She settled in to read, Radar beside her, taking up more than three-quarters of the couch as he gnawed on a beef pizzle.

Radar hopped off the couch and ran to the door before the doorbell rang. He pawed at the handle before Syd gave the command. Radar excitedly danced around Mark as he stepped inside and kicked off his shoes.

"Hey." She glanced at him.

"Did you miss me?" He grinned.

"Terribly," she said, not looking up from her book. "I thought you had a date."

"It was just a coffee date," he said on his way to the kitchen. "You didn't eat again."

"How do you know?"

"I know you. And I see I'm right. Last night's pizza box is right where I left it and there is no evidence of food preparation happening in this kitchen."

"Busy," she said, turning a page of the hardcover in her lap.

She heard him rifling through her cupboards. He returned to the living room carrying a glass of wine and a sandwich on a plate. He held out the plate to her.

"Peanut butter. Better than nothing," he said.

"Yes, Mom," she said, accepting it. "How did it go?"

"Meh." He sat beside her. Radar sat in front of Syd staring at her sandwich.

"Why?"

"She was nice. There was nothing wrong with her. We didn't have much in common and there was no, I don't know, no spark."

She nodded, her mouth full of sandwich.

He nodded at the book in her lap. "Another textbook."

She held it up so he could see the cover, "Chemistry and Thermodynamics".

"God. That's not even a little interesting. Why don't you read a fiction like normal people?"

"I'm afraid Branson is going to have me explain this stuff and my calculations. I'm refreshing my memory."

"You, refreshing your memory? Seriously."

"Seriously," she said, swallowing the last bite of sandwich to Radar's disappointment.

Radar found his beef pizzle and settled at Mark's feet. Mark took the book away from her.

"Syd, you're good enough."

"Who said I wasn't?"

"No one. That's my point. You have to stop striving and relax sometimes. You have this thing."

"What thing?"

"You're driven."

"Says the pot."

"And what happened to your curtains?"

"You need to ask?"

He looked at Radar and shook his head.

"You have to get past the coffee date stage," she said.

"If there's no fire then why lead somebody on?"

"Sometimes ignition takes a while." She pointed to the text book. "It says so in there. Maybe you need to give things a chance to smoulder."

"At least I *go* on dates," he said.

"I'm busy."

"You don't trust anyone."

"I trust you."

"That's different," he said. "Speaking of smouldering, is Branson single?"

"Yes, but it doesn't matter."

"You wouldn't break your rule for him?"

"Nope. Besides, he has the same rule."

"I don't believe it."

Radar pricked his ears then popped his head up letting the beef pizzle drop from his mouth. He sprang onto the couch. The sudden excited motion knocked Syd's arm, causing a wave of wine to leap from her glass.

"Hey, stop it." She stood, the book falling from her lap. She put her dripping wine glass onto the coffee table as Radar barked maniacally at the window and scratched at it through the already tattered curtains. She'd pulled his face from the window but hadn't yet pulled him down from the couch when they were all jolted by a bang and the sound of breaking glass. Sharp shards flew across her arm.

"Down!" she yelled as the old thin window pane imploded, sending icicles of glass like daggers raining onto them.

Before they could hit the floor, a flaming bottle whizzed past them. It smashed on the living room carpet, instantly igniting into a lake of fire. Radar broke free of her grip and leapt through the window.

"No!" Syd jumped out after him.

She ran, her eyes darting around for danger but still ensuring she didn't lose sight of Radar. She chased him down the middle of the road, then across the street. He disappeared into a dark driveway. She sprinted toward it, not slowing to make the turn. She heard a male voice yell, "No". She stopped in the middle of the dark backyard. She couldn't see him. Radar barked. Beside the shed. She ran into the black space between the shed and the wooden fence. She saw a flash of white skin beneath Radar's black body. She heard sirens.

"Don't move," she said. "You move a muscle and that dog will eat you."

"Okay, okay. Get it off me," he said.

"Do you have any weapons?"

"Nothing. I swear."

She commanded Radar to hold there. She jogged down the driveway to the sidewalk. She could see two firetrucks and three cruisers already at her house. Another cruiser flew down the street, on its way. She waved it down. It drove past her, stopped, and backed up. The constable got out of the car.

"Back here," she said.

He followed her to the backyard where Radar still had the suspect pinned. She let the constable handle the arrest. The suspect was just a kid really, maybe seventeen years old. The constable took him away.

Syd and Radar ran home as more cruisers flooded the street. She felt guilty for leaving Mark alone with the fire.

She asked the first officer she saw, "Where's Mark Lewis?"

"He stole a radio and went looking for you."

"Get on the radio and tell him to come back."

When she saw him jogging up the street toward them, she and Radar ran to meet him.

"I'm sorry," she said.

"What for?" Soot streaked his face.

"For leaving you."

"Nothing I couldn't handle. You okay?"

"Yes. You?"

They headed back toward her house, Radar trotting ahead of them, nose and ears up.

"Yeah. I see you found Radar."

"He caught the guy, a kid."

Mark smiled. "Good boy."

The fire crew packed up as the captain approached Syd. Radar trotted to the truck to get a pet from everyone.

"The fire was contained to the first floor," the fire captain said. "Using that fire extinguisher saved your house."

Syd looked at Mark. "You had to run past the fire to get that fire extinguisher."

"Couldn't let the house burn down," he said. "Where would I go for red wine?"

The captain said, "Not many people keep a fire extinguisher that size."

"I'm afraid of fire," she said.

The captain nodded. "If people understood how fast and how vicious it is, everyone would be afraid of it. Even firefighters respect it."

The forensics van pulled up behind the remaining fire truck. Her home was a crime scene now. She knew she and Radar wouldn't be able to stay there. She looked through the thinning crowd of uniforms for the staff sergeant. Spotting him, she approached him. Mark and Radar went with her.

"Will you let me stay in the house if I stay upstairs?" she asked.

He shook his head. "You know better. You won't want to anyway. Place reeks of gas, smoke, and burnt material."

She nodded. "I didn't think so."

"Can I at least go in and get some of my things?"

"Go ahead."

Mark said, "You can stay at my place tonight."

Dave from Forensics had already gone in and was busy taking photographs when she stepped inside. The sight of the damage to her living room and dining room felt like a gut punch. She noticed the Chemistry and Thermodynamics textbook on the floor, partially burnt and covered in soot. Her eggshell blue walls were black. Black, brown, and yellow stained the original plaster medallions on the ceiling. Soot covered the chandelier in the dining room, each icy crystal teardrop smothered by the black consequence of fire.

She walked up the staircase noticing the smoke damage like long black fingers reaching up the walls to the second floor. She tossed some things into a pillow case and went outside. Mark had just finished giving his statement. After giving her statement, she and Radar got into Mark's car.

"We have to stop and get food for Radar. I don't want to give him the stuff from in the house."

Mark nodded. "I wish we could question the kid."

"Me, too. But we're witnesses," she said. "What am I going to do with Radar tomorrow? He can't stay alone at your place."

"Bring him to work, I guess."

"Ecklund will have an aneurysm."

"But the chief likes you."

"I know, but still." She rolled down the window.

"Mrs. Linton loves him. Maybe she'll watch him."

She worried about tiny, gentle Mrs. Linton dealing with Radar's antics, but it was her best option. "We'll see what she thinks and how it goes."

# Chapter Five

With some trepidation Syd left Radar with Mrs. Linton in the morning. Syd was a mess herself. Her clothes reeked of smoke despite having been a storey away and shut up in the closet and now they were wrinkled from sitting in the pillowcase all night. Mark didn't own an iron. His whole apartment smelled of smoke from the off-gassing of their clothing.

Mark and Syd spent the first hours at the office working on the Anderson case. One of the women from Records went home and brought in some clothes for Syd to wear. They weren't Syd's conservative style and the satiny pastel blue blouse was tight across her shoulders, but there's that saying about beggars and choosers and looking gift horses in the mouth, and the clothes were suitable enough for court. She changed and drove to the courthouse.

By the time she got there it was already a droning grey hive, people flowing into and out of the doors, buzzing about inside, the waiting area packed with people whose mass of murmuring voices sounded like one long drone. She walked briskly through the courtroom, sat beside Branson, then had to immediately stand again as the clerk said, "All rise". Branson continued presenting the Crown's case. Late in the morning he explained the thermodynamics and calculations to the court. Syd felt relieved when he told the court he would be bringing in an expert witness; she knew she would not be that expert witness. Riker's smugness melted away. He leaned forward scribbling notes on his dog-eared dirty yellow pad, his scrambled yellow-grey-brown hair as wild as his scribbling.

Outside, during morning break, Branson asked, "Were you at a fire call?"

"Sorry." She cringed. "I can't get the smell off of me."

"Where was it?"

"My house."

He looked genuinely concerned, those green eyes of his focused on her.

"What happened?"

She explained. He listened.

Riker stuck his head out the back door. "Can I speak to you for a minute?" he asked Branson.

Branson waved for him to come out. Riker stepped outside, glancing at Syd but not acknowledging her.

Riker said, "My guy will plead on the fourth fire for a minimal sentence and you drop the other charges."

Branson laughed. "C'mon, man. I can't even respond to that."

"Short custodial," Riker said.

"You're joking."

"He has no record."

"He set seven fires. It's a miracle no one died."

"Longer custodial but with two for one credit for time served."

"Riker, you're wasting my time." Branson turned away, took a step, then turned back.

"He's alibied for everything else. It's reasonable."

"Alibied by his girlfriend who will do anything for him," Branson said.

Riker shrugged. "Still an alibi. Love is not a crime."

Branson shook his head. "I'm going to impeach her. I'll have him on everything."

"You're gambling."

Branson looked him in the eyes. "She's gasoline. He's the match. I'm going to bring them together and you will watch your defence go up in flames."

Riker clenched his jaw.

Branson said, "He's not walking out of here with just one conviction."

"Two."

"Five."

"Five?! I'll take my chances with your fiery cross-examination."

Branson took a long drag of his cigarette and blew it out slowly. "It has to be more than half."

"Four. Short custodial with credit," Riker offered.

"Four. No joint submission on sentence. You're the gambler here."

"Streng will bury him." Riker's wide eyes and slack jaw solicited mercy.

Branson shrugged. "Then be realistic."

"Four. We pick which ones. Pen time but lower range."

"Mid-range." Branson stared at him, resolute.

Riker exhaled. "Let me talk to him."

Riker pivoted and went inside.

Branson turned to Syd and said, "We'd better tell the clerk we're going to be delayed."

\*\*\*

Syd walked beside Branson as he rolled the trolley of evidence to the elevator. Riker's client had taken the deal.

"Stay for lunch?" Branson asked.

"Thank you, but I've got to get back to the station."

"Are you going to be able to go home tonight?"

"I'm pretty sure I can, yes."

"Let me take you to dinner." He held his hands up in front of him. "It's not a date. Trying to cook in a damaged kitchen won't be pleasant."

She wanted to say yes, but didn't want to leave Radar alone in a fire damaged house.

"And I don't have anyone to celebrate with," he said.

*Maybe Mark would keep Radar for a few more hours,* she thought.

"I would like to. Let me see if Mark will look after Radar. Can I get back to you?"

He beamed like the sun. It sent a little shiver through her.

"Do you have your personal phone with you?" he asked.

"I do."

"I'll put my personal number in it. It's private though."

He put his number into her phone. She walked to her car, letting herself bask in the warmth of the spring sunshine.

\*\*\*

She found Mark standing alone in their office, staring at the wall map of the city.

"Why are you back?"

"He plead out." She dumped her binder onto her desk.

He glanced at her. "Good deal?"

"I think so. Guilty on four." She stepped beside him and stared at the map with him.

"There's something we're not seeing," he said.

"Anything come from talking to her friends?"

He shook his head. "No one knows where she might go for that hour before her shifts. They're all certain there was no boyfriend."

"Hey, I want to ask you something," she said.

He didn't hear her. He stepped closer to the map. "Shit."

"What?"

"Look." He put his finger on the map. "It's been right in front of our eyes all along."

"What?"

"In each case except two, the victims were on their way somewhere but never got there."

"That's usually the case." She grinned but he didn't see it.

"But look. To get from where they were last seen to their destinations, they all would have had to have gotten on highway 421."

"The two exceptions?"

"The D.V. and Kaylee."

"But we don't know where Kaylee went. She could have gotten on that highway."

He nodded, tracing each possible route with his finger.

"You thinking trucker?" she asked.

"It's only a small stretch of the highway. Maybe. Or maybe tow truck driver."

"You think they all had breakdowns?"

He rubbed his hands over his head. "That does seem too coincidental. But we have to check. None of their cars were found. Where are the cars?"

"I can check other jurisdictions that highway runs through, see if anything related comes up that wasn't put into VICLAS."

He walked to his desk and pulled up a list of tow truck companies on his computer. "You check trucking companies. I'll check the tow trucks."

"Before I forget, can you keep Radar for a few hours tonight?"

"He's got no room to run around at my place," he said.

"No worries," she said.

Pete stuck his head in the door. "What's going on?"

"Nothing," Mark said. "What's up?"

Pete looked at Syd. "We found something at your place."

"Oh?" She looked at him.

"There were shoeprints in your front, back, and side gardens underneath the ground floor windows, all facing in. They don't match the kid's shoes. There were no handprints or nose-prints on the glass of the windows but I think somebody else was looking in on you, Syd."

"Radar shredded my front curtains yesterday. I thought he was just being Radar. Now I'm wondering if he was flipping out at the window because someone was there."

Pete nodded. "Could be."

"Thanks, Pete," she said.

Pete left.

Mark said, "I don't like that."

She shrugged.

"I'll watch Radar tonight."

"Thanks."

"Where are you going, anyway?"

"Dinner with Branson. And it's not a date."

He raised his eyebrows. "It's a date."

"No. He clearly stated it's not a date. We're going to celebrate our court win. He knows about my rule."

Mark shook his head. "He said it's not a date so he could get a date."

"If that's true, that's his problem. I'm the ice queen, remember."

"And he's an inferno."

"Well, let's just hope it's the kind of inferno that heats your house in winter and not Dante's kind," she said.

He smiled. "It's good for you."

"It's not a date."

He turned his attention back to his computer. "I'm going to visit a few towing companies."

She sat at her desk. "I'll check the other jurisdictions and then start working out which trucking companies have regular routes on that stretch."

"Just make sure you leave in time to get ready for your 'not-a-date'." He smirked.

\*\*\*

Syd felt overwhelmed walking through her damaged home. The smell was more overwhelming than the sight. The guys had boarded up her front window and ensured everything was secure before they left. She walked upstairs to her room to find something to wear for dinner with Branson. She didn't have much of a selection. She had work clothes, sports clothes, and one dress that she wore to weddings and funerals. She couldn't wear the dress. It might send an unintended message. She settled on work clothes, minus the blazer. She brought the blouse to her face. It reeked of smoke. She took the clothes to her dungeon of a basement and tossed them into the wash.

While she waited she rummaged through her papers in the back of her closet and found her insurance policy with the broker's card paper-clipped to the front. She was lucky the fire hadn't reached her important documents. She put the policy on her dresser, then went downstairs to the kitchen. She wiped the counters, having to rinse the black out of the dishcloth after every swipe. Filthy with soot smudges herself, she looked at the cupboards, walls, and ceiling, all coated in black. There was no point in cleaning counters. *I've just wasted my time. Maybe professional cleaning was covered by insurance,* she thought.

She went upstairs and showered. She took her small tray of make-up out of the bathroom cupboard and put it on the vanity. She stood looking at it, then put it back in the cupboard.

She and Branson met at a restaurant at the edge of the city. He was dressed semi-casual but looked just as radiant as he looked in a suit and tie. Casual Apollo.

They sat together at a small corner table. They talked about work first, then non-work topics. He laughed at her jokes. He had this giggle, like a little boy. It made you want to pick him up and hug him. Their time together was good, easy, like crawling into warm fuzzy pajamas on a winter night.

"There's nothing fake about you. No fake nails, fake eyelashes, fake laugh, fake interests."

She looked at him, processing what he was saying.

He looked at her appraisingly. "You don't wear make-up but you're pretty. I hope that's not too forward."

She almost laughed. "It's okay."

"And you don't throw yourself at me like other women."

She smiled. "That does happen to you a lot."

"People assume that men are okay with that, but it's uncomfortable."

She gave him a sympathetic look.

"If I'm going to be with someone I want an equal. Do you know what I mean?"

"I do," she said. "I'm surprised you don't already have someone."

"I did, but not any more."

"I'm sorry."

"It's okay. Going our separate ways was the right thing. She was an artist and I, well, I'm me. We were never a match. What about you?"

"My life is good the way it is," she said.

"Thus your rule."

"Oh, the rule is because I've seen other people use work as a dating pool and it always ends badly," she said.

"Maybe we shouldn't tell anyone about our dinner together," he said. "They might jump to erroneous conclusions."

"I already told Mark."

"Will he gossip?"

"Oh, no. He knows better."

Branson smiled. He raised his coffee cup. "Here's to non-dates."

"To non-dates," she said, and sipped her coffee.

They talked and laughed until they saw the waiter lock the front door. They stepped outside into the cool misty night. Branson offered her a cigarette. She took it, wanting to linger with him just a little longer. She spotted Brice Avery across the street talking to someone. He hadn't seen them. She stared at him, frowning.

Branson said, "You know those guys?"

"I know who they are."

"You don't like them."

"He sets fires."

"You do."

The remark broke her icy glare at Avery. She looked at Branson.

"What?"

"You do," he said, holding eye contact so intense it burned into her.

She didn't know what to say, so she didn't say anything.

# Chapter Six

In the morning Mrs. Linton agreed to keep Radar for the day again. Syd gave her some things for him to chew on and a super-sized box of dog biscuits with instructions to only give him two.

The first thing she did when she got to work was check the overnight calls. She wanted to see if there had been any fires near the restaurant, having seen Avery in the area. There were none. She called the insurance company. They emailed her forms to fill out. Mark walked in to the churr of the printer.

"What's that?" he asked, nodding at the printer.

"Forms to fill out for insurance."

"Geeze Louise, that's more paper than a homicide brief."

Inspector Ecklund walked in. "Another arrest has been made in connection to your fire. Another kid. The two of them learned from the internet how to make Molotov cocktails. There's no connection to Brice Avery."

"So the shoe prints outside my windows were from the other kid?"

"I didn't ask that. Ask Forensics."

"Okay. Thanks."

He left. Syd picked up the phone and called down to Forensics. Pete answered. She asked about a match on the shoe prints.

"Sorry, Syd. We don't know who the shoe prints belong to."

Mark looked at her, awaiting an answer. She shook her head.

"Thanks, Pete."

Mark handed her a cup of station sludge.

"We get anything from the tip line?" she asked.

"Just the usual," he said. "A lot of women think their husbands or boyfriends are capable of kidnapping and murder."

They spent the morning slogging through fruitless conversations with tow truck owners and trucking companies.

At one o'clock, Syd sat back in her chair. "This is impossible. You hungry?"

"Lebanese?" he said.

She nodded. "Call in the order. I'll drive over now."

"Your usual?"

"Yes."

She drove to the restaurant and found a parking spot out front. She stepped inside and, out of habit, looked around. At a table in the back corner sat Liza, beaming, across from Branson. Syd turned away quickly, facing the man behind the counter.

"Almost ready," he said.

She heard Liza's voice, "Sydney."

Syd cringed. She wasn't sure how she felt and she didn't want to face it, whatever it was, and didn't want to face Branson and Liza. She smiled and waved at Liza. Branson turned around. He waved her over. Reluctant but trapped, she walked to their table and said hello. Liza sat straight like a third-grader trying to impress the teacher as she nervously twirled a lock of blonde hair around her pink manicured finger. Branson moved his chair back an inch, putting some distance between himself and Liza.

"Join us, Detective LaFleur," he said.

Syd watched Liza's eyes dim at that.

"I can't. I'm picking up lunch for Detective Lewis."

The man behind the counter called out, "Ready."

"It was nice seeing you," Syd said. "Enjoy your lunch."

She paid for her order and went back to the station.

\*\*\*

"Interesting tip came in on Amelia Morrison," Mark said.

Syd put their lunch on the desk and started unpacking it. "The one you think is not connected?"

"Still gotta run it down."

She handed him a Styrofoam box full of salad. "Of course. Let's eat."

She dug into her falafel while he talked.

"Woman named Nancy called in saying she and Mr. Morrison were having an affair at the time of Amelia's disappearance. A couple of days ago they have a fight. She

65

tries to leave. He chokes her and tells her she's never leaving. Says his wife is buried in the back yard and he'll bury her, too."

"There are charges for that right there," she said.

"She doesn't want to make a report. We could probably get a warrant based on the tip. It's been done before."

"Let's give her a call," Syd said, picking up the phone.

"She's staying with her sister," Mark said.

He read the phone number to her. When a female answered the phone, Syd identified herself and asked for Nancy. The woman put down the phone and Syd could hear whispering. Another woman's voice came over the line.

"Hello, this is Nancy." Her voice was quiet.

"Hi, Nancy. This is Detective Sydney LaFleur from Major Crime. I understand you might have some information in relation to Amelia Morrison."

"It was a mistake," she said. "He was just trying to scare me, I'm sure. I shouldn't have called."

"I understand. I'm sure you understand we have to follow this up. I'd like to have a chat with you here at the station. You're not in any trouble. It would help us."

"No. I'm not leaving this house."

"Okay. I can come to you."

"No. No police here. You don't understand. If he finds out…" She cried.

"I understand why you're scared. We can get an order to make him stay away from you."

66

"That didn't work for Amelia. I don't want to report the assault. He won't go to jail and if he does he'll get out."

"I understand." Syd wanted to promise Nancy the police and courts would protect her, but she didn't want to tell her that lie. "How about this: I can drive over and pick you up myself. I'm in plain clothes and my car is unmarked. We'll talk about Amelia."

Nancy cried again. Syd could hear her talking to her sister. The sister picked up the phone.

"She's really scared."

"I understand," Syd said. "It sounds like she's torn."

"She is."

"I told her we could come pick her up. Do you think you could persuade her? If he's done something to Amelia we can't just let that go."

"Could I come with her?"

"Sure. You can come to the station with her, but not into the interview room."

"Just a minute."

Syd waited, hearing the muffled voices on the other end of the line.

The sister came back on the line. "Yes. Come pick us up."

"Okay. We'll be there in fifteen minutes."

Syd hung up, looked at Mark, and said, "We're on."

"Yes."

On the drive over, Mark said, "I think you should do this one. I'll have a casual chat with the sister, see what she knows."

67

She nodded. They drove the rest of the way in silence, each mentally preparing; no need for words.

She parked across the street from the red brick house, removed her lanyard from around her neck, and shoved it into her blazer pocket. She went to the door while Mark waited in the car, watching the neighbourhood, looking for any sign of anyone watching.

Nancy wore sunglasses. Syd noticed the marks on her neck, a bruised imprint in the shape of hands and two thumbs. Nancy and her sister sat in the back seat. During the drive to the station they didn't talk about the case. Syd and Mark made small talk with the women, wanting to put them at ease and build some rapport.

Syd took Nancy to interview two, a windowless room with two chairs, one on either side of an office table. A camera on the ceiling pointed toward the table and chairs. A box of cheap tissues sat on one side of the table near the beige wall. Nancy sat on one of the chairs, clutching her purse in her lap.

"Can I get you something?" Syd asked. "Coffee, tea, water?"

"I can have tea?"

"Absolutely. How do you take it?"

"Strong, just a little milk."

"Okay. Make yourself comfortable, well, as comfortable as you can in this place." Syd smiled at her. "Sorry, it's not exactly five stars."

Nancy gave a little smile in return. It was small, but genuine.

"I'll be right back."

She left and made a cup of tea in a real mug for Nancy and grabbed a coffee for herself. She returned to the interview room, put the tea in front of Nancy, and then sat across from her. Syd stated the date and time and identified both herself and Nancy for the recording. She informed Nancy they were being recorded and obtained her consent.

Syd said, "It's better to have it recorded. I can focus on you instead of writing piles of notes. You understand?"

"Yes."

Syd leaned back in her chair, holding her coffee, looking casual. "How's your tea?"

"It's good."

"I really appreciate you coming in. Every little bit of information helps."

Nancy nodded. She took off her sunglasses, revealing brown eyes full of blood red dots and splotches. Petechial hemorrhaging.

Syd leaned forward and reached her hand across the table. "You were choked pretty badly."

"Yes, but I don't want to report that."

"Okay. I'm making the comment out of empathy, one woman to another."

Nancy looked down at her lap.

"Nobody deserves to be treated like that. You didn't deserve that, Nancy."

Two tears fell into Nancy's lap. "Maybe I did. I had an affair. I ignored the warning signs. I believed him." She lifted her head and looked at Syd, eyes full of tears.

"Look, even though I don't know your story yet, I'm still certain that you don't deserve that treatment. No matter what you did it's never okay for someone to assault you and it's always the fault of the abuser."

More tears. Syd pushed the box of tissues in front of Nancy. Nancy took a tissue.

Syd leaned back in her chair and asked, "What things do you *want* to tell me?"

"I don't know."

"Okay. Let's start with Amelia. Tell me about her."

"I didn't know her. I only know what Ed told me and I know now that he was lying."

"Okay. Start there."

"He told me she kept accusing him of abusing her but that she was just doing that to hurt him."

Syd waited. Listened.

"He said she was crazy and he thought she was cheating. I felt sorry for him. We started having lunch together at work every day and then we started getting together after work, too. We'd go for a walk or a drink. He didn't want to go home. I don't know how it happened really. Over time we got close. I was in love with him before we started the physical affair. He said he was going to leave Amelia but he kept having excuses about why he couldn't. First he said he was afraid of her, that she would call the police and accuse him if he tried to leave her. Then he said he felt sorry for her, that she had a mental illness. Then it was worries about losing his reputation at church. I was getting fed up and starting to doubt he would ever leave. Then he said she'd take him for everything, take the house, all his hard work. I told him it didn't matter, that we could start fresh and build something together. He kept playing for more time. Finally I ended the affair. A week later he said Amelia had gone to her mother's place, but I didn't want to start up with him again only for them to get back together. I wanted a clean break, to get over him. Then he told me Amelia was missing. I felt sorry for him so I met with him and got roped back in again."

"When did he tell you she went to her mother's?"

"April fifteenth. I remember that because it was exactly one week before my holiday week off from work."

Syd thought about this. Amelia hadn't been reported missing for another week after that. That's why Ed's alibi seemed solid. It was for the wrong date.

Nancy paused, looking at Syd. "What if it's my fault? What if he killed her to be with me?" She put her face in her hands. "Oh my god, I couldn't live with that."

"It's not your fault," Syd said. "Did you suggest he kill her?"

"God, no."

"And you didn't kill her?"

"No!"

"So it's not your fault. And really, we don't even know she's dead."

"I think she is."

"Okay. Tell me what makes you think that."

"Because two days ago he told me he did it. He said he buried her in the yard."

"How did that conversation come about?"

"I was trying to leave him again. He told me nobody leaves him. I tried to walk away but he grabbed me." She pulled up her sleeves to show Syd the finger shaped bruises on her arms. "I tried to pull away from him and he grabbed me by the throat. Then he started choking me and said, 'I buried Amelia in the yard next to the dog. Don't make the same mistake she did or I'll bury you, too'."

Syd nodded. "Did you believe him?"

"Yes."

"Earlier today you said maybe he just said it to scare you."

"I told you that because I was afraid to talk to you."

Syd nodded. "I understand. You said you were trying to leave him 'again'. Had you tried to leave before? I mean aside from when you broke off the affair."

"Yes. I was at his house. This was after Amelia was reported missing and before I moved in. He'd been having temper outbursts, calling me names, throwing things. He shoved me. I ran out of the house and went home. He apologized, kept texting and calling saying he was so sorry. He sent flowers. He showed up at my apartment. He was making such a scene yelling and crying in the hallway I let him in. He cried and got right down on his knees and begged me to forgive him. He promised he would never do it again, said he knew he'd been awful but he'd do better. He said it was because of the stress of Amelia's disappearance and the police investigation. The police had searched his house and he was upset about it. I felt sorry for him again. I gave in and took him back. It was okay, good, for a while. He was attentive and loving and bent over backwards to make me happy. I believed it wouldn't happen again. When he asked me to move in with him, I agreed. Terrible mistake."

"Was that the only time?"

"That he hurt me or that I tried to leave?"

"Both."

"He hurt me other times. It started with just verbal stuff, and throwing things. Then he'd grab me or slap me or shove me. He didn't beat me like you see in the movies. A couple of times I thought about just walking out the door and never going back, but I'd already given up my apartment and we'd sold my car. He said we didn't need two cars. I was stuck."

Syd nodded.

"I was embarrassed, too. I didn't want anyone to know what was happening. I felt stupid for still loving him. I thought if I could just be patient a little longer, if I could be understanding enough, a good enough partner, I could help him. Maybe when what happened to Amelia was solved then things could get back to the way they were in the beginning. Maybe the Ed I fell in love with would come back."

"It's never black and white, is it," Syd said.

"No, and that's what people don't understand. They only see the bad and think the answer is simple."

"But it's not simple."

"Right. You understand."

Syd nodded. "I do."

"So I would tell him I wanted to leave and every time he would apologize and things would be okay for a while. But this time he didn't apologize. This time was different. I'm scared."

Syd sat forward. "You're right to be scared. I would be scared, too."

"You?"

"Uh-huh. Any thinking person would be scared. We can put him away just based on what you're telling me now, for his assaults on you."

"He'll just say I'm crazy or I'm lying."

"Nancy, I believe you. And I can tell you're not crazy."

Nancy exhaled. Her shoulders relaxed. She cried.

"How long have you and Ed worked together?"

"Three years."

"You both work at Enco, right?"

"Yes."

"Where is that, exactly?"

"Just off of Highway 421. It's the office building beside the furniture store."

"When you moved in with Ed were Amelia's belongings still in the house?"

"No. He'd already taken her clothes to the thrift shop."

"What about jewellery? Was any of that around?"

"Not that I know of."

"Was he one to give you jewellery? He ever bring anything home for you?"

"No, never."

Syd continued questioning, filling gaps, getting exact dates and details, looking for new avenues and closing off others. She wanted to ensure she had enough to put together a fulsome and accurate brief both for the assault charges and for the warrants she needed.

"Where is Ed now?" Syd asked.

"What time is it?"

Syd looked at her watch. "Just after four."

"He'll be home by now. He gets off work at three."

Nancy decided she did want Ed held accountable for the assaults on her after all. Syd arranged for Nancy to go down to Forensics so they could photograph and document her injuries.

Before she left the interview room Syd asked, "Are there any weapons in the house?"

"Yes. All over."

"What weapons?"

"Guns."

"Handguns, long-guns?"

"Both. He started collecting them about a month ago."

"Are they locked up in a gun cabinet or box?"

"No. They're all over the house."

"Okay. Any pets in the house?"

"No."

"Visitors? Anyone else?"

"No. No one."

"Okay. Thank you very much, Nancy. You have been a big help."

Mark met her in the hallway. "I watched the whole thing. I've got the Informations for the warrants already filled out. We just have to swear them."

As they strode the fifty feet toward their office she said, "I want to pull up his bank statements again. I remember a forty-five hundred dollar deposit dated a month before Amelia's disappearance. At the time he said there had been a lot of break-ins in the area so he'd gathered all the cash he had stashed around the house and put it in the bank. I think he sold her car."

"Right. She never went anywhere."

"He has guns all over the place," she said.

"Tactical."

"What about getting him to come here?" She pushed open their office door and turned to face him.

"If he thinks we're onto him he might destroy evidence if there is any in the house."

"Not like he can run out and re-hide a buried body. I'm thinking pretext," she said.

"We could tell him there was a robbery near his house. We could get the guys in robbery to call him in as a friendly witness, maybe offer a reward."

"That's good. I don't feel like getting shot at today."

"I'll call them."

"I'll call. Can you call Mrs. Linton and tell her we'll be late picking up Radar? And see how he's doing?"

"Sure."

"And somebody has to take Nancy and her sister home. I don't want her crossing paths with Ed Morrison in the building or parking lot."

"On it."

"Did you catch that bit about their office being close to the 421?"

"I did. I included it on the Information for the search warrant. We need to be able to scoop anything related to the other cases if it's there."

\*\*\*

Everything came together. Robbery convinced Morrison to come in. When he arrived Syd arrested him for the assaults on Nancy. She took him to custody and told him they would be searching his property. She asked him if there was anything he wanted to tell her ahead of time."

"That bitch is a crazy liar," he said, baring his teeth. "You already searched my property. This is harassment."

Syd turned and walked away.

She met Mark outside in the back parking lot where the team was assembled. They had their warrant and everything was arranged, including a cadaver dog, Forensics, Firearms, and uniforms. The Duty Inspector ordered the Command Van. They all rolled out to the Morrison place.

Officers cordoned off the property around the two-storey brown stuccoed house, including the sidewalk out front. Spectators appeared like cockroaches do when the lights go out at a tenement building. Syd and Mark stood beside the K9 officer's vehicle with the increasingly restless cadaver dog, a Belgian Malinois, still inside. The dog would do his thing first, before everyone put their scents all over the place.

A constable behind the yellow police line hollered, "Hey, Lewis, LaFleur."

"You're good to go," Mark said to the K9 officer.

Mark and Syd walked over to the officer who'd hollered for them.

The officer motioned to an elderly man in front of him on the other side of the tape. "This gentleman says Ed was digging up the yard, replacing the sod. But it was two weeks before the wife was reported missing."

The man said, "I didn't tell the police before because it happened before all of the hullabaloo about her missing. But now that I think about it I hadn't seen her for a while before that."

Syd took the man's statement.

In the short time that took, the dog had picked up a scent. Everyone watched the dog. Even the birds were quiet. Excitedly following the scent, the dog pulled the handler along the side of the house to the backyard. Keeping their distance, Mark and Syd followed. The dog indicated on a spot on the grass in front of the flower garden.

"Here," the handler said.

Cruisers had already blocked both ends of the street. Reporters and cameramen poured into the area, jockeying for position. A news helicopter flew overhead as digging equipment was brought in and tents set up. The area indicated by the cadaver dog would be excavated like an archeological site rather than dug up like a landscaping job. It would take a while.

A quiet excitement buzzed through the crew when they found bones, then subsided when they determined the bones were canine. The dog's skull bore an indentation in the shape of a hammer peen. A spider's web of fracture lines encircled the indentation and expanded outward, the final chapter of the story of the crime inflicted on the poor creature written in its bones. They collected the dog's bones. Mark told them to keep going, that Amelia would be buried near the dog. They worked under the tent and lights as darkness fell and Pete's team went back and forth from the house taking bags of potential evidence. When they uncovered a human body Mark called Amelia's mother to notify her before the press plastered it on the news.

It was two a.m. when they went home. They would need the few precious hours of sleep before they had to be back at work in the morning.

# Chapter Seven

Their first coffee filled morning hours in the office were quietly frenetic. They prepared the bail brief on the domestic violence and firearms charges, and laboured over the paperwork on the homicide investigation. Mark was still working on the latter when Syd left for court. They were requesting the Crown oppose bail. Syd wanted to be there to keep her eyes on it and let the Crown know there was more coming.

At the Crown's office she asked Eleanor, the Senior Legal Administrative Assistant, "Who's in bail court today?"

"A per diem. Do you need to speak with him?"

"I do."

"Is it about the Amelia Morrison case?" Eleanor asked as she led Syd down the carpeted hall to the law library.

"It is."

Syd stepped into the library where a thin-faced bearded lawyer sat at the long table, a tower of file folders on either side of him, the briefs he had to read before ten o'clock court. Eleanor scurried down the hall toward Branson's office.

"I have another one for you," Syd said to the lawyer.

He glanced up from the file he was reading. "Put it on the pile."

He continued reading what was in front of him.

"This will be a hearing," she said.

He ignored her.

She plopped the Morrison file on top of the one he was reading. He looked at her, not hiding his feelings of irritation.

"Hello," she said. "Detective Sydney LaFleur, Major Crime."

"Oh," he said, his scowl changing to surprise.

"We want bail opposed on this one. We expect to be charging him with second degree murder."

"But you haven't yet."

"There's enough in there already for a successful bail opposition."

"You're a lawyer too?" He rolled his eyes and pushed her file aside.

"Detective LaFleur." Branson's voice, putting on a show of cheeriness and familiarity. He'd come in behind her. "What do you need?"

Eleanor hollered, "A solid Crown in bail court," as she passed by pushing a cart full of files.

Keeping a straight face, Syd watched the corner of Branson's mouth turn up slightly.

"Let me have a look at the file," Branson said.

Syd snatched up the file and she and Branson walked down the hall to his office. As soon as they got inside, Branson shut the door.

"Eleanor is going to get herself in trouble one of these days, but that was kind of funny."

Syd smiled.

"He probably deserved it," he said. "This morning he asked her to pick up his dry cleaning. Unbelievable."

"The file," she said. "It's domestic violence and firearms. Accused is Ed Morrison, Amelia Morrison's husband. We found a body buried in his yard late last night. We're pretty sure it's hers. We need you to keep him in."

Branson put the file on his pristine desk. He'd dispensed with the piles of boxes that lined the wall previously. He'd properly moved in to the space. He stepped outside his office door and spoke to Michael Cortez, the Crown whose office was directly across the hall.

"Can you do my pleas in 104 this morning?"

"Eleanor already brought me the files," Michael said.

Branson closed the door and sat at his desk across from Syd.

He smiled and whispered, "I had fun on our non-date."

Without wanting to, she smiled back at him. He opened the file.

"I can wait downstairs," she said, suddenly wanting the energy boost nicotine would give her.

"No, no. Stay. In case I have questions."

He read. She sat quietly, looking around. The spacious office was notably devoid of any personal objects, save for a pressed shirt and an extra tie hanging on the coat rack. The big plant in the corner near the window pre-dated Branson. She remembered it from when this office belonged to George. Thick law books lined the shelves but there was nothing else. She thought it odd his degrees weren't hanging on the wall. Everyone had their degrees on the wall.

He pushed the file aside. "Good work, Sydney."

"And Mark, and a lot of other people," she said.

He nodded. "Well, let's go down and see if he's even got a surety."

Bail court hadn't started yet when they walked into the loud crowded courtroom at ten after ten. It never started on time. Duty counsel walked in with a handful of paper and stepped toward the per diem Crown. Branson intercepted him.

"Does Morrison want a hearing today?" Branson asked.

"I think so. Riker is back there drumming up business for himself. He's talking to Morrison now."

Branson and Syd gave each other a look.

"All right," Branson said, "we'll be out back. Will you send someone to get us when he's ready?"

Duty counsel looked at the sheaf of paper in his hand then gave Branson a wearied look.

Seeing this, and having overheard everything, the court constable said, "I'll radio Sgt. Wilkinson when I see Riker. He'll get you."

Syd nodded to him in appreciation. Branson left the Morrison file on counsel table and he and Syd walked to the back door. She felt along the top of the doorframe for her stash.

"I took it," Branson said, holding out a cigarette from his pack.

"What if you weren't here?" she asked, taking the cigarette and pushing the grey door open.

"Then you'd have to come find me." He grinned like a teen-aged boy.

"Is that a ploy?"

"Maybe." He smiled brighter.

She lit her smoke and leaned with her back against the wall. He did the same beside her.

"You could have had lunch with Liza and me," he said. "It wasn't a personal lunch. I'm just trying to get to know everyone."

"You don't have to explain yourself to me," she said.

"I know. I'm just telling you."

"Okay. I was busy anyway." She stared at the parking lot across the street, not wanting to keep on this subject.

"I see that. Did you get things sorted out with your house?"

"Not yet."

"Do you need help?"

"I'm okay, thanks. There's a restoration company in there and my Aunt Mary is picking out new furniture for me and having it delivered."

"You have an Aunt Mary who orders your furniture?"

"Everybody should have an Aunt Mary," she said.

Sergeant Wilkinson stuck his head out the door. "LaFleur."

"Hey, Wilkie."

He looked at her. "Nice job."

She smiled. "A team effort."

"The weasel is in court." He gave her a wry smile.

"Weasel one, two, or thirty-seven?" she asked, knowing he was referring to Riker.

He laughed and walked away. She and Branson went back to bail court. The still grouchy per diem Crown sat at counsel table looking at his notes while Riker stood hovering beside him, trying to get his attention. The court clerk emphatically arranged and rearranged papers in front of her, muttering about never starting on time. The court constable smirked, keeping one eye on the melodrama and the other on the members of the public wandering in and out of the room. Branson and Syd approached Riker.

"What's happening with Morrison?" Branson asked.

"It's difficult to talk to my client when I don't get the bail brief in time." Riker shot Syd a sour look.

"So no hearing today," Branson said.

"I didn't say that. His girlfriend is here to act as surety."

Surprised, Syd looked around the room for Nancy.

"His girlfriend can't act as surety; she's the victim," Branson said.

"The alleged victim is no longer his girlfriend. He has a different girlfriend."

Syd pulled her notebook out of her pocket.

"Who?" Branson asked.

Riker provided the basic information about the proposed surety. Syd jotted down her name, date of birth, and address. She left the courtroom and hurried through the congested public waiting area, then down the hall to the police room.

She handed her open notebook to Wilkinson. "Run this for me."

He turned to his computer and typed in the information. "No record. Disturbance call at her address a month ago."

"Pull it up."

She stepped around the desk so she could read over his shoulder. He pulled up the report. A neighbour had called police about a loud argument and a woman screaming. Responding officer found a couple arguing. The couple claimed no assault had taken place. The man who the proposed surety had been arguing with was Ed Morrison."

"Why do these guys all have multiple girlfriends?" Syd commented.

Wilkinson shrugged. "They get away with it."

"Print it for me?" she asked.

He hit 'print'. She grabbed the report and took it to Branson. Court was in session. She and Branson stood in the back of the courtroom while he read it. He smiled. He took it to the front of the courtroom and handed it to Riker. Syd wanted to walk up there to watch the look on his face and hear the whole whispered conversation, but she stayed put. Branson walked back to Syd and they stepped through the doors into the public waiting area.

"Tomorrow," he said. "Riker thinks a second surety will help."

"By tomorrow he'll be charged with murder."

"Then tomorrow he'll be remanded again. We'll be going to Superior Court. I'm going to take this one myself just to burn Riker."

Syd grinned.

"Come to my house after work. Not a date," he said. "I need some interior decorating advice."

"I can't. I'll be working late as it is and I have to give poor Radar some attention. Besides, you don't want interior decorating advice from me." She smiled. "I'll give you my Aunt Mary's number if you want."

"Maybe that was just a ploy," he said, giving her a mischievous smile.

"See you in a couple of days," she said, as she walked away.

She got back to the office just in time to leave again. They were going to search Morrison's office.

"Your insurance adjuster called," Mark said during the drive over. "They've approved the restoration and cleaning company but they're sending more forms to fill out."

"What a pain in the butt."

She filled him in on what happened at court. He filled her in on the information he'd received so far from the search of the Morrison property. Forensics would take a while to determine if anything was linked to the other missing women.

The search of Morrison's office turned up nothing useful. Most of their day was filled by paperwork and dead end interviews related to the missing women.

\*\*\*

Radar opened the front door of Mrs. Linton's apartment. He jumped on Syd, licking her face and wagging his tail. He dropped down, ran around in circles, then jumped on her again. She kissed his black and gold furry head. She stepped inside and closed the door. The whole place was redolent with the aromas of molasses and cinnamon. A chewed up blue fuzzy slipper lay in the middle of the chocolate coloured carpeted living room floor.

"Hello," Syd called out.

"Mrs. Linton, a grey wisp of a woman, emerged from the kitchen wearing a floral apron and wiping her small arthritic hands with a yellow tea towel.

"Hello, dear," she said. "You've come to take Radar from me."

Syd smiled. "I have. Thank you so much for taking care of him."

"Oh, he was a big help. You know, he can get the mail and answer the door."

Syd smiled.

"There are some men in the neighbourhood who come every day asking me for money."

Syd furrowed her brow, concerned. Radar tugged at the towel in Mrs. Linton's hand.

"Go lay down, Radar," Mrs. Linton said.

To Syd's astonishment, Radar immediately loped to an armchair beside a basket full of knitting. He lay in front of the chair.

Syd asked, "What men?"

"Oh, Radar took care of them," she said.

Syd inhaled, worried about what Radar might have done.

Mrs. Linton shuffled to her brown striped couch and sat down. "Radar answered the door yesterday, and today the men didn't come back. Have you eaten supper, dear?"

"I'll get something at home. These men, did you give them money?"

"Oh, no, dear. Mark told me to never give out money. He's a good boy."

Syd relaxed and smiled. "Yes, he is."

"And Radar is a good boy, too."

Radar's ears perked up.

"He ate all of his cookies," Mrs. Linton said.

Syd's eyes widened. "The whole box?"

"Yes, two at a time just like you said."

Now Syd understood why Radar had been so good. She glanced at him and shook her head. She took him home, then took him for a run. When they ran past Liza's house she noticed Liza, her hair in a ponytail, kneeling on the lush grass in front of her garden planting pink petunias. Syd ran, taking in the pale greens of newly unfurled leaves, the winged red of robins, and the air thick and redolent with aromas of newly dug gardens and freshly mown grass, while the sun lingered, casting a warm rosy hue over all. Oh, the promises Spring makes. She breathed in the fragrant promise, not thinking about how Spring's kiss moves baby buds to open and blossom while failing to warn of the blazing summer sun that sears the tender flower. She ran, breathing in the promise, revelling in its sweetness. She ran, feeling the burn in her muscles as she pushed herself. Fire.

# Chapter Eight

"Got news," Mark said. "Body was Amelia Morrison."

"That was quick." Syd looked away from her computer screen to look at him.

"Broken hyoid and the back of her skull was smashed in," he said.

"Like the dog she was buried next to," she said.

"Yeah." He shook his head.

"Bet he was choking her and smashed her head against the wall," she said.

"Or the floor," he said.

She nodded. "Well, we'd better go tell her mother."

\*\*\*

When they got back to the office, they spent the rest of the day buried in paper and silence.

Syd leaned back in her chair and rubbed her eyes. "The paper," she said.

"Yeah. Goodbye to another forest."

Mark chugged back the cold dregs at the bottom of his coffee cup. "This is the stuff they don't show in the movies."

"Because no one would watch," she said.

Branson knocked on the side of the door. Mark and Syd both sat up straight, surprised. Crowns never visited the police.

"I hope I'm not disturbing you." Branson smiled tentatively.

"Not at all," Mark said. "Come on in."

Mark smirked. Syd shot him a look that said, 'shut up'. That only made him grin outright.

"I came to talk to Pete about hockey and thought I'd stop and say hello. I got lost. This place is a maze."

Syd smiled. "If a suspect tries to run away in here, he'll get lost."

Mark put his feet on his desk. "I didn't know anyone was going to hockey tonight."

"Pete said the same thing. You're all pretty busy."

"You and Pete are friends?" Syd asked.

"I wouldn't say that. We have hockey in common. He says you play a mean game, Syd. Maybe that's where 'Ice Queen' comes from."

Mark laughed.

"Hey," she said. "I'll take that."

"I thought I'd see you in court today, Syd."

"It was just a remand, wasn't it?" she said.

Branson nodded.

"We laid the new charges on Morrison today," Mark said.

"Okay. Tomorrow will be a remand too, then," Branson said. "It will go to Superior Court. Will one of you walk me out so I don't get lost again?"

"Syd will walk you out." Mark smiled and turned away, pretending to look at his computer screen.

Syd led Branson downstairs and to one of the back doors closer to the parking lot than the main entrance. They stepped outside. This was the door the chief used. There was a little patch of lawn on each side of the concrete walkway that curved out to the parking lot. Branson offered her a cigarette.

She glanced around for the chief. "Sure, why not."

He stood close enough to her that she could smell his cologne. She stayed put, letting the clean aroma waft across her nose. They merely made small talk, but somehow it still felt intimate. He had this way of making people feel special yet still wanting. She'd noticed it at court. People liked him, gravitated to his warmth. Everyone knew he could also be icy and they seemed to prefer the danger of the fire over the desolation of the psychic arctic tundra.

She walked him to his car before his smoke was done, worried he'd drop the butt in front of the chief's door. They stood beside his car, not saying anything substantial but both wanted the interaction to last a little longer. The parking lot suddenly became busy. Shift change. People stared. It was time to go.

\*\*\*

The following day Syd and Branson walked the block from Superior Court back to the Crown's office in the Provincial building. The warm air did nothing to thaw his inexplicably chilly demeanor. She would have gone straight to the car and back to the station but he'd asked her to come back to the office to talk further about the Morrison case. She wanted coffee. The Crown's office had one of those machines with the pods of specialty coffee. She wondered if she would get one, though, given Branson's mood. She'd thought he'd brighten after he won the bail hearing but he hadn't.

She sat in the white chair facing his desk. He closed his office door. He sat in his cushiony leather chair behind his desk, leaned forward, resting his arms on the desk, and held eye contact with her. She felt her stomach knot. She didn't like not knowing what was going on, not being able to predict things. This hot and cold thing from him threw her off kilter.

"I want you to break your rule," he said.

She felt heat rush to her face, her breath fail for a second. Her body wanted to shift in her chair. She willed it to be still. She blinked.

"That sounds nice but, uh, I, uh..."

He held eye contact, listening, waiting. Those eyes burned into her soul.

"That wouldn't go over well with work," she said. "And there'd be the gossip."

He nodded. "I've thought about that. Crown Attorney and Major Crime Detective. Every accused would claim conspiracy against them."

"And if it didn't work out it would be awkward," she said.

"Oh, it would work out." He sat back, relaxed in his position. "I've considered the facts, run through the variables. We're a good match, Sydney."

She stared at him like you stare at an icy lake before diving in. This lake was unfamiliar and she didn't know how deep it was.

He straightened. "Coffee?"

"Yes, please."

"Vanilla," he said.

He left the room before she could answer and returned a few moments later with coffee for both of them. He shut the door behind him.

"We'd have to keep it a secret," he said. "That's if you agree."

"And if it doesn't work out?"

"I have no doubts."

"You should."

He shook his head. "When I'm with you, no matter whether we're working or just talking, I feel like I'm home."

She nodded. She felt the same way.

"And there's this spark, no, fire, between us that keeps growing," he said.

She stared at him, unable to assess both him and herself at the same time. She said, "The question is whether that fire will consume me."

"It could consume both of us."

"Fire is dangerous," she said.

He nodded.

"So will you be my safe haven or will you be the end of me?" she asked.

"I could ask you the same thing."

She stared at her coffee cup knowing she was about to do the most reckless thing she'd done in her life.

"Yes," she said.

His eyes lit up. He beamed. Apollo shining down on her.

"So now what?" she asked.

"A date?" he said.

"When?"

"There's something I have to do tonight. Tomorrow night? Seven o'clock? I'll pick you up at your house."

"Sounds good," she said. "You know, there's always the chance I will have to work late. It goes like that."

"I understand."

***

She stopped at the coffee shop on Vine. Standing in line she stared out the window. Such a nice neighbourhood. Did Kaylee disappear from here or somewhere else? What was around here that might lure a young woman for an hour before every shift? Who frequented here?

The barista interrupted her thoughts, "Can I help you?"

"Oh, yes." Syd remembered the last order she'd bought for Records. She gave that order and remembered to get something for Mark.

She stopped at Records on her way up to her office.

"Oh, Syd. I was just about to call Detective Lewis," Lori said.

Syd pushed the box of coffee trays across the counter.

"Thanks. I have something you might be interested in. It's just a one page report, no further action, but it struck me as odd," Lori said.

"Tell me."

"A young woman came in with her Aunt Mary. She had a breakdown on highway 421 last two days before Kaylee Anderson went missing. Anyway, a tow truck pulled up behind her to help, except she never called a tow truck. She has CAA so a tow would be covered and she wanted to use them. She explained this to the guy and he got really insistent. She felt uncomfortable so she locked herself in her car and called CAA. Everything turned out okay but her aunt pressed her to report it. They came in today. Stood right there in the lobby to give the report. I overheard the whole thing. Do you think it's something?"

"Maybe," Syd said, thinking about Mark's theory of a tow truck driver.

"I printed it out for you," Lori said.

"Thanks." Syd took the report

She walked into the office and handed Mark the coffee.

"Ooh, froofie coffee," he said.

"Froofie?"

"Yeah. Froofie. We drink that battery acid. Lawyers drink froofie stuff. You've been hanging out at the Crown's office too much. Don't go soft on me, LaFleur." He lifted the plastic lid off the cup.

"Records brought something to my attention," she said.

He took a sip of coffee. "Oh, this is g-o-o-o-d." He took another sip.

She laughed. "Don't go soft on me, Lewis."

She handed him the report. He looked at it.

"This is a shit report," he said, tossing it on the desk. "Why are there so many shit reports?"

"Probably thought it wasn't anything." She shrugged.

"Someone came to the police thinking it was something. They took the time to report it. The least we can do is write a decent report."

"I hear you. I think sometimes they think why bother if it's going to come to nothing or end in a plea deal anyway."

He had that look on his face, the one that said a rant was about to burst out of him. "You know why so many of our cases, I mean you and me, you know why so many end in guilty pleas?"

"Because we investigate as if everything is going to trial," she said.

"Right. And we write good freaking reports."

"Excellent reports," she said.

"Yeah. Excellent."

"You done now?"

He smiled. "Yeah, I'm good."

"Phone call or interview?"

"They were just here, right?" he asked.

"Yes."

"Phone call. And write a decent frickin' report."

She picked up the phone and called the complainant, Danielle Sawyer. When she was through with the call she looked at Mark and smiled.

"Always listen to your Aunt Mary," she said.

"I'm listening."

"Complainant made a stop at the Outlet Mall. Had her breakdown right after that."

"Full of young women," he said.

"Perfect hunting ground."

"Let's go."

# Chapter Nine

They sat with the acne-faced lone security guard in the cramped windowless office at the mall reviewing video from the day Ms. Sawyer had her car trouble. They saw her park and go into the mall. Ten minutes into the video they saw a security guard walk through the parking lot. It didn't seem unusual until he reached into his pocket and then crouched down beside her car on the driver's side, out of view of the camera.

"Back up. Let's look at that again," Mark said.

The watched over and over but couldn't see what, if anything, he'd done to the car.

"He did something to the tire," Syd said. "She had a flat tire."

Mark nodded. "Maybe. A leak might not have been noticeable until she hit the highway."

Syd asked the bug-eyed security guard for the name of the guard on the video.

"Henson. He quit."

"When?" Mark asked.

"Wednesday."

"The day of your press conference," she said.

"Okay, let's keep watching," Mark said.

They watched until they saw Danielle Sawyer walk to her car.

Both Mark and Syd said, "Stop" at the same time. They'd both seen it.

"Go back to the video of the front doors," Syd said.

There, in perfect resolution, was Kaylee Anderson walking out of the mall two days before she disappeared. Syd looked at the timestamp. 10:40 a.m.

"Shopping. She was going to the mall before her shifts," she said.

"There were no purchases on her credit or debit," Mark said.

"Some women like to go and just look."

"How far back do you keep your video?" Mark asked the guard.

"I dunno. A long time I think. It gets stored on the cloud."

Syd listed the dates each of the women disappeared. "Can you get those?"

"I think so, yeah," the guy said.

"Try April eleventh starting from ten o'clock in the morning."

He was able to pull it up. They scoured all the camera angles.

"There," Mark said, pointing at the corner of the screen. "Felicia Williams. I'm sure that's her. We need the videos for all of these dates."

The guard said, "I don't know if I can..."

"Get your supervisor on the phone," Mark said.

The guy made the call. Mark spoke to the supervisor and was able to secure the footage they needed. They would need a court order for Henson's employment records or even an address. That wasn't going to stop them from getting what they needed sooner.

He asked the guard, "What's Henson's first name?"

"Mitchell."

"Are you guys buddies?"

"No."

"Do you know where he lives?"

"I think Strathcona, somewhere around that gas station attached to the burrito place."

"What kind of car does he drive?"

"A dark green Crown Vic. It's old."

"Have you talked to him at all since he quit?" Syd asked.

"No."

"How do you know he quit?" she asked.

"I got called into work on my day off because he didn't show up for work. He just never came back."

"Okay, thanks, buddy," Mark said.

They walked out of the mall, keeping quiet until they got out of earshot of the members of the public.

"Hot damn!" Mark said as soon as they got to the parking lot. "Finally we got something."

It was easy to find Henson's address. They ran his name from the car. He had no record. As Mark pulled out of the mall Syd wrote down Henson's address and let dispatch know where they were going. They drove to the house, situated in a run-down neighbourhood, where Henson lived in the apartment on the second floor. Mark went around to the back of the house to see if there was another exit in case Henson decided to run. He came back around front shaking his head.

"No exits, no movement," he said.

Syd knocked on the front door. No answer. She pulled it open, looking up the shadowy narrow stairwell. It smelled of dust and crumbling plaster. At her feet lay a pile of mail.

"Looks like he's away," she said, picking up the mail and shuffling through it.

She left the mail in a pile behind the door. In single file they walked up the stairs quickly but quietly, listening, ready for anything. A stairwell is a bad place to be if things go sideways. Mark banged on the door at the top of the stairs. No answer. He banged again.

"Police," he bellowed.

They listened. No footsteps or telltale noises of anyone there.

"You hear that?" Syd whispered.

He listened. "Ah crap. Flies."

"Want to go in?" she asked.

"Not really."

Mark stood at the door while Syd went back down the stairs. She knocked on the old wooden door of the ground floor apartment. A rotund balding man in his sixties opened the door.

Syd showed her identification. "Are you the landlord for upstairs?"

"Yes."

"Is your tenant Mitchell Henson?"

"Yes. What's going on?"

"When was the last time you saw him?"

"I never see him. I heard him walking around up there maybe last week. Or maybe it was two weeks. Why?"

"We're concerned about his welfare. Do you have a key for his apartment?"

"Don't you need a warrant?"

"Not if we think someone is lying in there hurt."

"Oh. Okay." He shuffled away and returned with a key labelled #2 with masking tape.

He walked up the stairs slowly, hanging onto the rickety railing, huffing and wheezing with his laborious ascent. She walked behind him willing him not to fall or have a heart attack. He unlocked the door then stepped back onto the top stair.

Mark opened the door. Hot air thick with the stench of rot hit them in the face. The volume of the buzzing flies grew louder. Syd and Mark cautiously stepped inside. They quickly and methodically cleared the apartment for the presence of threats. In the small kitchen they found the source of the flies. On the counter sat a decomposing thing covered in maggots and flies. The single sink overflowed with dirty dishes sitting in fetid water. The kitchen garbage, also overflowing, teemed with flies.

Syd nodded toward the decomposing thing on the counter. "Chicken?"

"I think so."

They stepped out and closed the apartment door. Mark handed the landlord his card.

"If Mr. Henson comes back, or if anyone else tries to go in there, call us right away."

The landlord asked, "Is he okay?"

"We don't know," Mark said. "But he's not in there. We'll be back."

They knocked on some neighbours' doors trying to shake loose more information. No one had seen him lately. One of them said he thought Henson had a brother named Lucas living in St. Catharines. None of them had seen him with any women or male friends. None had seen a tow truck in the neighbourhood.

Once they were in the car Mark said, "We don't have enough for a search warrant."

"Nope."

"We saw him apparently tamper with one complainant's car. Two of the other missing women were at his workplace just before they disappeared."

"Sure. When the J.P. asks me what we're looking for I'll just say, 'goin' fishing Your Worship'. Besides, I didn't even see a computer in there, did you?"

Mark shot her a look. "I think he's our guy and he has an accomplice."

"I think you're right. You want to sit on the apartment?"

"Nah. He's not coming back."

"Want to drive out to St. Catharines?"

"Yeah."

He took the exit toward St. Catharines. She rolled down her window. All she could smell was the maggoty stink of Henson's apartment clinging to them both.

"If Danielle Sawyer doesn't identify anyone in the photo lineup, maybe she can sit with Pete and do a composite if that doesn't turn up anything," she said.

"I was thinking that, yeah."

The red brick apartment building on Geneva Street where Lucas Henson lived was easy to find. They took the stairs. A pungent cocktail of cooking smells filled the second floor corridor but it still didn't replace the maggoty rot smell stuck in the back of Syd's throat. Lucas didn't seem surprised when Syd and Mark identified themselves and said they were interested in speaking with Mitchell.

"I knew sooner or later someone would come," he said, holding the door open only a crack.

"What makes you say that?" Mark asked.

"Because I know my brother. He's slick but not as smart as he wants everyone to think he is. I figure he's going to get into a fight or smack a woman and someone is going to call you guys."

"Has he smacked a woman in the past?" Mark asked.

"Girlfriends when we were teenagers. I don't know about now. But weak men don't change, do they. Our father was like that."

A woman laden with grocery bags walked down the hall. She stared at them.

"Would you mind if we came in?" Syd asked.

Lucas glanced over his shoulder. It set them on edge.

"Umm…" He glanced over his shoulder again.

"If you've got drugs or something in there we don't care," Syd said. "We're not here for you."

"Oh. Oh, no, there's nothing like that." He pulled open the door and let them in.

A woman and a little girl, maybe three years old, sat at the glass coffee table colouring. The woman looked at Syd and Mark. She picked up the little girl and scooped up some crayons and the colouring book.

"We'll go in the other room," she said.

The little girl's big brown eyes looked at Syd over her mother's shoulder. The girl smiled and said, "Hi, lady."

Syd smiled and waved at the child.

Mark's eyes darted around the room. Lucas invited them to sit down.

"It's okay," Syd said. "We won't be here that long."

"When was the last time you spoke with your brother?" Mark asked.

"Has to be more than two years ago. We don't have a good relationship."

"Are you friends on social media? Have mutual friends?" Syd asked.

"No."

"How about other family members? Is there someone he would go to for help?" Mark asked.

"It's just the two of us. Our parents died in a fire when I was twelve and he was nine. They think Mitch started the fire. We went to foster care after that. I got a good home. He didn't. He was never able to get close to anyone."

"Sounds rough," Syd said.

He shrugged. "I'm doing okay. I feel bad for him but, well, I have a family to protect."

Mark nodded. "Thanks a lot for talking to us. I hate to ask, but there's one more thing. Just so we can dot our i's and cross our t's, will you let us have a look around the apartment to make sure he's not here?"

Lucas nodded. "Yeah, okay."

Syd and Mark looked through the apartment. There was no sign of Henson having been there.

Mark gave Lucas his card. "If you hear from your brother or if there's anything else you think might help us, give us a call."

"What did he do?" Lucas asked.

"We just want to talk to him," Mark said.

They left and got back in the car.

"All that way for nothing," Mark said.

"I don't know," she said. "We eliminated a possibility and gained some insight into who he is."

"Yeah, you're right. Let's go home. We'll get back at it tomorrow," he said.

"You want to come over for a movie?" she asked.

"Can't tonight. I have a date at eight."

"Eight? You're not going to make it on time. What is her name?"

"Jolene."

"Internet?"

"Yeah. She seems nice. We'll see. I'll come over tomorrow night."

"Can't tomorrow night," she said.

"What, you have a date with a textbook?"

"No." She turned her head to look at him. He glanced away from the road for a second to look at her.

"Then what?"

"You can't tell a living soul."

"Branson," he said. "I'm right."

"You are."

"It was only a matter of time. The two of you are like dynamite together.

"That's what I'm afraid of," she said.

"Ha. I got you to admit it."

\*\*\*

Syd and Radar ran down Liza's street. A black Mercedes drove past them. She turned to get a look at the plate, but it turned a corner before she could catch it. She knew Branson's plate number. It was a habit of hers to look at license plates and, with her memory for written material, she memorized them all without trying. She remembered Branson sitting in that cozy corner with Liza at the restaurant. Was he visiting her? She turned, doubled back, and ran around the corner where the Mercedes had turned. It was gone. Should she ask Branson about it? No. There were other black Mercedes on the roads. And how would it go if she questioned him like that before their first official date? There was no commitment between Syd and Branson and her curiosity would come across as jealousy. She would have to let go of her need to know everything all of the time.

# Chapter Ten

Everyone showed up at dawn. Mark, Syd, Pete, and two uniforms would be searching the side of Highway 421 starting from the Outlet Mall and going in each direction on both sides of the highway. Each person was assigned a stretch of highway. It was mid-morning when Hammond, a rookie, got on the radio.

Hammond: There are bales of hay over here. They've broken down and it's covering the ditch.

Pete: You have to rake the hay, Hammond.

Hammond: Seriously?

Pete: Yes. I'll come and help you.

Hammond: Why are there bales of hay on the side of the road?

Syd: It's for the stray cows.

Hammond: Stray cows? On the highway? You're shitting me.

Syd: I shit you not. Sometimes cows wander away from their farms. The hay is there so they have something to eat until the farmers find them.

Pete: It's true. Do you see any cows?

A second later, Hammond: No. Will they charge at me for being at their hay pile?

Pete: Just keep your eyes peeled.

Hammond: Hurry up then.

Syd couldn't help but laugh. She imagined the looks on the other guys' faces and laughed out loud.

At noon, PC Tam got on the radio. "Got something. Cellphone."

Pete answered he was on his way. Syd wanted to go, too, but she stayed focussed on her stretch of highway. It wasn't five minutes later when her eyes followed a line of broken bits of plastic from the gravel shoulder to the ditch where a smashed cellphone lay partially covered by the grass. She stood still, scanning the area. She spotted a glint of gold from the gravel six feet in front of her. A section of the gravel ahead looked disturbed. That could be from anyone or anything, but she didn't want to disturb it. She took out her cellphone, took a picture of the glinting gold, then looked at the photo, zooming in. It looked like an earring. She reported the information over the radio. While she waited for Pete she took pictures of the grassy area beyond the ditch, and again zoomed in on each photograph. In one of the photos a black strap protruded from the grass between the trees. It looked like a purse strap. She waited until Forensics took over.

Both bug-bitten and parched, Mark and Syd headed back to the station.

"We're hot again," he said. "We're going to get them."

"Which drive-thru for lunch?" she asked.

"I don't care."

After grabbing some burgers and fries they parked in the side lot at the station and got out of the car, each holding a brown and red take out bag. They heard yelling.

"Mark Lewis! Mark Lewis!"

A brunette wearing a short skirt and red heels, carrying a red purse marched toward them.

Mark smiled at the woman and said, "Hi, Jolene."

"Don't hi Jolene me."

Mark looked confused.

Jolene said, "I came here to tell you I'm not speaking to you. You're a player, a rotten player. I'm never speaking to you again. You hear me?"

Mark, still wearing a look of bewilderment said, "Okay. I have no idea what I did, but I'm sorry."

"I told you don't speak to me. You led me on, you player. And who is *she*?" she said, pointing at Syd. "Never mind. Don't speak to me. I'm not speaking to you."

Jolene thwapped his shoulder with her purse. He held the take out bag up in front of his face as she thwapped him again, causing the bag to break and fries to tumble to the asphalt like hot pick-up sticks.

Syd stepped between them. "Hey!"

Jolene straightened her skirt and strutted away. Two cops heading into the station with brown paper cups walked past Mark and Syd.

"Spicy," one of them said.

"Shut up," Syd yelled at them.

The two kept walking, snickering to each other.

Syd picked Mark's still wrapped burger off the ground. "What was that about?"

"I don't know."

"C'mon. You must have some idea."

"We went for drinks last night, had fun, then went back to her place. She drank more there. She wanted to mess around. She was pretty drunk, so I said no."

Syd nodded.

"She got mad about it. I explained to her I couldn't be a hundred percent sure she was consenting, that I didn't want to take advantage of her state. She got offended by the way I explained it. Then she accused me of playing games. She was really drunk, Syd."

"She's wrong."

"Yeah. Do you think she'll come around?"

"No, man! Forget her. You dodged a bullet."

"Yeah, I guess you're right." They started walking again. "But she *is* spicy." He grinned.

\*\*\*

Syd gave Mark her fries. He devoured his burger as he went through their messages. Syd found Henson's social media and scanned through it.

"Look at this guy," she said. "He's all about himself, all about trying to look powerful."

Mark looked. Syd stole a fry from his desk. Henson's account was full of photos of himself in his security guard uniform and selfies at the gym.

114

"What gym is that?" she asked.

Mark squinted at the picture. "Can't tell."

"I bet Lundy would know," she said. "Maybe he could join that gym, make friends with Henson. "If Henson is still around. I'm thinkin' he's not. I'm gonna go talk to Lundy."

Mark took the photo to Lundy while Syd worked on compiling a list of his 'friends' from social media and then finding phone numbers and addresses for those people.

"Lundy recognized it," Mark said when he returned. "It was part of a chain of fitness centres that closed down four months ago. He sat down and scrolled more through Henson's social media. "Hey, check this out," he said. "The security uniform in this photograph is different from the security uniform for the mall."

"When was it posted?"

"A year ago," he said.

She frowned. He zoomed in on the patch on the uniform.

"First Security," he said.

"Well, maybe he made a friend while he worked there," she said as she googled it. "It's a small company."

"If they had a falling out maybe they'll be more willing to cooperate with us," he said.

She shrugged. "We can't sit around hoping for the BOLO to bring results."

Pete stuck his head in the door. "Hey, the cellphone we found near that earring belonged to Felicia Williams. The other one belonged to a guy, a Thomas Bright."

Syd sat up, thinking. She could see the name 'Thomas Bright' in black and white in her head. She closed her eyes and let it come to her. She could see the entire document. She opened her eyes. "Thomas Bright is Andrea Green's boyfriend. She's one of our missing. There was something wrong with her phone so she borrowed his on the day she disappeared."

Mark said, "So the guy smashes or tosses the phones on the side of the highway so we can't track where they are."

But only two of the phones pinged there. The other ones were elsewhere," Syd said.

Pete left. Mark pulled up the map showing the radius within which the phones pinged.

"We should ask for a geographical profile," she said.

"Yeah, I was thinking the same thing. I'll ask. We should go see Felicia Williams' mother."

"We should show her photos of the earring and purse, see if she can identify them. I'd like to talk to her before the press figures out what we were doing out on the side of the highway," she said.

They visited Felicia's mother. She confirmed the purse and the earring belonged to her daughter. As the realization of what that likely meant set upon her, she shook with grief.

You never get use to watching someone's heart shatter before your eyes. You never get use to watching the trauma irreparably tear them apart while you stand there helpless to change it. Mark and Syd walked back to the car, silent under the weight of it. It was always strange to hold two disparate sets of emotions, feeling the sombre ache for the family, and feeling fired up at having a lead to chase, a puzzle piece in place. Sometimes Syd dreamt about the desperate pleading eyes of family members, pleading to bring their loved ones home, pleading for answers, pleading for the answers to be wrong, pleading for justice that would never come because their loved one could never be brought back to life.

They went straight from the Williams' house to one of the addresses on Henson's Facebook friend list. It happened to be nearby. The man they spoke with said he actually didn't know Henson well. They'd gone to the same high school but never interacted even back then. They had similar conversations with other 'friends'.

They stopped by the office of the security company whose uniform Henson had worn in his photo posted a year ago. First Security operated out of a converted old wartime house in the north end of town. The only person there was a young woman behind a desk in a sparsely decorated front office. She didn't know Henson. The owner was away on vacation in Europe and wouldn't be back in the country for a few more days.

They sat in the car, silent for a moment.

"I'm out of addresses and phone numbers," she said.

"He has a hundred friends and nobody knows him," he said.

"We could try the gyms. He works out somewhere," she said.

"Maybe get his picture out on social media, say we think he's a witness to a crime and we need to talk to him," Mark said.

"Media is your bailiwick," she said. "Whatever you think. There's already a province wide BOLO."

"I hate those media decision meetings," he said. "They are as much about politics as anything else."

He started the car. "Danielle Sawyer is coming in tomorrow. Maybe she'll identify the tow truck driver. I think they're in it together."

"So what do you want to do?"

"Go back to the office. See if anything has come in for us. Then maybe call it a day. I'm so tired I can't think straight.

\*\*\*

*Why am I so nervous?* Syd thought. She didn't like this feeling. Her cellphone buzzed.

Mark. "I'm across the street. Can I come in?"

Syd texted back. "You're an idiot."

Mark: "Hey! Don't say that."

"Radar, go answer the door."

Radar bounded to the door and opened it. Seeing Mark coming up the walk, Radar bolted outside to greet him. Syd heard them come in as she futilely rummaged through the fridge for a pre-dinner snack.

"Why'd you call me an idiot?"

"Because you're asking permission to come in."

"I know you have a date. I didn't want to bother you."

"You're family." She walked to the dining room so she could see him. "Let's get something straight. You are always welcome in my house no matter what else is going on. No guy is going to mess up our friendship."

"I was just trying to be respectful," he said.

"I know, and I love you for it, brother. Any guy interested in me has to know what he's in for."

"Are you talking about me or Radar?" he asked, smiling. "I thought I'd hang out in the yard and play with Radar. I'll be gone before you get back home."

"That's perfect," she said.

"And you should start locking your front door. We still don't know whose shoeprints were outside your windows."

"Ah, it was probably someone casing the place and Radar scared him away."

Mark shook his head. Radar ran to the door. He opened it just as the doorbell rang.

"Radar, come," Syd called.

He ignored her. He stood in front of the open door barking at Branson. Mark stepped to the door, grabbed Radar's collar, and pulled him back.

Stunned, Branson said, "Hi."

Syd walked to the door. Branson looked at her quizzically. She smiled at him.

Mark said, "Have fun."

She and Branson got into his Mercedes.

"Does Mark live with you?" he asked.

"No. He's just there to hang out with Radar. It's not good to leave a dog alone so much."

They drove toward the restaurant in silence. It was an uncomfortable silence, awkward. *'Maybe this was a mistake'*, she thought. Branson pulled over.

"Something wrong?" she asked.

He looked at her. "Yes."

Her stomach knotted. She braced herself for whatever was coming.

"I feel uncharacteristically nervous," he said. "It's going to ruin our dinner."

"Oh. What do you want to do?"

"I want to get it over with," he said.

"Pardon?" She suddenly wanted to flee.

"I don't want to sit through dinner waiting, thinking about the first kiss. I want to just do it so I don't have to think about it," he said.

"Ohh, I see," she said. "Like now?"

"Yes."

"Okay."

He touched her cheek and leaned toward her. Their lips met. He was gentle and soft. It was electric heat and cool relief at the same time. He smiled.

"Better?" she asked.

"Yes." He pulled the car back onto the road, smiling.

He was right. The awkwardness and nervousness was gone. In spite of the lead up to their first kiss being nothing like the movies said it should be, it was still wonderful. They talked about everything under the sun, besides work.

He laughed easily. She liked that about him. After dinner he drove her home.

"Do you want to come in?" she asked.

"I do. Will Radar bite me?"

"No?" She said it like a question.

Radar settled after barking at Branson for a few minutes, but still made sure he stayed by Syd's side. On the dining room table sat two wine glasses beside a bottle of Shiraz with a note taped to it.

"Enjoy yourselves. Stay up late. Don't even think of coming to work early. Mark."

"He loves you," Branson said.

Syd smiled. "Clearly he likes you. Shall I open the wine?"

"I want to stay sober," he said, moving closer beside her.

Radar wedged his head between them. Branson touched Syd's arm. Radar jumped on him, knocking him away from her. Branson staggered back, eyes wide. Syd's heart sunk.

"I'm sorry. He's protecting me. It will take him a while to get use to you."

Branson took a big breath, then exhaled. Syd felt heat in her cheeks. *Maybe it's for the best,* she thought. *I'm not relationship material anyway, especially for a man like him. He would have high standards, high expectations I could never meet. And there's not a domestic bone in my body.*

Branson said, "Are you okay?"

"Yes. A little embarrassed," she said.

"I'll just have to make friends with the dog."

She gave him a half smile.

"Let me make dinner for you," he said.

"You cook?"

"I'm a good cook. I like it."

"Okay," she said, her normal smile returning.

He walked to the door.

"Soon," he said. He blew her a kiss and walked out.

She opened the wine, poured a glass, and took it to the coffee table. She plopped onto her new velvety navy couch. Aunt Mary had even sent contrasting canary yellow throw cushions. Radar found a bone and settled beside her.

# Chapter Eleven

She was speeding down a dark deserted street. The traffic lights ahead turned from yellow to red. She stepped on the brake but the car continued to race ahead. She pulled the emergency brake. It had no effect. The car flew through the red light. She saw flames up ahead and didn't want to go there. She wanted to steer away but there was nowhere else to go. She heard Radar barking in the distance. The barking grew louder, closer. She opened her eyes to see two brown doggie eyes staring back at her. He barked at her. She reached over the side of the bed and pet him. The first rays of dawn glowed through the thick white curtains.

She put Radar on his tie-out, then started the coffee maker. She heard a dog bark out front but didn't hear Radar bark in return like he always did. She opened the back door and looked outside to check on him. She didn't see him. She stepped outside. Radar was gone. A surge of panic burst up in her chest. She ran down the driveway, looking down the street in both directions. She spotted his wagging tail sticking out of a flower garden two doors down. Still wearing her cotton pajamas with prints of baby tigers all over them, she ran down the street barefoot.

"Radar, come."

He poked his head up out of the flowers and then turned around, crushing a row of impatiens under his big paws. He bolted from the flower bed and ran in circles on the neighbour's lawn before deciding to obey Syd's command. A two foot length of his tie-out dangled from his collar. She took him home and unclipped the broken tie-out.

She examined it. It had been cut. She examined the other end still in the yard. Radar didn't bite or break his tie-out cable. There was no doubt it had been cut. She remembered the shoeprints Pete had found around her house. She walked the perimeter of the house and property. She saw no new shoeprints, nothing disturbed, nothing breached. Who would cut his tie-out and why?

She went back inside. She fed him, showered, then played a training game with him. She took the broken tie-out to work with her.

Mark didn't look away from his computer screen as she walked in.

"I told you not to come in early," he said.

"Radar tried to protect me."

He looked away from his screen, putting his full attention on her. "No. How bad was it?"

"Considering it's Radar, not that bad."

"Blood?"

"No blood."

"Then it's fine," he said.

She dropped the length of cable onto his desk. "Somebody cut his tie-out between last night and this morning."

He picked it up. "You sure he didn't bite it or break it?"

"Look at it. There are no teeth marks on the plastic coating. The cable inside is cut clean."

He looked closely at it, furrowing his brow. "That *is* a cut. You want Pete to look at it?"

"Nah. I'm not even sure why I brought it in. It's bugging me."

"I'm calling Pete," he said, picking up the phone.

She shook her head, but it was too late. Mark was already asking Pete to come up. He hung up.

"Pete says to get our lazy butts down there if we want to talk to him."

He picked up the broken cable and walked out. She followed him down to Forensics. Mark explained his concern to Pete.

Pete looked at the cable. "I won't get anything from that."

"Cut marks?" Mark said.

Pete shrugged. "What am I comparing them to? I can check your windows for prints again, though, Syd. That serial rapist struck again, not far from your neighbourhood."

"What serial rapist?" she asked.

"Guy has been attacking women in their own beds while they're asleep. I'm surprised you don't know about it," Pete said.

Mark and Syd had been so busy they hadn't done their usual socializing, so hadn't heard anything.

Pete continued, "It's the same thing every time. No signs of forced entry, but somehow he gets in, attacks them while they're sleeping, uses something from the victim's own house as a ligature."

"Shit," Mark said.

"Yeah. Sex Assault is pretty concerned about him," Pete said.

"He's going to kill someone sooner or later," Syd said. "You have physical evidence?"

"Yeah. Guy wears gloves, so no prints. He uses condoms but must not realize he can leave DNA in other ways. We have fibers, hairs, and epithelials."

"That's great," she said.

"Except there's nothing in the databank to compare the DNA with. We'll get him, though. Just a matter of time," Pete said.

Mark turned to Syd. "Lock your damn door."

"What happened with Radar has nothing to do with this," she said.

"You don't know that," Mark said. "Maybe those shoeprints around your house were from him casing your place. He sees Radar going crazy and decides to go somewhere else. He comes back and cuts the tie-out hoping you'll lose the dog."

"I don't know," she said.

"Why does someone cut a dog's tie-out?" Mark asked.

"To get rid of the dog," Pete said.

Syd thought about it. A rapist coming to her place would be making a big mistake. What disconcerted her was the thought of harm coming to Radar. He didn't comprehend the danger of cars. He thought they were giant toys to lunge at and chase.

"Guess who the victim was last night," Pete said.

Syd and Mark looked at him, waiting for him to tell them.

"Liza."

"Liza? Our Liza from court?" Syd asked.

"One and the same," Pete said.

"Oh, no. How is she? Do you know?" she asked.

"Night shift had the call. Sounds like she was pretty messed up. Her sister came and got her this morning. I think she's going to stay there for a few days."

\*\*\*

Syd and Mark spent part of the morning making calls, trying to track down Henson. When they ran out of people to call, they turned their attention to the mall footage. Danielle Sawyer, their complainant who'd had the frightening encounter with the tow truck driver came in at noon. She looked carefully through the photos Mark had put together. She didn't identify anyone. Henson's face was in the line-up but there was not a flicker of recognition in Ms. Sawyer's eyes when she looked at it. Mark arranged for her to go to Forensics to get a composite done using their FACES program.

"Want to go back to Henson's place, see if he's been back?" Mark said.

"He won't be there," Syd said.

"We got nothin' else."

"Sure. We can pick up food on the way and eat it in the car," she said.

They sat in the car across the street from Henson's house eating subs on stale buns.

"You know," Syd said, "Henson is missing, too."

"Yeah. Maybe his accomplice did something to him."

"It did look like he left in a hurry." She pulled a string of wilted lettuce out of her sub and put it on the paper wrapping in her lap. "Looked like he was in the middle of prepping a chicken for dinner and suddenly left."

"Could be it's not us he's running from," he said.

"It's us."

"But we don't know that, right? We have a couple of things going on here. He's a suspect and he's missing."

"No one has reported him missing," she said. "We're reaching."

Mark called Henson's brother who agreed that, yes, his brother is missing and he's concerned about his safety and would like the police to look for him.

Mark turned to Syd. "Now he's officially missing. Between those two things we've got to have enough to at least get his phone and bank records."

"Theoretically. What would you put on the Information?"

He wiped his mouth with the napkin, staring straight ahead. "The truth. I think I could write it up."

"Well, you do write decent reports." She smiled.

"Excellent reports," he said, grinning. He nodded, thinking. "Yeah, I think I could get enough on the Information."

"You're swearing it then," she said. "And it depends on which J.P. you get."

"Okay. Let's knock on doors first, since we're here. Dot the i's."

"And cross the t's," she said. "Okay."

On speaking to neighbours and the landlord, and finding Henson's pile of mail untouched, they found exactly what they expected, which was nothing. They went back to the station. Mark did the paperwork. He took the Information over to the courthouse while Syd stayed behind going through surveillance footage. She checked her phone, hoping to see something from Branson. There was nothing.

Mark phoned her from his car.

"Did you get it?" she asked.

"If you mean shit, then yeah. The J.P. said we were working the system. You want froofie coffee?" he asked.

"Vanilla."

"Okay." He hung up without saying goodbye.

\*\*\*

129

Syd and Radar jogged past Liza's house. She noticed a bit of yellow police tape caught around the stem of a pink petunia in Liza's garden. Other than that, the house looked like it always did, no neon sign telling of the horrendous crime that occurred there. The cute little house with its enclosed veranda and perfectly planted pink petunias in the front garden was not what you'd imagine as the scene of a soul destroying crime. It was another place on Syd's mental list. Places around the city weren't mere places like most people perceived them. They weren't just the mall, the school, a middle class neighbourhood; they were an abduction, a rape, a sudden death. Even on days off you couldn't escape the darkness. You know it's everywhere. You can't forget even if you try – especially if you try.

Syd went home, showered, and took her already opened bottle of wine to her backyard, the bottle meant for her and Branson that she would drink alone. She checked her phone again, hoping for a text from Branson. Nothing. She fired up the barbeque thinking of him. Fire.

She had the same thing every Friday night: steak, potato, and asparagus. She ate it outside in her backyard. Her sorry looking weedy gardens cried out to be tended to. She walked to the garage to get her gardening tools. She stood there staring at them, thinking about Liza happily planting her petunias, Liza putting care into her home, her sanctuary, only for it to be violated, smashed, by someone who cared nothing about her humanity. Syd shook her head, turned, and walked out of the garage. She closed the door.

Mark stopped by on Saturday afternoon. He informed her they wouldn't be having their usual Saturday movie night.

"I have a date," he said.

"Ooh, on a Saturday. You must like her."

He smiled. "Saw her last night."

She grinned. "Two nights in a row, ooooh."

He shrugged, grinning. "There was a spark."

"Fire?"

"Smouldering, like you said. I really like this one. We clicked."

"What's her name?"

"Amy. I'm taking her to that nice restaurant on Third."

She listened as he told her about Amy. He looked happy. She was happy for him and told him so as he was leaving.

At ten o'clock that night she decided she had to do something with her phone. She'd been compulsively checking it, hoping for a text from Branson. She turned it off and threw it in the linen closet. She and Radar sat in her t.v. room upstairs watching movies. She fell asleep there.

\*\*\*

Syd was dreading it. She tried to get out of it, but she had to go. She had a meeting with Michael Cortez, the Crown whose office was directly across from Branson's. It was Wednesday afternoon and she'd still heard nothing from Branson. She didn't want to run into him. She opened the back door, listening for footsteps and voices. The stairwell was empty. She went up to the Crown's office hoping Branson was busy downstairs. Eleanor buzzed her in.

As Syd started down the hall toward Michael's office, Liza burst out of Branson's office. Athough Liza wore sunglasses, Syd could see her face was wet with tears, red with emotion. Liza wore a pink silk scarf around her neck. Syd guessed it was to hide the ligature marks. Liza flew past her and fled out the door. Syd hurried to Michael's office and closed his door behind her. They had their meeting which was about an older case going to trial, neither saying a word about what they'd just witnessed.

She got back to her office to find Mark staring, zombie-like, at his computer.

"You look like the undead," she said.

He rubbed his eyes. "We're getting nowhere."

"Do we have a composite of the tow-truck driver?"

He picked up a black and white computer generated photo printout off his desk and handed it to her. The likeness was of a bald Caucasian man with a thick neck, high cheekbones, and small eyes.

"Is it public yet?" she asked.

"They did a media release but that's all. They didn't connect it to our missing women," he said.

"Tips?"

"Guy called in saying he saw bright lights in the sky the night before Kaylee disappeared. He's sure it was aliens and that's what happened to all of the women."

"You going out with Amy tonight?"

He brightened. "Yeah."

"Maybe we should go home at a reasonable hour for a change," she said.

He smiled. "Now there's an idea. I think I'll have a cup of tea with Mrs. Linton before my date."

"I think I'll take Radar to the beach," she said. "Watch the sunset and then go for a late run."

\*\*\*

Syd left her phone at home. She and Radar had fun at the beach. It felt good to get out into the fresh air, to be amongst the living. It felt like walking out of a dungeon. She took Radar for a night run, avoiding Liza's street, but still running in the neighbourhood. She found herself looking around for the serial rapist despite knowing she wouldn't be successful. She didn't know what he looked like. He could be anyone.

She got ready for bed at eleven, a nice, normal hour. She would finally get a real night's sleep. She turned on her phone to see how much battery life was left. She had a notification. She opened it. It was a text from Branson.

"Where r u?"

The text had been sent at nine o'clock. Dammit. The one time I go anywhere is when he finally decides to text.

# Chapter Twelve

She texted Branson in the morning. *"Sorry. Phone was off."*

She waited a few minutes for a return text that didn't come. She went to work.

Mark quietly hummed a tune as he walked through the door of their office.

"You're happy," she said.

He smiled. "Amazing what a little fun and a decent sleep will do. Anything come in?"

"Henson's old employer is back from his vacation. He says we can come in any time this morning. Want to go talk to him?" she asked.

"We got nothing else," he said.

The receptionist at First Security led them into Al Weeks' office. Al, a stocky man with a well-groomed grey goatee, stood and offered his thick hand in greeting.

"What can I do for Major Crime?" he asked as he sat behind his solid but well distressed wood desk.

"We're looking for Mitchell Henson," Syd said.

She and Mark sat in the hard fake wood chairs on the other side of Al's desk.

"Last I heard from him was a year ago when he came to pick up his final paycheque."

"Do you know where he was going?" she asked.

"Nope. Didn't ask."

"Was he friends with any of the other employees?" she asked.

"No. Nobody liked him. To be honest, I was glad he left."

"Why is that?" she asked.

"There was something wrong with him. He made people, especially women, feel uncomfortable. But no one could come up with a solid reason for a complaint. He showed up on time and did his job, so I couldn't just fire him."

"What kind of words did people use to describe his behaviours when they told you he made them feel uncomfortable?" she asked.

"Creepy. Almost everyone said creepy. And 'bad vibe', 'off', 'wrong in the head'."

"What was your gut feeling?" she asked.

"If I found out he was a serial killer I wouldn't be surprised. Is he? A serial killer?"

"Not that we know of," Mark said. "We want to talk to him about a case."

Syd asked, "Can you describe a behaviour that gave you that gut feeling?"

"He needed to be in control. The security business if full of people like that but this was different. He'd push to get his way. He wanted to be my second in command here.

I appreciate ambitious people, but the way he did it, it was by being pushy, not by doing a good job. And the way he looked at women, like he was looking at dinner. I didn't trust him. But, like I said, he didn't do anything I could fire him for."

"Where was he living when he worked here?" Mark asked.

"Strathcona. Near that burrito place."

"What reason did he give for leaving?" Syd asked.

"He didn't. But I think it was his girlfriend."

"Tell us about that," she said.

"He'd started to unravel. Still came in on time, did the job, but he looked tired all the time and had a shorter fuse. Her disappearance really got to him."

Mark looked up from his note-taking. "Disappearance?"

"Yeah. She went missing."

"What's her name?" Syd asked.

"Wendy Slogget. I called her 'slugger' once and he got hot about it, so I never forgot after that. I've printed off his work records and resume for you. You can have everything I've got."

He picked up a blue file folder from the corner of his desk and slid it across to them. Mark and Syd leaned forward and leafed through it.

"Was Ms. Slogget ever found?" Mark asked.

Al shrugged. "Don't know."

"Has he been in contact with any of the other employees?" Mark asked.

"No. Like I said, no one liked him."

"Can you ask around, see if anyone has any information that might shed light on where he might be, where he likes to hang out, who his friends were?" Mark asked.

"I don't think they'll know. Henson kept to himself. But, sure, I'll ask around."

Syd gave him her card.

"Thanks for your help," Mark said. "If there's anything else you can think of, give us a call."

"You're welcome. I hope you find what you're looking for." Al stood and walked them out.

When the door closed behind them, Mark said, "Holy shit."

Syd said, "The look on your face when he said the girlfriend went missing. I almost asked him for a ladder."

"A ladder? What?"

"To climb up and pull your eyebrows down off the ceiling." She smiled.

"Well, yeah, of course."

From the car they looked for information on Wendy Slogget. There were no reports of her ever having been missing but there was a report filed by her in respect to criminal harassment.

"See," Mark said. "A shitty report. This should have come up when we looked in the system for Henson but it didn't because his name isn't in the report. Who writes a report on harassment and doesn't even include the guy's name?"

"Someone who writes a shitty report? Maybe the officer didn't want to hurt Henson's work prospects?"

Mark shook his head. "Let's go to her last known address."

Syd agreed and they drove over.

The woman who answered the door of the two-storey family home said she'd moved in ten months ago and she didn't know the previous owners. Mark and Syd knocked on neighbours doors, looking for someone who knew the Sloggets.

Two houses down a red-headed woman in her late fifties answered the door. She said, "Yes, I knew them."

"Are you still in touch?" Mark asked.

She squinted her eyes and pursed her lips.

"We're looking for Wendy Slogget. She's not in trouble," Syd said. "We want to ask her about her boyfriend, Mitchell Henson."

The woman's eyes widened for a second before returning to normal. She pushed the screen door open. "You'd better come in."

They stepped inside. She led them to her spotless kitchen where they made their introductions and sat at the table covered by a white tablecloth with a festoon of yellow flowers printed along the edges. The woman's name was Kate Ogilvie.

"Mitchell Henson is not Wendy's boyfriend, not any more. He's the reason the Sloggets moved away," Kate said.

"You have our full attention," Mark said.

"Would you like a cup of tea?"

"No thanks," Syd said.

Kate continued. "Mitch and Wendy dated for about five months. Wendy hadn't dated much before that so she was easily enchanted by Mitch. He was a couple of years older, had a job and a car. Wendy really liked him. Anne, her mother, liked him too in the beginning."

"But that changed?" Mark asked.

"Yes. Mitch started complaining when Wendy spent time with her friends. He wanted her to spend all of her time with him. Anne thought this was unhealthy. She encouraged Wendy to keep her friends. Mitch put so much pressure on her to leave her friends behind, Wendy promised she'd spend less time with them."

"Pressure how?" Syd asked.

"Oh, he complained, then threatened to break up with her if she didn't do as he asked. She was so enthralled by him she did what he wanted. Then he would check her phone, demand she account for every phone call."

"How do you know this?" Mark asked.

"Anne told me. She was over her for tea all the time, talking about it, worried. She finally told Wendy she wasn't allowed to see Mitch any more. That backfired, though. Wendy was an adult and wasn't going to stand for her mother telling her what to do. It made Wendy want to be with him even more. Wendy and Anne got into screaming matches over it. I could hear them all the way from here. Anne told her, 'my house, my rules', so even though they had those arguments, Wendy wasn't seeing

Mitch, but I would see him in the neighbourhood all the time, driving by, hanging around across the street. And there kept being little fires at the Slogget house."

"Fires?" Mark said.

"One time on garbage night their recycle bin was on fire on the sidewalk. Another time their garbage bins attached to the side of the house caught fire."

"Anyone in the house smoke?" Mark asked.

"No. But Mitch did."

"Was that all of the fires? Just the two?" Syd asked.

"No. There was another one. Half of their front porch went up in flames."

"Did the fire department come for any of these fires?" Syd asked.

"Just the porch one. They said it was caused by careless smoking, but, like I told you, they didn't smoke. They had to tear down the porch. That's why the porch over there is cement now."

"Did anyone question Mitch about it?" Mark asked.

"No, but Anne was convinced it was him. Wendy wouldn't believe it. She didn't want Anne saying anything to the police because it might hurt Mitch's career in security to have questions like that on his record. Wendy thought the accusations were unfair, that Mitch was misunderstood. She threatened Anne that she would move out and move in with Mitch if Anne wasn't going to let her see him. She was old enough, so there would be nothing Anne could do. Anne was afraid Wendy would make good on her threat and then she wouldn't be able to protect her daughter at all. She was beside herself with worry. She finally agreed to let Wendy see him but only at the house. Once they were back together, no more fires."

"Did Wendy go missing at some point?" Mark asked.

"No. But Anne told Mitch Wendy ran away. It was true in a sense but it was Mitch who Wendy was running from."

"How did that come about?" Syd asked.

"He got mean. It started with him criticizing her clothes and make-up. He criticized her weight. Poor girl believed him and went on a diet. She had a beautiful figure, no reason to diet. Then he started calling her names, demeaning her. She finally broke up with him when he twisted her arm behind her back."

"And did he go away?" Syd asked, knowing the answer, but wanting Kate to tell her.

"No. He got worse. Showing up all the time, following her around when she was out with her friends. He even showed up at their church and tried to ingratiate himself with the people there. Anne and Wendy called the police. Anne wanted him charged but the police said he had a right to go to the mall or stand on a public sidewalk or go to church. So it continued. The final straw was the dog."

"Dog?" Mark asked.

"They had this little dog. One of those things with the long hair and flat face. Really cute. Anyway, one day Anne goes outside to bring the dog in from the backyard and he's not out there. She goes around front to look for him and the poor thing is laying on the front lawn with his head bashed in."

"Did she report that to anyone?" Mark asked.

"No. After the police didn't do anything about Mitch the first time, Anne and Wendy figured there was no point in calling them. There was no proof Mitchell had done it. But that's when Anne sent Wendy away to live with her aunt in Niagara Falls."

"Wendy's aunt or Anne's aunt?" Mark asked.

"Anne's sister," Kate said. "Anne told Mitch Wendy had run away. He kept hanging around, watching. Anne sold the house and moved to Niagara Falls herself shortly after that."

"Do you have Anne's address or phone number?" Syd asked.

"Yes." Kate picked up her phone from the table, scrolled through it, and read out Anne's number.

Syd dialled the number. Anne answered. Syd identified herself, explained they were looking for Henson, and asked if they could come and talk to her." Anne agreed and gave Syd the address. They thanked Kate. Mark left his card with her. They got in the car and headed to Niagara Falls.

"We're hot again," Mark said.

"Warm maybe," Syd answered.

"We're gonna get him," he said.

Anne lived alone in a well-kept house on Second Avenue, a wide old street lined with big old maple trees and where everyone had flower gardens. She told them the same story Kate had told.

"So you don't know where he is?" Anne asked them, worry in her eyes.

"Not yet," Mark said.

"Who did he hang out with?" Syd asked.

Anne shook her head. "I don't think he had friends. He only ever went to work and our house."

"How did Wendy and Mitch meet?" she asked.

"He was a security guard at the strip mall near our house. There's an ice cream shop there Wendy and her friends liked to go to. They met there."

"Where is Wendy living now?" Syd asked.

"She has her own apartment on Morrison, right across from the police station. It's not far from here by car."

"Does Mitch know where she is or where you are?" Syd asked.

"God, I hope not. Me and my daughters all have unlisted numbers. We moved away to get away from him."

"Do you think Wendy would talk to us?" Mark asked.

"Oh, I'm sure she will. I know she's working today. She won't be home until after six. I can call her and tell her you're coming."

"Thank you," Mark said.

He left his card with her and they left.

"We have an hour to kill," Syd said. "Want to find food?"

"Yeah, and caffeine."

They drove around and found a restaurant on Victoria, a two minute drive from Wendy's address. The place was old, with red stools at the counter, glass cabinets full of pies, and red vinyl padded booths along the wall. They slid into a booth.

"Hey, look at this," Syd said, pointing to a mini jukebox selector attached to the wall. "Only a nickel. Does anyone carry change any more?"

"Probably been here since 1960," he said.

She flipped through the selection of songs. "They haven't changed the music selection since then, either."

"I hope she knows the name of even one of his friends," Mark said.

"Why did Ecklund argue against a press conference, against getting Henson's photo circulated more widely?"

"Because he's Ecklund."

The waitress plopped two plastic covered menus on the table and walked away. Mark picked one up and perused it.

"They have all day breakfast," he said.

She looked. "They have onion rings."

The waitress came back with scratched glass tumblers full of water and took their order. Syd ordered the burger and rings. Mark ordered the hungry man breakfast.

When the waitress walked out of earshot Mark said, "If Wendy agrees, we could still charge Henson with the harassment and the assault on her and get an arrest warrant. As it is, even if we find him we have nothing to keep him on."

She shrugged. "Bet she won't want to. And we still have to find him."

"You think he might come here? Look for her?"

"Maybe he never stopped looking for her. Something made him leave in a hurry," she said.

"Maybe all the media coverage about Kaylee spooked him. Or he had a falling out with his accomplice."

"Or something else entirely that we don't know about yet."

The waitress put their coffee on the table.

"He's going to need money," Syd said.

"Between the time he quit his job at First Security and the time he got the job at the mall, what did he do for money?" Mark said.

"I wish we could get at those bank records." She sipped her coffee. "Wonder if he has picked up his final paycheque from his mall job."

"Probably direct deposit," he said.

"If we could get them to manually issue a cheque he would call them looking for his money. We could be waiting for him when he goes to pick it up," she said.

"Worth a try." He pulled his notebook from his pocket. "Here's the number."

She looked at it and let it deposit itself into her memory. "I'm going step outside and call them right now."

The air felt hot and dry in contrast to the cold air conditioning of the restaurant and the late afternoon sun blazed down unmitigated by any breeze. The squat buildings, devoid of awnings or overhangs, offered no shade, nor was there a single tree to offer respite. Maybe that's why there were no pedestrians; a landscape of concrete, asphalt, and brick, unfriendly to sentient creatures, was populated by moving cars taking their human occupants somewhere else. Syd stood roasting, breathing the smell of hot asphalt and thick car exhaust as she dialled the number and listened to the recording that informed her that the office would be closed until 8 a.m. When she stepped back into the cold shelter of the restaurant their food was already on the table. She sat and bit into her burger, suddenly realizing how hungry she was. Mark looked at her with the question on his face. She shook her head and shoved a greasy onion ring into her mouth.

"What if we're looking at this all wrong?" she said. "What if Henson has nothing to do with Kaylee's case?"

"You think we're tunnel-visioned?"

"Not really. But then again, we might not know it if we were."

"Okay. Let's consider that. We do have to dot our i's," he said, dunking his well buttered toast into the runny egg yolk on his plate.

"And cross our t's," she said.

They discussed gaps in their knowledge and possibilities of other scenarios and suspects until it was time to go.

They walked up the creaky painted wood stairs to Wendy's apartment on the second floor of the old house across from the Niagara Regional Police station. They heard the clicking and sliding of several locks. Wendy opened the door. The petite brunette invited them in. Mark and Syd shot each other a look. Wendy looked like Kaylee Anderson. They sat on a loveseat in her small, sparsely decorated living room. Wendy sat curled up in the corner of a plush chair that didn't match the loveseat, hugging her knees to her chest.

"Is he here?" Wendy asked.

"We don't have reason to believe that," Mark said.

Wendy exhaled audibly and relaxed the stranglehold on her knees.

"Back in November a friend of mine slipped and told him we moved to Niagara Falls. I've been scared ever since," she said.

"Have you or your friends or family seen him or heard from him?" Syd asked.

Wendy shook her head.

Mark said, "We talked to your mom. She didn't mention your friend's slip-up."

"I didn't tell her," Wendy said. "I don't want her to be worried."

"Does your landlord live downstairs?" Syd asked.

"No. They live in Toronto. Other tenants live downstairs."

"You could show them a picture of Mitch and tell them to call police if they see him in the neighbourhood," Syd said.

"I threw away all my pictures of him. The police won't do anything anyway."

"There's already a harassment report on file. And now we're interested in him. The police will do something this time." Syd unzipped her binder and pulled out a sheet with Henson's picture on it. She handed it to Wendy. Wendy looked at it and put it face down on the coffee table.

"Okay," she said.

The rest of the interview revealed nothing new and Wendy was wholly uninterested in pursuing charges for the previous incidents. She wanted to get on with her life without the intrusion of anything having to do with Mitchell Henson.

Standing outside, Mark said, "Police station is right there. Wanna go tell them we're here?"

"Sure. I can use their washroom before the trip home," she said.

They walked across the street to the station. They introduced themselves. Syd went to use the washroom, leaving her binder with Mark. She returned to find him laughing with the sergeant.

Before they left the sergeant said, "We'll post that photo on the board there," indicating to the bulletin board covered in wanted posters on the wall in the foyer.

They traipsed into their own office just before 10 P.M. Mark checked messages while Syd took her personal phone from the desk drawer and turned it on. There were two texts from Branson. Her heart jumped at the sight of the notifications.

The first text, sent at 1P.M. said, *"Dinner tomorrow?"*

The second, sent at 8:10 P.M. said, *"Where r u?"*

She texted back. "Yes to dinner. On my way home from work now."

# Chapter Thirteen

By 8a.m. Syd was on her fourth cup of coffee and had checked her phone as many times. She tossed the phone in her desk drawer and called Henson's mall employer from the land line. They hadn't yet deposited his final pay but they refused to issue a manual cheque.

At two o'clock Mark said, "If you're going to check your phone constantly, just leave it on and put it on the desk."

"I'm not checking that much."

"You are."

She handed him the phone. "Put it in your drawer."

He did. "This is not like you, Syd."

He was right. This wasn't like her. Branson had effectively hooked into her in a way no one else ever had. She liked his intelligence and his compassion for people, the way he fought for victims in court. Like any sane breathing woman she found him attractive, but the hook wasn't physical, although his piercing and haunted eyes did play a part. Those eyes could look straight into her soul yet keep the secrets of the man who beheld her psychic nakedness. There was a vulnerability behind those haunted eyes, a mystery in need of unravelling, beckoning her, almost daring her, the mystery unravelling the detective.

The workday was one of dead ends and tying up loose ends on other cases. At two-thirty, Syd's phone buzzed inside Mark's desk drawer. He grinned. Mischief danced in his eyes.

"Just give it to me," she said.

He opened the drawer and picked up her phone. She shot him a look that said, 'don't you dare'. He handed the phone to her.

It was Branson. "Great. Your place."

She responded, *"What time?"*

\*\*\*

Still full of energy when she got home, she considered taking Radar for a run. Branson hadn't responded to her text to give her a time. She figured most people have dinner at five or six. If she ran Radar she wouldn't have time to shower by then. Then she realized her assumption that they'd have take-out was an assumption. What if he expected her to cook something? She looked in her fridge. Condiments, a mushy tomato, a soggy half-eaten falafel sandwich, and a jar of pickles was all that stared blankly back at her. Branson would have to be satisfied with take-out and red wine.

She showered and put on decent clothes, foregoing her usual track pants and tee. There was nothing to do while she waited. Her books had been ruined by the fire and water and if she sat upstairs watching t.v. she wouldn't hear the door. She thought about tending to her sad garden but she would get filthy. She settled on playing training games with Radar. It would be good to get him mentally tired. When, by seven-thirty Branson hadn't shown up she checked her phone. No texts. She felt hungry and irritated. Already dirty and sweaty anyway from playing with Radar she gave up on waiting and changed into her track pants. At seven-forty-five she ordered a pizza and started on the yard work, figuring she'd work until the pizza arrived, and get some more done afterward before the sun set. Branson hadn't responded. He probably wasn't coming. She left the back gate open and put Radar on his tie-out. He would alert her when the pizza guy pulled in.

She was well covered with dirt when Radar barked at eight-fifteen. She walked through the back gate expecting pizza. Branson's Mercedes was in the driveway. He stepped out of the car and smiled at her. The irritation she'd felt disappeared, mostly.

With Radar still barking at him, Branson walked to his trunk and pulled out a shopping bag with "Everything Pets" written across it.

"I stopped and bought Radar a toy," he said. "I thought we could be friends."

What was left of her irritation quickly melted away.

"That's great," she said, walking down the driveway. "Go ahead and give it to him."

He pulled the toy from the bag, a big blue plush bear with long floppy arms that Syd knew wouldn't last the night. Radar stood in the driveway as far as the tie-out cable would let him go, watching Branson and the toy with interest. When Branson tried to approach, Radar barked and lunged. Branson glanced at Syd, a look of uncertainty on his face. She made Radar sit and wait. Branson approached slowly, holding the toy, Radar eyeballing him. As soon as he could, Radar snatched the toy and ran to the backyard with it.

"He's tough," Branson said.

"Believe it or not, you made progress."

He went back to the trunk and lifted out two bags of groceries.

He smiled at her. "I need directions to your kitchen."

She led him inside. As he unloaded groceries she said, "What do you want me to do?"

"Nothing. I'm cooking. Did you forget we had a date?"

She felt suddenly embarrassed.

"I'm going to run upstairs and change. Be right back."

While she got herself cleaned up she chided herself. Of course he is this late. He had to work, go home, and go shopping at two different places. By the time she returned to the kitchen he already had a salad made and two chicken breasts sat soaking in a marinade. The pizza had arrived and sat on the counter beside the microwave. *Now for sure he's going to think I forgot our date,* she thought. She decided to not mention anything about the pizza.

She stood beside him. "Wow, if you hang around you'll be good for my waistline."

He slid his hand across her back and around her waist. "You have no problems in that department."

He turned to her and kissed her. It was a long kiss, one she might have wished would go on forever except for the fact she couldn't breathe. He stroked her cheek and looked into her eyes with those stunning eyes of his. She stood frozen and melting, her feet fused to the kitchen floor by his radiance, his touch, his scent. Dark Apollo had her, a mere mortal, in his supernatural grasp.

Radar, still outside, barked once.

Branson said, "You said you have a barbeque?"

"Yes, and a fire pit. Out back."

He picked up the bowl of marinating chicken. "Lead the way."

"Hold the bowl over your head," she said.

"Why?"

"Trust me."

They walked out back. Radar hopped at the bowl of chicken hoping Branson would drop it. Branson turned on the gas and pressed the barbeque igniter.

"Oh, sorry," she said. "My igniter is broken. There should be a barbeque lighter there."

He clicked the igniter again, looking underneath at the mechanism. "I can fix that for you."

"You can?"

"I can pick up the part on the weekend," he said.

Dinner was fantastic. Radar was well-behaved for the most part, having no choice but to accept this strange new person in his space. He destroyed the plush toy.

"Sorry," she said as she picked bits of fluffy stuffing from the grass.

Branson insisted on doing the clean-up. Syd helped, unable to let him do it alone. Radar weaved between them. When they sat on the couch, Radar hopped up and parked himself between them. Whatever plans Syd and Branson might have had in mind, Radar had ideas of his own on how things would be in his house.

They stepped out onto the front porch to say goodnight. He pulled her into him.

"Look," he said, pointing to the front garden.

She turned. Fireflies danced throughout the garden.

"Perfect," she said.

He kissed her just long enough to create a minor electrical storm. He left.

She went to bed, fireflies dancing in her head.

\*\*\*

She woke to the sound of her phone buzzing. She looked at it, expecting it to be work. It was a text from Branson.

"I'm disappointed this morning."

She smiled and sat cross-legged under the first rays of the morning sun in her bed looking at her phone, Radar beside her, biting her hair. She texted back.

"Why?"

Branson: "I woke up without u beside me."

She sent him a smiley face. She hopped out of bed and jumped into the shower singing.

***

"Hot damn!" Mark said when he hung up the phone. "We're going to Rick's towing."

Syd stood and followed him out. They strode down the hall together.

"The composite?" she asked.

"Yeah, someone recognized it," he said.

She stopped at the elevator.

"Stairs," he said. "Quicker. Besides, it stinks. I think someone on night shift had sex in there."

"Again?" she said as they jogged down the stairs.

***

Outside of Rick's Towing they met with Jay, a lanky guy in blue jeans with a cigarette hanging out of his mouth.

"You recognized the guy?" Mark asked.

"Yeah."

"What's his name?"

"I don't know, but he tried to steal a job from me. It's the same guy," Jay said.

"Tell us about that," Syd said.

"I got dispatched to a job and when I got there this dude was already there hookin' up the customer's car. I told him it was my job and he said he was already takin' care of it. I was pissed, man. This business is already competitive without some fake trying to steal a job. Anyway, we started arguing. He turns to the customer and he asks her who she wants to tow her car. He smiles at her with them good teeth of his, not like me, see." He smiled to show them he was missing two front teeth. "And he's dressed all nice, too. Of course she tells him she wants him to take her. Well, I know there's somethin' wrong with the whole picture, ya' know. I mean the guy was wearing one of them golf shirts and there wasn't a speck of dirt or grease on him. And his hands were clean, man. He was no tow operator."

"So what happened?" Mark asked. "Did she go with him?"

"I go up to the lady and I tell her, look, somethin's not right here. Look at his truck. There's no name, no towing company on it, no phone number, nothing. Somethin's not right. So the lady changes her mind, says she'll come with me. Well, it nearly came to fists with the guy. I got in my truck and talked real loud to dispatch sayin' I needed the cops right away. That's when the guy decided to leave."

"When was this?" Syd asked.

"About three weeks ago. Dispatch can tell ya' exactly."

"Where?" she asked.

"Highway 421, just before the York Street exit."

"Did you happen to get a plate number?" Mark asked.

"Hell, yeah. I took a picture." He dropped his cigarette butt onto the cracked grey asphalt and stepped to his truck and retrieved his phone. He found the picture and held it out to them. It showed a white tow truck with a non-commercial Ontario plate.

"Can you text this to my cellphone?" Mark asked.

"Sure."

"And don't delete it from your phone," Mark said.

Mark gave him his cell number and Jay sent the picture. They spoke with Jay's dispatcher who gave them the date, the time the customer called, the time Jay called in, and the name, address, and phone number of the customer. Syd called the customer, a Dana Kristoff, and arranged for her to come to the station.

"We're hot," Mark said as Syd pulled onto the busy road.

"Yes, I think we might be," she said.

"We should hit all the tow companies again, bring the composite," he said. "Those guys would notice a tow truck with a plate like that."

"Most people sitting on the side of the road needing help might not notice that, or even notice the plate at all," she said.

"Probably not," he said while he ran the plate.

"I think it's time to press Ecklund to do more than a milquetoast media release. We have to warn people, especially women, not to take help from a tow truck if they didn't call for it," she said.

"Plate comes back attached to a green Honda Civic, stolen three years ago," Mark said.

"Let's hold back the plate and truck description from the public," she said. "Just put out the composite and say he might be driving a tow truck."

"Yeah. It's harder to change his appearance, easy to change what he's driving."

"A tow truck with a non-commercial plate will get the attention of any patrol who sees it," she said.

They didn't stop for lunch, didn't want to spend the time. They worked their way through towing companies. No one else reported a similar experience as Jay but they all agreed to circulate flyers amongst their drivers.

Mark conducted a video recorded interview with twenty-one-year-old Dana Kristoff. Syd watched.

Mark showed Ms. Kristoff the composite.

"That's him," she said. "He was nice. I was glad he got there so fast."

"How long was it between the time you called and the time he got there?"

"Just a minute or two. I figured they have trucks on the highway already and that's why he got there so fast. I didn't know he wasn't who my car club called until the other man showed up."

"Where were you coming from when your car broke down?"

"I was coming from my sister's place."

"And where is that?" he asked.

"Oh. She lives in Port Dalhousie."

"Did you take any detours or stop anywhere on the way?"

"Oh, yes. I stopped at that big mall."

Syd picked up the phone and arranged to secure the video from the mall for the date and time Dana Kristoff was there.

Jay the tow truck driver probably saved Dana's life. They didn't tell Dana how close she'd come to losing it.

# Chapter Fourteen

Syd walked into her house to find a pair of her good slacks crumped on the living room floor. She noticed a sock on the staircase. She followed the trail of evidence to her bedroom, the scene of Radar's crime. Every piece of clothing in her closet was on the floor or the bed. The clothes hamper lay on its side, empty. She felt guilt. Radar was alone too much. He was probably bored. She called Mark.

He answered said, "You miss me already?"

"Yes. I never see you any more. You've changed, Lewis."

He laughed. "What's up?"

"Do you think Mrs. Linton would take Radar on a regular basis if I paid her?"

"Probably. Might be a problem picking him up in the middle of the night when we're late."

"Will you ask her for me? He's alone too much."

"Yeah, sure."

She found her sweatpants and t-shirt in the wreckage of Radar's tornado, then picked up the rest of the clothes and tossed them all on the bed. She took Radar for a run. They ran past Liza's house. The house was quiet but Liza's car sat in the driveway. Weeds grew between the petunias, threatening to strangle them.

She ran back home, showered, and changed back into her work clothes. She took Radar to the pet store and let him pick out a new toy, knowing that wouldn't fix the problem or assuage her guilt.

When they got home Radar hopped out of the car with his new chew toy in his mouth. Instead of trotting toward the house like he usually did, he stood beside the car. He dropped his toy. He sniffed the air. He turned and ran toward the street dragging her behind him. She looked around trying to figure out what he was after. She saw Branson's car parked down the street. She let Radar lead the way to his car.

Branson rolled down the window and smiled at her.

"Hi. I was just about to text you," he said.

"Did we have a date?" she asked.

"No, but I was hoping we would," he said, giving her his pretending-to-be-innocent smile.

She laughed. "Okay. You might as well come in."

After stopping in the driveway so Radar could collect his toy, they went inside without any Radar related incidents. Syd put away his leash and Radar sprawled out across the living room floor to bite his toy.

"So that's the trick," Branson said. "Something to bite."

She smiled. "Have you eaten?"

"No."

"Pizza okay?"

"Sure."

She pulled out her phone and placed the order as she walked to the kitchen. She grabbed the open bottle of wine from the fridge, then reached into the cupboard for wine glasses. He caught her around the waist.

"Hey, slow down for a second," he said.

She turned to face him.

"Hi," he said.

"Hi," she said. She felt out of breath.

He kissed her, then wrapped his arms around her. Just as she was melting into him he stepped back.

"Um, were you getting dressed in your kitchen?" he asked.

"What?"

He pointed toward a spot on the floor in the corner. They were looking at her bra sitting on the kitchen floor.

"Oh, my god," she said, snatching it up off the floor.

She scrunched it up and held it against her chest, trying to hide it as if he hadn't already seen it. It wasn't even a pretty one. She didn't own any pretty ones.

"Radar," she said.

"Radar wears your bras?"

"No. He got into my clothes."

She ran up the stairs and tossed it on her bed with the rest of the clothes. The third stair from the top of the staircase creaked. Branson was at the top of the stairs. She hurried out of her room and shut the door behind her. He was in the hall.

"Is that your room?" he asked, coming closer.

"Yes, but it's a mess. Radar…."

He kissed her. Part of her wanted to stay there with him and part of her was screaming, *don't let him open that door!*

He opened the door.

She felt the heat in her face and wasn't sure whether it was a result of his kiss or her embarrassment. He stepped into the room and pulled her in after him.

"I'm sorry it's a …"

"Shh." He put his finger to her lips. He smiled. "It will be more fun."

He threw himself backward into the mountain of clothes. She climbed the mountain and put her arms around him. He looked into her eyes like he was searching for something.

He whispered, "Who are you?"

She knew in that moment she'd been captured completely. He kissed her. They were on fire together.

Then the earth shook. The earthquake's name was Radar. He'd jumped onto the bed to join in this strange game. Branson bolted upright. Syd tumbled onto the floor. Radar dug furiously into the clothes, burying his head, then emerged joyful and hopped around in circles on the bed.

"Sorry," she said as she pulled herself up from the floor.

He smiled weakly. "We should have closed the door."

"He can open doors," she said.

Radar leapt from the bed and tore down the stairs.

"Oh, no," she said. "The pizza guy."

She raced down the stairs but it was too late. Radar had the door open. He ran outside. She flew through the door in time to see the poor pizza guy running toward the sidewalk.

"Radar, down!" she yelled.

Radar dropped to his belly. The pizza guy turned around and faced Syd, ashen-faced and wide-eyed. Radar stayed put while Syd retrieved the pizza. Branson walked outside barefoot with his shirt hanging open and gave the guy a fifty dollar bill as an extra tip which was really compensation and a bribe.

After they'd eaten, Branson and Syd sat on the couch, Radar between them. Syd burst into laughter. Branson laughed at that. The rest of the evening went without incident. Radar let Branson play with him while Syd did laundry so she would have something to wear to work in the morning.

***

They got the call just before two. Mark put the call on speakerphone so Syd could hear. The caller was Paul Kroger, retired cop and head of security for the casino in Niagara Falls.

"I had a guy in for a job interview this morning. At lunch I went to the police station on Morrison to meet up with a buddy for a bite. I always look at their wanted posters while I'm there. I saw the picture of your guy, Henson. I was pretty sure it was the same guy, so I checked his resume when I got back to the office. It's Mitchell Henson."

"What's the address he has listed on the resume?" Mark asked.

"He says he's staying at the Yellow Rose Motel here until he can find an apartment."

Syd said, "Can you get a hold of him and tell him you want him to come in for a second interview? We're going to come down there, but if we miss him or he's not really at the Yellow Rose we can pick him up in your office."

"Can do," Kroger said. "What time do you want me to make the appointment for?"

"Nine," Mark said. "If he knows he has to be up early maybe he'll go back to the motel and not be prowling the city all night."

"Okay. I'll let you know," Kroger said.

Mark called Niagara Police to let them know what was going on and that he and Syd were coming. Syd called Mrs. Linton and told her she might not get home at a reasonable hour to pick up Radar.

They drove to Niagara Falls. They spoke to the manager at the one-star motel who told them Henson had left in the morning and hadn't returned yet. She hadn't seen anyone other than Henson coming or going from the room. Mark gave her his cellphone number and asked her to call him right away if she saw Henson or anyone else come back to the room. She promised she would. Mark and Syd parked at the restaurant directly across the street where they could watch the motel parking lot and Henson's unit. They waited.

Just after six, Mark said, "Hey. Is that him?"

She looked. There was Henson walking down the street on the same side as the restaurant. He cut across the restaurant parking lot toward the doors, walking right behind their car. Syd and Mark opened their car doors at the same time. They approached Henson, one on either side of him. Henson looked at each of them. His eyes darted around. He was clearly thinking about running.

"Don't bother," Mark said. "We want to talk to you."

"I haven't done anything," Henson said.

"We need you to come to the station and talk to us," Syd said.

"You're talking to me right here."

"We need to show you some things," Mark said. "We can't do that here."

"I know my rights," Henson said. "You can't force me to talk to you. I don't have to go with you when I'm not under arrest."

"Suit yourself," Syd said, reaching for her cuffs.

"Hey, you have no reason to arrest me."

"I'd say murder is a pretty good reason," she said.

Henson's face blanched. "Don't arrest me. I'll talk to you, but I have a job interview in the morning."

Syd stepped to the car and opened the back door.

Mark asked, "Do you have any weapons on you?"

"No," Henson said.

Mark checked. Henson slid into the back seat.

They were intentionally silent during the ride back.

About twenty minutes into the drive Henson said, "Can I get a lawyer?"

"You're not under arrest," Syd said. "What do you need a lawyer for?"

"You guys are making me nervous," Henson said.

"We haven't said a word to you," she said.

Mark said, "You can call a lawyer if that's what you want. I'll even lend you my cell phone and you can call right now. But you know what a lawyer is gonna tell you, right?"

Mark glanced in the rear-view mirror at Henson.

"A lawyer is going to tell you to remain silent. Then all this will take ages and you won't make it for your job interview."

"That's right," Syd said. "And it's not like on t.v. where the lawyer can sit in the interview with you anyway. The lawyer just tells you over the phone to remain silent and then goes back to his glass of expensive scotch and waits for you to go to jail and get him a Legal Aid Certificate."

They waited, letting Henson think about it.

Mark said, "So do you want my phone?"

"No," was all that Henson said.

# Chapter 15

They left him in interview one and walked down the hall.

Mark said, "If he doesn't talk we can't even get him on a mischief to property."

"He doesn't know that," she said. "And you're good at this."

"How do you want to do it?" he asked.

"I think you go in. He hates women. He won't respect me."

"Yeah, but he'll be afraid of you," he said.

She paced with her hands on her hips, thinking. "I say you try the buddy route first. I think he wants to be you. He might open up."

"I'm good with that," he said.

They wanted Henson to stew for a few more minutes. Syd watched him via the video feed while Mark gathered what he needed. Henson looked around the room nervously, arms crossed. He shifted in his chair, uncrossing his arms and leaning back. He rubbed his palms against his thighs. He sighed visibly. He shook out his arms and shoulders, then repositioned himself with his arms on the table. He crossed and uncrossed his legs. He rubbed his forehead with the heels of his hands.

Mark walked into the interview room and put a bottle of water on the table in front of Henson. Henson looked at it suspiciously. Mark sat across from him and started the interview the usual way, with the date, time, location, etcetera.

"Until recently you worked security at the Outlet Mall, right?"

"Yes."

"Was it a good job?"

"Yeah, I guess." Henson relaxed slightly.

"Pay's not great though, eh."

Henson smiled slightly.

"Guys in security are underappreciated," Mark said.

"Yeah."

"We're hoping you can help us. We think you might be a witness to something we're looking into."

Henson let out a long slow breath and uncrossed his arms.

"I want to know if you recognize this man," Mark said, sliding the composite across the table to Henson.

Henson leaned forward, peeking at the picture. He leaned back.

"No. I don't know him." Henson crossed his arms again.

"Maybe you've seen him hanging around the mall."

"No."

"Why did you quit your job at the mall?"

Henson shrugged. Mark looked at him, waiting. Henson shifted in his seat. Mark waited, holding his gaze on Henson.

"Sick of it." Henson shrugged again, looking down.

"We were at your place on Strathcona."

Henson raised his eyes.

"We were worried about you. You left in a hurry," Mark said.

"Well I'm fine."

"What made you leave in such a hurry?"

"I wasn't in a hurry."

Mark leaned forward. "Look, if this guy or someone else is a threat to you, we can help you. But you've got to tell us what's going on."

"Nobody's threatening me." Henson puffed out his chest. "There's nothing going on."

Mark leaned back. "You're telling me you were halfway through making a chicken dinner and decided to just walk out the door and move to another city for no reason?"

"What's this got to do with anything?" Henson said. "That's my business."

"I'm just trying to make sense of what I'm seeing," Mark said.

"What do you care?"

"I've got six missing women and I need to know what happened to them."

"I have nothing to do with missing women. I was at work. You can check."

"You were at work when all six women went missing?"

"Yes."

"That's interesting. I didn't say when they went missing."

"It was all over the news," Henson said.

"The dates and times they went missing weren't specified on the news," Mark said.

"The last one was."

"Right. The last one was, but not the rest of them."

"I'm always at work. I was probably at work." Henson uncapped the water bottle and took a swig.

"So why'd you run?"

"I didn't run. I told you, I was sick of everything."

"Listen man, I'm trying to help you here and you're making it difficult," Mark said.

"I don't need help."

"I thought a guy like you, career security, would be a friend to the police. I thought we were on the same side, man. I need to find this guy and I know you know who he is."

"I can't help you." Henson took another swig of water.

Mark put a photo of Danielle Sawyer in front of Henson. "Have you seen her?"

"No."

"She was at the mall when you were working. Are you sure?"

"I've never seen her."

"Then why did you mess with her car?"

"I didn't."

Mark slid a still shot from the mall surveillance in front of Henson. It showed Henson kneeling beside Sawyer's car. Henson looked at Mark and swallowed.

"I was picking up a nail. I noticed it by her tire and so I picked it up," Henson said.

"How stupid do you think I am?"

Mark waited. With the side of his index finger Henson wiped sweat from his upper lip.

"You put the nail in her tire. From the cameras at your work you saw her park her car and get out. You went out there and put the nail into her tire and then called your buddy, this guy." Mark pointed to the composite.

"I didn't do anything. I picked up a nail," Henson said.

Mark shook his head. "I thought you were one of us. I was wrong."

Letting Henson see the look of disgust on his face, Mark stood and walked out. He walked into where Syd was sitting.

"Good final remark to him," she said.

"People lie to me every damn day and I still hate it," Mark said.

"You gonna give him a chance to redeem himself?" she asked.

"Naw. Let him see he's not going to get chances to play games with us. You go in."

"Want to give him five to stew?" she asked.

"No. Keep the pressure on. Turn up the heat," he said.

She walked into the interview room and pulled the chair from across the table to the side of the table, closer to Henson. She slapped a picture of Kaylee Anderson onto the table in front of him. She sat down. He pushed the photo away. She pushed it back.

"Why are you showing me a picture of Kaylee?" he asked.

"Where is she?" Syd demanded.

Henson threw up his arms. "I don't know."

"Yes you do," she said.

"No. I don't."

She noticed his adam's apple go up and down as he tried to swallow his stress. She slapped down a photo of Felicia Williams.

"Where is she?" One by one, she laid out the photos of each of the missing women. "And her, and her, and her, and her."

He crossed his arms, hugging himself, and sat back in his chair, putting distance between himself and the pictures.

"Where are they?" She kept her voice stern and loud but made sure she didn't yell.

He lurched forward and with a sweep of his arm knocked the pictures away, scattering them. "I don't know!" he yelled.

She was unfazed.

She put the composite in front of him. "What's his name?"

"I don't know him." Henson picked up the water bottle and hugged it to his chest like a child with a teddy bear.

"Don't lie to me, Mitch. We know you know him. We know the two of you were in it together."

Henson shook his head. She picked up the photos of the missing women and placed them face up in front of him again.

She pointed to the photo of Heather Wakefield. "Look at her."

Henson glanced at the photo and looked away.

"Her name is Heather. She was a single mom. Her little boy is in foster care now. He's four years old. He's in the system now. He has nobody. Where is she?"

Henson closed his eyes and shook his head.

"Open your eyes, Mitch. Look at this young mom. That four-year-old boy *can't* close his eyes, can't escape what he's going through."

Henson kept his eyes closed.

"That four-year-old is braver than you, Mitch. You can't even open your eyes and look."

Henson opened his eyes and looked at Syd with rage and hatred and fear. She could smell the fear. She picked up the photo of Kaylee.

"Look at her. You know, she looks a lot like Wendy Slogget."

Henson's eyes widened. His breathing sped up so much he was almost panting.

"What," Syd said, "Did you think we didn't know? Do you think we'd track you down, drive all the way to Niagara on a hunch? We know more than you think, Mitch."

Henson stared at her like a scared rabbit.

She leaned forward and tapped the composite with her finger. "We know it was his idea."

The water bottle in Henson's hand made a crackling sound as he gripped it tighter.

"Mitch, you know he's going to point the finger at you. He's going to say it was all your idea, that you did it all and you forced him to go along with it."

Crackling of the water bottle.

"Really, I don't care," she said, leaning back, looking nonchalant. "We know what he's driving and every cop in the province is out looking for him right now while we sit here. They're going to catch him no matter what. Once they do, then we don't need to keep talking to you. He'll tell us it was all you and you go to jail and I really don't care."

Henson melted in his chair like a snowman in July.

"If you give us something now, then we can tell the judge you helped us. Now's the time, Mitch."

Henson trembled.

"Open your eyes, Mitch. He's gonna make you go down for him. Four-year-old boy without his mother. Where's his mother, Mitch?"

Henson put his arms across his stomach and bent forward. "I feel sick."

177

"You gonna puke?"

"I dunno. Maybe."

Syd left the room, grabbed an office garbage can, and returned, putting it in front of him. He leaned over the can. She picked up the photo of Heather and held it in front of his face.

"Where is she?"

He shook his head.

"Is she dead?"

He nodded. He retched. He vomited into the garbage can filling the room with the stench of it.

"All right. We're getting somewhere," she said. "Do you need more water?"

He nodded.

"Do you want something to eat?"

He shook his head.

She picked up the garbage can and walked out. Mark met her in the hall carrying a bottle of water and a chair for himself. Syd left the puke can in the hall and she and Mark stepped back into the interview room. Henson looked up at Mark, then hung his head.

"He's mad at me," Henson said.

"Who is mad at you?" Syd asked as Mark put his chair down across the table.

"Beaufort."

"Your accomplice," Mark said, sitting down.

"Yeah. That's why I ran. I thought he was going to kill me."

"Why was he going to kill you?" Mark asked.

"He thought I was gonna talk. I guess he was right 'cause I am talking."

"It's the right thing. Get it off your chest," Mark said.

"That's not why. It was Kaylee." He rubbed his face with his palms and looked at the ceiling.

"What about Kaylee?" Mark asked.

"She reminded me of Wendy. I didn't want to kill her."

"Did you kill her?" Mark asked.

"No."

"Did someone else kill her?" Syd asked.

"Maybe not yet. I don't know," Henson said.

"You're saying Kaylee is alive," Mark said.

"Could be. He keeps them alive until he finds a new one. He makes the new one watch. He likes it when they're scared. He records it," Henson said.

"Where is Kaylee now?" Mark asked.

Henson hesitated.

"You've come this far. Save her life," Mark said.

"Probably in the basement."

"The address," Syd said.

"I don't know the address."

Mark stood up. "Aw, come on, man!"

"It's on Denton Avenue, right at the end of the cul-de-sac. The house has white siding and a blue door."

179

# Chapter Sixteen

The sunset turned the sky flaming orange. They raced into it, sirens screaming, through the pretty west end neighbourhood, tires squealing as Mark flew around the corner into the quiet cul-de-sac. The house was just as Henson had described it.

A small army of officers surrounded the house. Police rammed in the front door and made entry. The odour of bleach, and what that meant, hit Mark and Syd immediately. Three officers ran up the stairs to the second floor as Syd and Mark stepped into the barren whitewashed living room. Other officers went ahead of them toward the kitchen at the back of the house. The place was devoid of furnishings.

In the middle of the living room stood two lights on top of poles, the kind you see on professional photo shoots. Clear plastic tarp covered half of the varnished wood floor. Mark nodded toward the kitchen. Syd looked to see what he meant. A door on the left wall stood just inside the kitchen. Aside from a sliding lock at the top, it appeared unsecured.

Syd heard the noise. It was a small sound, a little 'poof' like a pillow falling off of a bed. She heard a hiss.

"Trap!" she yelled as the chemical smell hit her nostrils.

It was too late. Fire flared up everywhere. It rolled across the floor and licked up the walls. In a second it climbed the doorframe between the living room and kitchen and ran across the top of it. Heat filled Syd's lungs. Officers yelled. Mark ran through the flaming doorway to the kitchen. Syd followed him through the fire.

He slid open the lock and yanked the basement door open. He and Syd went through the door. She pulled it shut behind them, the metal knob burning her hand as he pounded down the wooden stairs. She ran after him, yelling Kaylee's name.

She heard him yell, "No!"

With her hand on her weapon she rounded the corner at the bottom of the stairs, nearly bumping into him. Against the wall near the rusty water heater laid a heap under a pale blue sheet. Two blue hands in cuffs protruded up from the sheet, attached to a u-ring bolted to the cement block wall. They ran to the heap. Syd stood with her back to his, scanning the shadowy basement, while he pulled back the sheet from the body. It was Kaylee Anderson. He knelt beside her and checked her breathing.

"She's alive," he said as he pulled out his handcuff key.

Syd got on the radio. "We got her. Need rescue."

"They're coming. Hang on," came the reply.

"Shit," Mark said. "My cuff keys don't work." He grabbed at the u-ring and tried to work it free.

"Need bolt cutters," Syd radioed.

She tore through the boxes in the basement looking for something Mark could use. There was nothing in the boxes but women's clothing. She ran to the closest window and tried to open it. It was nailed shut. She tried the other windows, all sealed. She heard sirens and yelling outside. She heard breaking glass. She heard creaking above her. She looked up. The boards of the floor above were shrinking as the fire desiccated them. Hot embers fell through the cracks as blue flames wrapped around the boards over her head. She smelled burnt human hair. She ran to the smashed window where an officer knelt and looked in.

"She's cuffed to the wall. Mark's keys don't fit. We need something to cut the cuffs," she said.

He ran off. She looked at Mark who was on top of Kaylee, using his body to protect her from the raining embers. A flaming board fell from the ceiling landing beside them. Syd ran to it and kicked it away. It instantly melted the side of her shoe.

She yelled into the radio. "Ceiling is gone. We're out of time! Bolt cutters!"

She saw a firefighter's boots outside the window. The window was too small for anyone to get in there wearing gear. He handed giant cutters to her through the window. She ran back to Kaylee and cut the cuffs as burning material rained down onto her skin, into her hair, and down the inside back of her vest. Mark lifted Kaylee even before Syd had completely cut through the metal. He ran to the window with her. The firefighter had just put his jacket across the bottom of the window frame to protect her from the broken glass. Syd supported Kaylee's head and neck as they lifted her toward the window. Firefighters pulled her through and ran with her to where paramedics were waiting at a safe distance. A firefighter and another officer helped Mark and Syd through the window.

Syd gulped in the fresh air, but her lungs still felt on fire. Both she and Mark coughed up black and brown mucous as they were escorted away from the inferno. The orange light of the sun was gone, replaced by flames and red flashing lights that cut through the night and reflected off the wet pavement. Paramedics loaded Kaylee into an ambulance while news cameras rolled.

Syd looked at Mark as a paramedic tended to him, his pant legs full of holes, the back of his vest melted. His hair was frizzed from being burnt, his red scalp visible in one spot. Her concern for him trumped her own physical pain. She didn't realize she was as much of a mess as he was. When she held out her blistered hand to the paramedic she was surprised to see blood flowing from a gash along the inside of her forearm. She didn't know when that happened.

"Did everyone get out?" she asked.

The paramedic didn't know.

Her left pant leg had fused to her calf. She was covered in small burns and couldn't get the heat out of her lungs no matter how hard she coughed.

Mark stepped into a tiny room in the E.R. where a doctor sat stitching Syd's arm.

"How is everyone?" Syd asked.

"Smoke inhalation, all of them. Lundy got burns on his leg, but they're all going to be okay," Mark said.

"How is Kaylee?" she asked.

"She might lose her hands," Mark said. "She's going to survive, though."

"How are you?" she asked.

"Itching to get back to work."

"Me, too."

A voice outside the door said, "You're going home, the both of you." The chief.

He stood facing into the room, filling the doorway, a stern look on his face. His dark dinner suit with its triangle of white handkerchief poking from the breast pocket fit his large torso well.

"Hiya, Chief. What are you doing here?" Syd asked.

"Checking on my officers, of course," he said.

"There's an accomplice we have to go find," Mark said.

The chief shook his head. "They're doing it now."

"Who?" Mark asked.

"OPP spotted his truck. Instead of pulling him over they followed him and called us. He led them to a warehouse in the north end."

"Then we have to go," Syd said.

184

The chief shook his head. "They have it. Do you actually think you're fit for regular duties right now?"

"We still haven't done any paper," she said. "They'll need it in the morning for bail court."

The chief raised one of his grey eyebrows at her. "LaFleur, were your ears injured?"

"No, sir. "

"You and Lewis are going home. Get some rest. That's an order." He turned as if to walk away, then turned back. "Good job today," he said. He left.

\*\*\*

Branson was waiting in her driveway when she got home. "I saw you on the news," he said. "How are you?"

"Pretty good. Kaylee is alive. You should have seen the way Mark shielded her with his own body," she said.

"Isn't that his job?"

"Whether or not it was his job doesn't make it any less heroic," she said.

"Yes, of course."

She held up her right arm to show him the bandages on her hand and arm. He hugged her, then walked into the house with her. He cared for her. He stayed the night and never really left after that.

\*\*\*

Mark and Syd both showed up early for work in the morning. There was too much to do to take time out to rest. They still weren't done with Henson and there were reams of paperwork to complete. The station was abuzz with talk of last night's events. Forensics was still on-scene at Beaufort's warehouse. He'd been charged with kidnapping, forcible confinement, administer noxious substance, choking, and sexual assault to start with for his crimes against Kaylee Anderson. He insisted he would not speak to investigators and was doing an excellent job of remaining silent. Syd and Mark would not be able to press him excessively with questions but they were confident they already had enough for a conviction and the searches would turn up more evidence.

Pete poked his head in the door of their office.

"What are you doing here?" Mark asked.

"Hey, I've come up here because you two never get off your lazy butts to come downstairs."

"No, really," Mark said.

"I'm on days. Night shift has the search. They're gonna keep going," Pete said. "They found body parts."

Syd sat up straight. "I want to go."

"We can't. Besides, we can't do anything there," Mark said.

"This 'not fit' stuff is b.s.," she said. "We're fine."

"Neither one of you are fit to be on the street," Pete said. "Look at you. Next time you're gonna do something to injure a hand, at least have the sense not to injure your gun hand."

"Sure, Pete, we'll remember that for next time," Syd said.

"You're the goddam Bobsey twins, both of ya' with your right hands bandaged up." Pete shook his head.

"Do they know who the body parts belong to?" Mark asked.

"No. They found them in barrels. They know there's more than one person."

Syd thought about all the families. The media coverage would be tough for them, the social media commentary brutal. They would have to endure the waiting for the identifications, the needing to know, the hoping it isn't true, then the agony of their loss and the horrendous circumstances. They would have questions that couldn't be answered. They would think about their child's last moments, terrified, suffering, alone in the grip of monsters. Losing a child is out of the natural order of things. Suffering the loss of a daughter or son might be the worst thing a person can suffer, but homicide and suicide made that unimaginable pain even more profound. Then, if things went well, the monster would be held accountable. There would be a trial and the families would have to hear in cruel dispassionate detail what their loved one endured. Any scabs of healing would be ripped apart and new wounds inflicted. And even if there was a conviction, and even if the monster was locked up, none of it would bring their children back. They would shake in stunned shock and electric nerve jangling realization as their every illusion shattered, the universe falling in sharp shards around their feet, a hundred thousand burning icicles stabbing and slicing on their furious reality of descent. None would ever again be afraid of monsters or believe in fairy tales, for they would know with harsh certainty that we write about monsters because they are less frightening, we write about monsters to distance ourselves and deny our own nature, to insulate ourselves from the morbid monstrous unbearable reality that the monsters are us and the things that go bump in the night also go bump in the day and go bump within our very souls, that the most fearful things of all sleep beside us and reside within us. The only magical thing, the only thing to get resurrected would be pain. Grief sears the heart. Homicide is hellfire; it burns forever.

"Syd!" Pete's voice.

"What?"

"Are you hearing this?"

"Sorry," she said.

Pete shook his head at her in disdain.

"Did they find the videos?" Syd asked.

"What videos?" Pete said.

"I think he was recording what he did to them," she said.

"We'll find everything. Everybody wants this done right," Pete said.

"Thanks, Pete," Mark said.

When Pete left Syd said, "What did I miss?"

"Beaufort was running a chop shop out of the warehouse," he said. "Where were you a minute ago?"

"We have to talk to the families," she said.

"Yeah," he said quietly. "We do."

# Chapter Seventeen

Radar was on his tie-out in the backyard. Syd laid face down on the couch while Branson changed the dressing on her calf. He talked about his day. He mostly complained about people not doing their jobs properly and how he had to pick up the slack. He cracked jokes about Riker that she couldn't help but laugh at.

"You know," she said, "I *can* change this dressing by myself."

"You can do everything by yourself," he said. "But I want to. One of the things I like about us is our devotion to one another."

She considered his remark. She couldn't think of anything she did for him that qualified as devotion. She felt a pang of guilt. She thought she should do more for him.

She heard Radar open the back door, then the click of his nails on the kitchen floor. She sat up. Radar trotted into the living room dragging a three foot length of red tie-out cable from his collar. She unclipped the cut tie-out and dropped it on the kitchen counter on her way to the back door. She ran outside, looking for signs of anyone around. It was puzzling. After the previous incident with his tie-out being cut, she'd developed the habit of checking it every day. Branson had put Radar out this time, but she'd already put him out an hour ago and had checked it then. It couldn't have been cut while Radar was attached to it; he wouldn't have let anyone that close to him. It had to have been done in the last hour but if there had been anyone outside, Radar would have heard it and barked at the windows. He hadn't. Maybe she hadn't checked carefully enough. Maybe it was only partially cut so it would break when Radar pulled on it.

She walked the perimeter of the property, then the house. There were no signs anyone had been there. She picked up the other end of the tie-out. Maybe Pete could find out if it had been cut by the same tool as last time.

When she went back inside she found Radar tossing a roll of gauze around the living room, then chasing it. Branson wasn't there. The contents of the first-aid kit lay scattered across the coffee table and floor. She cleaned up the mess. She offered Radar a toy in trade for the gauze but he knew it wasn't a fair deal. He gave it up only when he heard Mark at the door. With great enthusiasm he greeted Mark.

"Hey." Mark smiled.

Syd smiled back. Branson walked down the stairs.

"Hey, Branson. How are ya'?"

"Fine, thank you," Branson said without returning Mark's smile.

Mark stepped into the living room. Branson stepped into the foyer and put on his shoes.

Mark said, "Was I interrupting?"

"Of course not," Syd said.

"Where's Amy tonight?" Branson asked.

"Working," Mark said. "Look, if you guys are busy I can take off."

"No," Branson said. "I was just leaving."

Syd knew this hadn't been the plan. Branson had talked about devotion not ten minutes ago and here she was failing already. He picked up his keys. Her heart hurt. She felt like she was losing something. He walked out the door.

Mark turned to her and said, "What's with him?"

She dropped her shoulders in defeat. "I think I'm not doing enough for him."

"You're not serious."

She flopped onto the couch. Radar sat at her feet. Mark shook his head. He walked to the kitchen, returning with a bottle of wine and two glasses. He sat beside her and filled a glass for her.

"Did he say that to you?" he asked.

"No. Well, I think he just said it by leaving," she said.

"So you're a mind-reader now?"

"With him I have to be."

"And that's a problem," he said.

She sipped her wine and tried not to sulk.

"What is it he wants you to do for him that you're not doing?"

"I don't know. He's hot and cold and I can't figure it out."

"Syd, you know who does that shit? Teenaged boys."

"I don't think that's fair," she said.

"Yeah, it *is* fair. You guys never go anywhere. He never tells you when he's going to be here but then wants to know why you're not here when he wants you, so you never go anywhere. You don't come to hockey any more. You don't come for drinks after work. That's not like you. He has you on a string."

"There are plenty of times when I'm late or have to cancel with him because of work," she said. "It's not fair for me to expect him to be precise when I'm not."

"That's different. You can't help that. What he's doing isn't about work. It's manipulation. What would you say to a d.v. victim who gives up her friends and her time for a guy?"

"Geeze, Mark. He's not hitting me. He's not demanding I give up my friends."

"Oh yes his is. He's just more sophisticated about it."

She stared down at her wine. "Why does this hurt so much? It's stupid of me. He hasn't done anything terrible. He's everything anyone could want."

Mark put his hand on her arm. She looked at him.

"It hurts so much because he's messing with your head. If he punched you in the face it would all be obvious but he's wormed into your brain. He found your weakness and he is exploiting it."

"What weakness?" She gulped her wine. "Everybody knows I'm the ice queen. I have no weakness."

193

Mark raised his eyebrows at her. "We both know you're no ice queen."

She let her shoulders fall. She nodded.

"You think you're not good enough but you're wrong."

"Then why do I have to work so much harder than the guys? I have to be perfect. Perfect. One mistake and that's what everybody sees. And when I do something perfectly, they find something else to point to, like ice queen, as proof I'm not quite good enough." The cabernet in her glass threatened to leap out with the shaking of her hands. She put the glass on the coffee table and continued her rant. "But *they* can screw up six ways to Sunday and it's okay. Why?"

"Because we live in a shit system. Not just work. Everywhere."

"What am I supposed to do with that?"

"Stop. Fuck those guys anyway."

"Easy for you to say. You're not the one who will be denied a promotion," she said.

"You going for Inspector?"

"No. I'm just sayin'. And how does this help me with Branson?"

"You stop. Syd, you're terrific already."

"But I'm not. I'm nothing close to the ideal woman," she said, picking up her wine glass.

"What is that supposed to mean?" he asked.

"I don't wear the pretty clothes and make-up, I'm not sweet, sometimes not even nice. I'm not soft. I eat take-out all the time and only do housework when I absolutely have to. I swear like a, well, a cop. I drink, I smoke. My sense of humour is morbid as hell."

He smiled. "I know. It's great."

She let out a half-laugh.

"Look," he said. "Branson has to accept who you are or find someone else."

"But I don't want him to find someone else. I've finally found someone who makes my heart race *and* gets my brain going. That's rare." She poured more wine for both of them. "Besides, there's nothing wrong with compromising or trying to better yourself."

"Syd, he wants a swooning fan-girl. You're not that. For God's sake don't try to be that."

"He says that's not what he wants," she said.

"Great. Then just be your regular self."

"But that's not enough."

"Ha!" he said.

"Oh, shut up, Lewis."

He sat back with his wine and a satisfied grin. She looked at Radar, resting contented at her feet.

"Radar has been good. I think being with Mrs. Linton every day is good for him," she said.

"I saw the broken cable on the counter. Is that new or from before?"

"New."

She explained to him what happened. He agreed they should ask Pete to have a look.

"Let's go out," he said.

"Can't drive anywhere," she said. "We've both had two glasses of wine."

"We'll take Radar to the park."

Radar perked up his ears.

"Wanna go to the park, Radar?" she asked.

Radar ran to his leash and brought it to Syd.

# Chapter Eighteen

Syd stared at the images on the screen. The sounds of their cries burned into her soul. She knew they would echo there forever. Mark sat beside her rubbing his forehead and cringing, his eyes glassy. They were watching the porn found on Beaufort's computer.

Syd swallowed the sick rising in her throat and focussed on making the notes they would need for court and any potential further investigation. She sat stony-faced but she felt like giant hands were reaching into her chest and wringing out her heart. She could put herself in the position of those women. They watched frame after frame of horrendous violation, the absolute destruction of human beings, their helplessness and horror, the pain, the desperation, the terror, and the sense of utter aloneness. In frame after frame the monsters masked as men gleefully thought of new ways to inflict torture. It was clear that Beaufort was the dominant one but Henson participated in all of it. Every one of the missing women was on the vile video collection, irrefutable evidence of Beaufort and Henson's egregious depravity. Frame after frame Syd took notes. She wouldn't turn it off, wouldn't take a break. These women suffered this; the least she could do was bear witness. That and make sure she and Mark hadn't missed anything, make sure what they sent to the Crown was perfect.

It was Mark who said, "Turn it off. I feel sick. I need a break."

The phone rang. Mark picked it up.

He held out the receiver to her, "For you."

She stepped to the desk and answered, "LaFleur".

"Sydney? This is Liza, from court."

"Hi, Liza."

"I was wondering, well, I see you run by my house sometimes."

"Uh-huh."

"Well, I'm wondering if maybe you could stop by. You could bring your dog."

"Um, well.."

"It's not about the, the incident. It's personal," Liza said. "I need advice."

"I don't think I'm to one to be giving personal advice," Syd said.

"But I think you are. I know we don't really know each other well but I need help and I don't know who else to call."

"Okay," Syd said. "I can come by after work. I think I can get out of here by five-thirty or six. Is that okay?"

"That's great."

"Give me your number in case I'm delayed," Syd said.

Liza gave her the number.

Mark said, "Let's go for a walk, just around the block. I need to see a tree or people doing ordinary boring things." Syd and Mark walked down to the lobby. Leena Davis from the Sex Assault Unit was just walking in.

"Hey, Davis," Syd said. "You making any progress on that serial rapist?"

Leena shook her head. Syd and Mark walked around the block in silence, breathing in car exhaust fumes but still glad to be outside. Syd looked at her phone. One-forty-five. Branson would be on his lunch break now. No texts from him. Apollo eclipsed.

At one minute to two, Syd's phone buzzed. Branson.

"I missed waking up with u."

Syd: "Me too."

Branson: "C u tonight?"

Syd: "Yes. But later. I'm seeing Liza after work."

Branson: "There's always something with u."

Branson: "I thought we could talk. Work it out."

Syd: "We can."

Branson: "I made reservations for us for 6. I know u wanted to go out. I'll cancel. C u another time."

Syd: "No. I'll cancel. We'll go out. We'll talk it through."

Branson: "Pick u up at 530"

Syd: "Okay."

Syd called Liza and arranged to meet her the following night instead.

After a sickening, gut-wrenching, afternoon of Beaufort's videos, Syd picked up Radar and went home. Mark went to Amy's.

Six o'clock came and went. No Branson. She called his cell. It went straight to voicemail. Had she misunderstood? Was she to meet him at the restaurant? She realized he hadn't said where he'd made the reservations. Doubting her memory, she looked back over their texts. No, she hadn't misunderstood. Had he been delayed at work? She called the private line to his office. No answer. She called the station and asked if there'd been any personal injury accidents in the city. Nope, nothing serious. She realized she didn't know Branson's family. She had no one to call to see if they'd heard from him. They'd been in a bubble, carefully constructed by him, and to which she'd acquiesced. It slowly dawned on her that this was a game. Hot and cold. Apollo rising and shining up her; Apollo hiding behind the earth, withholding his warmth.

\*\*\*

She had to go talk to Michael Cortez, the Crown across the hall from Branson. They didn't have an appointment so she wasn't surprised to find his office empty. She stuck her head into Branson's office. He wasn't there. The crisply ironed white shirt wasn't hanging from the coat rack where it lived. She walked to Eleanor's desk.

"Michael isn't in his office," Syd said.

"Oh, sorry. He must have gone down the back stairs. He'll be in 104."

"Is Branson in today?" she asked.

"He's in 101."

"Thanks, Eleanor."

So Branson was alive. She took the stairs and went to 104 hoping she'd get a chance to speak to Michael before his court started at ten. She went in and approached him. Anna, the court clerk, stood in front of him rolling her eyes and shaking her head.

"What's wrong?" Syd asked.

"Liza. She didn't show up and didn't bother to call. She's not answering her phone. She's probably out getting her nails done while we scramble to get in another reporter."

Syd asked, "Has she ever done this before?"

"No."

"Then why are you saying she's off getting her nails done?" Syd said.

"You don't have to be rude. It's not like it's any of your business anyway," Anna said.

Syd turned to Michael and spoke to him about what she'd come in for in the first place. She stepped outside of the courtroom and called Dispatch. She requested a welfare check at Liza's address.

Syd and Mark got the call at eleven-thirty. The officer sent to Liza's hadn't seen any signs of a problem. He'd heard water running inside the house so figured she was probably just in the shower and that's why she hadn't answered the phone or the door. He left and returned later to check again. Still hearing water running he knew something was wrong so he made entry. He found Liza's body.

Syd and Mark drove to the scene. Pete was already inside working. An officer stood at the yellow tape. Syd and Mark surveyed the area as they walked to the officer. Syd noticed a squirrel in Liza's front garden. It picked up a single pistachio from the ground between the petunias. The squirrel shoved the nut into its cheek and scurried away.

"Damn squirrel just compromised our scene," she joked.

"What?" Mark said.

"A squirrel took a pistachio and ran away with it."

Gesturing to the constable, Mark said to Syd, "You wanna make him capture the squirrel and retrieve the evidence?"

An image of the poor guy chasing the squirrel popped into Syd's head. She might have smiled at that under different circumstances.

They put on shoe covers and walked up the steps into the screened veranda. Beside a padded wicker chair sat a small wicker table covered in magazines. Healthy plants sprung from colourful pots on every windowsill and flowed from hanging planters. Syd walked the length of the veranda. No spider's webs, no dirt, all of the screens were intact. As she walked past the table of magazines, she noticed something written in black pen inside the petal of the flower pictured on the front of the top magazine. It was in Liza's handwriting. Syd had seen her writing in court. It said, *"poison flower"*. The flower in the magazine photo looked like the ones Syd had in her own front garden. Syd crouched to look at the other magazines without touching anything. She wanted a better sense of who Liza was. Nobody is only their work persona. The magazines were a mix of gardening and women's magazines.

Mark pointed to the floor in front of the door. A square patch of the green painted wooden floor was darker than the rest of the green.

"Welcome mat?" he said.

She nodded. "Pete probably took it."

They stepped into Liza's living room. Nothing seemed out of order. The place was spotless, marks from the vacuum cleaner still on the baby blue carpet. They heard Pete clear his throat upstairs. They went up. He was in the bathroom, hunched over the tub looking at the body.

Syd stood in the doorway. A pink towel sat in a heap beside the tub. Beside that, Liza's mottled feet dangled over the edge of the tub. Her naked body was sprawled on her back widthwise in the tub, her head and neck in an unnatural position. Syd looked at Liza's lifeless hand lying palm up in an inch of water, her nails short and unvarnished.

Syd asked, "Has anything been moved?"

"No. But I put the plug in the tub. Shower was running cold. I turned it off and plugged it. I'll collect the water but I don't expect to find anything," Pete said.

"Does the lividity look right to you?" she asked.

Pete looked at the body. "I think so. Looks like she was getting out of the shower, slipped and fell backwards and hit her head."

Syd looked around the bathroom, her eyes stopping every few inches to take everything in before moving on.

"This scene has been staged," she said.

"What are you seeing?" Mark asked.

"It's what I'm not seeing," she said, "look at the vanity."

Mark and Pete looked at it.

"Looks like she was getting ready for work," Pete said, "She has her toothbrush and toothpaste out, deodorant, hairbrush, jewellery, and that giant tray of make-up."

"And what's missing?" Syd asked.

Pete shrugged.

"Lotion. Face cream, specifically," she said.

"Maybe she doesn't wear face cream," Pete said.

"Most women who wear make-up put on a face cream first," she said.

"Oh, you can't know that," Pete said.

"Liza would. She was particular about how she looked. She got Botox at age twenty-six for heaven's sake. I'm telling you, she would have a face cream out. Somebody else put this stuff here to make it look like she was getting ready for work and slipped and fell. The water is a forensic counter-measure. Do you reach for your towel before you turn off the shower?"

"No," Pete said, "But people do weird things. You're serious about the face cream?"

"Yes."

"Well, that's why they pay you. I do a thorough job no matter what kind of case it looks like."

"I know you do, Pete," she said. "Did you find her fingernails yet, or clippings?"

"Haven't seen anything like that yet," he said.

"Hey," Mark said. "Did you already take the doormat from the veranda?"

"No. There wasn't one. I noticed that, too. I took a photo. I'll take her vacuum, too, just in case. If this was a homicide we'll get the bastard."

Mark and Syd left Forensics to their work and stepped outside. Spectators hovered beyond the police line. Two people had set up lawn chairs across the street and sat with drinks in their hands watching like this was some kind of movie, not the very real tragedy of a young woman who had been robbed her life. Syd wanted to yell at them to go home and watch C.S.I. on t.v.

She and Mark approached them and took their names. They didn't even live in the neighbourhood. They hadn't seen anything that might help the investigation. They'd heard the call on a scanner and decided to come on down. Syd and Mark looked at the small crowd in front of the police tape. The officer there would get the names of everyone who approached. Syd and Mark looked for any spectator who was hanging back.

They went door to door, questioning neighbours and asking for doorbell and security camera footage from those who had such devices. Nobody had seen or heard anything. Nobody saw visitors at Liza's. A lot of people weren't even home. Mark left his card in their doors and wrote down those addresses. They would go back and keep going back until they spoke to everyone.

One neighbour they spoke to made the hairs on the back of Syd's neck stand up. He lived on the street perpendicular to Liza's house. Standing on his front porch Syd looked to her right and had a clear view of Liza's place. Mark knocked on the door. A clean-cut forty-something man answered immediately, like he was already behind the door, waiting. He wore shorts and a faded rock concert t-shirt that barely covered his beer paunch. His square face shiny with sweat, he stepped outside, closing the door behind him.

"Is Liza okay?" he asked. He reeked of cheap cologne.

"Do you know her?" Syd asked.

"I know everyone," he said. "I know you."

"Pardon?"

"You run by here all the time. You have that German Shepherd. He's a bruiser. Bet no one bothers you with him around."

"How often did you speak to Liza?" she asked.

"Oh she liked me. I'd stand and talk to her while she worked in her yard. Friendly girl." He smiled. Something about him made Syd's stomach turn.

He continued, "She sat out in that front porch thing of hers all the time. I told her, you know, she shouldn't sit out there at night. With the light on it was like she was on display. You never know who is watching. And that screen door to the porch doesn't even lock."

"How do you know that?" Mark asked.

"Because one time I noticed a magazine on the steps. She was at work, so I opened the screen door to put the magazine inside her porch for her. I'm a good neighbour."

"When was this?" Mark asked.

The guy shrugged. "Couple days ago."

"Do you remember which magazine?" Syd asked.

"No."

"If you saw it again would you recognize it?" she asked.

"Oh yeah," he said. "On the cover it had a picture of a blonde in a skimpy outfit. Lots of cleavage." He looked and Mark and moved his eyebrows up and down.

"When you were picking up her magazine for her, did you go right inside the porch or just throw it in the door?" Syd asked.

"Well I had to, to put her magazine in there. I told you." His facial expression had changed to mild annoyance.

"Did you maybe walk around in there?" Syd asked. "Check the locks on the doors, make sure everything was okay?"

"Everything was okay," he said.

"You didn't answer my question," she said. "Did you look around inside the veranda? Touch anything?"

"No."

"Where did you put the magazine?" she asked.

He pressed his lips together. "Inside the door."

"The screen door," Mark said.

"Yes."

"Ever been inside the house?" Mark asked.

"No." He crossed his arms.

"You said she was friendly, that she liked you," Mark said. "Did you like her?"

"Yeah. Is that a crime?"

"Not at all," Mark said. "I just thought if she liked you and you liked her, maybe she would have invited you in. Maybe the two of you went on a date one time." Mark smiled at him.

He uncrossed his arms. "Naw. She was friendly and she liked me, but in that other way she was stuck-up."

"She turn you down?" Mark asked.

"No," he said, contorting his face like he'd just been insulted.

"Okay," Mark said. "I had to ask."

"Did she have many visitors?" Syd asked.

"Just some woman and a little kid," he said.

"Anyone else? Anyone hanging around outside maybe?" she asked.

"No. And I would know. Like I said, I'm a good neighbour. I watch. Sometimes I'm out at two, three o'clock in the morning watching the neighbourhood. I know everything that goes on. Like those people over there," he pointed to a house across the street. "That guy is having an affair while his wife is at work. I know everything."

"Do you have a security system?" Mark asked.

"Baseball bat." He laughed.

"Cameras?"

"Naw."

"Okay. Thank you for your help. What's your name?" Mark asked.

"Why do you need my name?"

"To cross you off our list," Mark said.

"Hal Hogart. Like Bogart but with an 'h'," he said. "Get it? Hogart, Bogart? Humphrey Bogart? You know him?"

"We get it," Mark said. "We'd like to arrange for what we call 'elimination prints'. You have a reasonable explanation for why your fingerprints are there…"

"Yeah, I told you."

"Right. So we'll print you so that we don't waste a lot of time tracking down the prints at the scene when they're yours and you have an explanation. It helps us cross you off our list."

"No way. That sounds like some sort of set-up."

"It's routine," Mark said.

"Well too bad," Hogart said.

Mark handed him a card. "If there's anything else you can think of to tell us, give us a call."

Hogart stood looking at Syd like he was waiting for something. "Don't I get your card?"

"You can reach both of us at the number on the card Detective Lewis gave you," she said.

"Maybe I'll see you when you run by. You can stop by sometime. I have cold beer, or wine if you like that, whatever you want. You can even bring that dog. I have dog treats in the house," he said.

Suppressing a sick shiver she asked, "What kind of dog do you have?"

"Oh, I don't have a dog. I just like them. I keep treats for the neighbourhood dogs."

She smiled. "Thank you. Call us if you remember anything else."

"Okay, well, maybe I'll catch you some time." He smiled. "Get it? You run. Run, chase, catch." He laughed.

"We get it," Mark said.

They walked away. When they were out of earshot Syd said, "I feel like I need a shower."

"Yeah," Mark said. "What a creep."

"He had such an absence of insight that he made that sick joke right in front of you," she said.

"He probably thought I'd think it was funny," he answered.

They walked back under the police tape, fewer spectators around now. They put on fresh shoe covers and went into Liza's house just as the coroner pulled up outside. They went upstairs.

Pete was in Liza's bedroom.

"You done in there yet?" Syd asked.

"Not quite. Not a single fingerprint in here, not even Liza's. We're going to take the clothes laid out on the bed, the bedding, and her laundry."

They looked at the work outfit carefully laid out on Liza's neatly made bed.

"Do you lay your clothes out like that?" Mark asked Syd.

"Pfft. No. I reach into my closet and whatever falls off a hanger is what I'm wearing," she said. "But I'm sure some people lay their clothes out."

Mark and Syd waited in the hall for Pete to give them the okay.

Syd told Pete, "There are magazines in the veranda. There should be fingerprints that don't belong to her on at least one of them. The neighbour touched it, said he put it inside. He's a creeper."

When Pete was done, Mark and Syd stepped into Liza's bright bedroom. No matter how many times they did this, they were always aware they were walking into people's intimate spaces, rummaging through their secrets. The sheer white curtains on the east facing window welcomed the morning sun that reflected off the white walls with their border of tiny painted pink roses. The bed with its brass headboard nestled between two polished rich brown wood nightstands that matched the four drawer dresser. On the dresser beside a small wicker basket full of colourful bottles of perfume stood a picture of a little girl. On the wooden frame in pink painted letters were the words, 'I love my Aunt'. The room smelled of perfume and freshly laundered sheets, and something else. Sweat. Male sweat, specifically.

"He spent time in here," Syd said. "I can smell him."

"All I smell is perfume," Mark said, his eyes slowly scanning the room.

But to Syd, that faint smell overrode everything in the room. His smell was stench shattering the crisp clean white sanctuary with sooty breath of death, stealing Liza's dreams, and all hope, abducting innocence and peace, destroying life itself, reducing it to ashes from which no phoenix would ever emerge.

Mark picked up Liza's cell phone from the nightstand. He looked at the last call."

"Last call was from you, Syd."

She felt a surge of guilt.

"She wanted me to come by, wanted to talk. I cancelled on her."

"What did she want to talk about?"

"I don't know. She said it was personal. We rescheduled for tonight."

"Where were you last night?" he asked.

"I picked up Radar and went home."

"What then?" he asked.

"I sat around with Radar and watched t.v. Are you checking my alibi?"

"Think about it, Syd. You were her last contact before she died."

"Except for whoever killed her."

"Let's get this out of the way, Syd. Who saw you at home?"

"No one." She stared at him. "Oh, wait. The pizza guy. I ordered pizza. And I was making phone calls. You can check. Ease your mind."

"My mind doesn't need easing when it comes to you. If you say you were home, then you were home. But a defence lawyer might make a big deal out of this. Someone other than me is going to check your phone and talk to that pizza guy. I don't want anyone accusing you, or me, of anything wrong."

"Okay."

Mark turned his attention back to Liza's phone. "The call before yours was to a Melissa."

He called the number from his phone. Syd heard him identify himself and ask the person how she knew Liza.

Then he asked, "When was the last time you saw her or spoke to her?" Then, "Okay. We need to come and talk to you."

When he was finished with the call he said to Syd, "You're off the hook. Melissa is her sister. Liza showed up there at five o'clock yesterday and stayed for supper. She left at seven."

Syd closed her eyes and exhaled.

Pete stepped out of Liza's spare bedroom. "There's no vacuum in this house."

"He took the vacuum," Syd said.

"Maybe she didn't have a vacuum. Maybe there was a cleaning lady," Pete said.

"If she had a vacuum and it's missing, that's a hold-back," Mark said.

Syd and Pete agreed.

Syd added, "And we hold back the missing acrylic nails and whatever comes back from the coroner's office.

When Pete gave the okay, Syd and Mark looked through the spare room. In the drawer of the antique desk they found bills, receipts, and old greeting cards Liza had kept. The cards were all from family members. Wrapped in a long elastic band they found warranty information and 'use and care' manuals for every appliance in the house, including the latest model of Dyson vacuum. They took the Dyson manual as evidence.

They left to go do the notification.

# Chapter Ninteen

After Melissa's initial shock and outburst of grief subsided a bit, they were able to ask some questions. They sat in her spacious toy filled living room.

"Was she having any problems with anyone?" Mark asked.

Melissa shook her head. "Not that I knew of. There was that, the rape. Do you think the guy came back and killed her?"

Both Mark and Syd shook their heads.

"We're not even sure yet that it was a homicide. We have to see what the coroner says. We're treating it as suspicious until we know otherwise," Mark said.

"Did she have a boyfriend? Someone interested in her?" Syd asked.

"She said she didn't but I'm not so sure," Melissa said.

"She wouldn't have told you?" Mark asked.

"Usually, yes, but lately something was off. She was secretive. It made me wonder if she had someone and maybe he was married. But then again, she hadn't been herself since the rape."

Syd nodded. "Was she one to keep a diary?"

"I don't think so. Her big thing was her garden and her niece." Melissa broke down. "What am I going to tell my daughter? She's six. She adored her auntie. How do I explain this to her?"

"Do you know her friends? Is there anyone she might have confided in?" Syd asked.

Melissa wiped her eyes. "She pretty much kept to herself, spent a lot of time here. She took my daughter to dance class every weekend. Excuse me."

Melissa stood and walked away. They could hear her blowing her nose in the next room. She came back and sat on the edge of her recliner.

"She did say she was going to talk to a police officer she knew. There was some issue at work she was struggling with. She said there was this policewoman she really liked who might help her sort it out."

Guilt tumbled down onto Syd like a collapsing brick house. Should she tell her? Yes.

"That was me," Syd said. "I was going to see her this evening."

Melissa looked at her. "Oh, I wish it was yesterday."

More bricks tumbling down.

"Did she say who at work she was having an issue with?" Syd asked.

"No. Never."

"Can you think of anyone, even if the idea is remote, anyone who might hurt her?" Syd asked.

Melissa shook her head.

"Did she use a cleaning service or a grass cutting service?" Syd asked.

"No. She took care of everything herself," Melissa said.

"Any other services where someone would be in the house? Any repairs recently?" Mark asked.

"Not that I know of."

"Anyone have a key to her house?" Syd asked.

"No."

"Did she have a doormat, like a welcome mat or something?" Mark asked.

"She did. Inside the veranda just in front of the door to the house," Melissa said.

"What did it look like?" he asked.

"It was one of those bristly things. It had a design of hummingbirds etched into it and the logo for Urban Paradise in the corner."

Syd recognized the name 'Urban Paradise'. They'd found numerous receipts from the popular gardening store at Liza's.

"Did she still have it the last time you were at her house?" Mark asked.

"Yes."

"When was that?"

"Four days ago."

They explained elimination prints to her and asked if she would make herself available for fingerprinting. She agreed.

Syd offered to have a team from Victim Services come over. Melissa declined. Syd left her card.

In the car Syd said, "I have to tell you something."

"Okay."

"The reason I cancelled with Liza is because Branson wanted to talk things out. He said he made reservations somewhere for six last night."

"So did you work it out?"

"He never showed."

Mark looked at her, then put his eyes back on the road. "Have you talked to him?" he asked.

"No yet, no."

She explained the whole thing to him, including the calls she'd made.

"Do you think he's capable of killing her?"

"Of course not. But everybody is capable under the right circumstances."

He nodded. "Yeah, they are. And a Crown would know enough about forensics to take counter-measures."

"But it's stupid to kill a co-worker. He's not a stupid guy," she said. "And he cares about his career and reputation."

"True. But what if she threatened that?"

"I still don't think so. He has enough power he could just get her fired. People hardly ever believe the woman, or they view her as conniving," she said.

"Maybe that's why she wanted to talk to you," he said.

"Why not talk to someone who knows everyone at court better, someone who has power over there? She got along with Cortez. All the J.P.'s liked her."

"Are you thinking it's a cop?" he asked.

"I'm thinking we have to not assume anything. Nobody is above suspicion. We hold back more details than usual."

"Let's see what we get from the interviews of her coworkers, and what shows up on security footage from her street. We'll ask everyone what kind of car they drive," he said.

Syd remembered seeing the black Mercedes in the neighbourhood a few days prior. She told Mark about it as they pulled into the parking lot across from the courthouse.

"Geeze," he said. "Anything else?"

"Not that I can think of."

They stepped through the doors of the courthouse just as they were being locked for the day. Mark spoke to Liza's supervisor. Syd stood in the public waiting area. The rows of hard seats bolted to the floor were all empty and only a handful of people walked through the space, most on their way out. Branson stepped out of court 101 with a court constable. He noticed her. He stood looking at her, green eyes beckoning across the chasm. She looked back at him, giving him nothing but the cold blue stare of the ice queen. She walked out. She waited in the car for Mark. Her phone buzzed even before they got back to the office. She ignored it.

They stopped downstairs at Forensics and found Pete hunched over his desk looking at Liza's fashion magazine through a loupe.

"The neighbour who handled that magazine refused to provide elimination prints," Mark said.

Without looking up, Pete said, "Well he provided his prints to us on this magazine." He sat up and rubbed the back of his neck. "Beautiful prints. Four fingers on one side, a thumb on the back. Look."

Syd and Mark stepped forward to look. On the front cover of the glossy fashion magazine, in black and grey, were four fingers so clear that they could see some of the ridge detail with naked eyes. The three of them smiled.

"Just the magazine?" Mark asked.

Pete rolled his chair back. "It's interesting," he said. "I found no prints at all inside the house. Whoever was in there spent a lot of time cleaning up. Even in scenes that have been cleaned I can usually find something, but not this one."

Mark looked at Syd. "You were right. Counter-measures."

"That's not all," Pete said. "The inside of the veranda was *covered* in prints."

"Maybe our guy didn't bother with the veranda because he knew he didn't touch anything in there," Mark said.

"Maybe he didn't spend time in there, knew he'd be seen," Syd said.

"Why not wear gloves?" Mark said. "Why go to so much trouble to clean up instead of wearing gloves?"

Pete shrugged. "Maybe it wasn't planned."

"Did he clean the entire house?" Syd asked.

"Every inch," Pete said.

"Maybe he had to," she said. "Maybe he was there before, maybe a regular visitor, so he knew his prints and hairs would be all over."

"Boyfriend," Mark said.

Pete said, "But why bother? He could just say he was the boyfriend and that would explain anything from him in the house. It's hard to forensically clean a place."

"Maybe he doesn't want anyone to know they were together," Mark said.

"Like if he was married," Pete said.

"Or in a position of power," Syd said.

"Her direct supervisor is female," Mark said.

"Well, I know she preferred men," Pete said. "You don't think it was a judge or J.P. do you?"

"We don't know," Mark said. "We have to keep quiet about this one, none of the usual talk."

Pete nodded.

Syd looked at Pete and said, "How do *you* know she preferred men and not women?"

He laughed. "Didn't you see her making googly eyes at Branson Oleander?"

"Everybody saw that," she said.

"Maybe it was a jealous judge," Pete said, only half-joking.

"What other prints did you find in the veranda?" Syd asked.

"I haven't got that far yet. A lot of them had the same whorl and loop patterns as these ones," he said, referring to the magazine, but until I look at the ridge detail I won't know. Just a minute."

He stood up. He retrieved an acetate with a print he'd lifted.

"I got this one from the window that looks into the living room from the veranda," he said as he sat down with it.

Mark and Syd waited while Pete compared that print with the ones on the magazine.

"This one is a match to the baby finger of the one found on the magazine," Pete said.

"Creep was looking in her window," Mark said.

"And he lied to us," Syd said. "I think we should go have another talk with him."

"Thanks, Pete," Mark said.

They drove back to Hogart's place.

When he answered the door he stepped outside and shut the door behind him like he'd done earlier. He smelled of beer.

"I told you before I'm not giving you my fingerprints," he said.

"Too late," Syd said. "We have them. And you know what else we have?"

He looked at her, his jaw clenched.

"We have your prints all over inside of the veranda."

"So? I told you I was in there," Hogart said.

"To put the magazine in there," she said.

"Right," he said.

Mark said, "You told us that's all you did. You lied to us."

"No I didn't."

"You were looking in her window," Mark said.

"Everybody looked in her windows. I told you. She put herself out there on display."

"She wasn't putting herself on display," Syd said strongly, working at keeping her anger in check. "She was sitting in her own veranda, her own home, like she had every right to do."

"Your prints were found on the window inside the veranda," Mark said. "Can you tell us something that will explain that, make us understand?"

"So what?" I was in her veranda. I told you that. That proves I didn't do it," Hogart said.

"How's that?" Mark asked.

"Because if I did it I wouldn't have left fingerprints."

"So you would have outsmarted us," Syd said.

"Yeah."

"So help us out here. What do you think you would have done better than the killer to outsmart us?" she asked.

"I don't know. What did he do?" Hogart asked.

"Well, what would you have done?" she asked.

"I would have worn gloves and a condom for sure. I wouldn't have left my prints all over the place. That's how you can tell it wasn't me."

223

"Because your prints were there," Mark said.

"Right."

"What do you mean, 'condom'?" Syd asked.

"To not leave DNA," Hogart answered in a tone that said she was stupid.

"Was she raped?" Syd asked.

"Wasn't she?" Hogart said.

"Would you be willing to provide a cheek swab so we can eliminate you as a suspect?" she asked.

"Don't you need a court order for that?"

"Not if you consent," she said.

"I'm not consenting to that," he said.

Mark said, "Why not prove it wasn't you? You afraid your DNA will be in her house?"

Hogart shook his head.

"Let's go inside and talk about all this," Syd said.

Hogart crossed his arms. "Nobody's going inside."

"Okay," Mark said. "We're going to find out everything sooner or later, Mr. Hogart."

Hogart stood with his arms crossed watching them walk away. Mark leafed through his notebook.

"Let's knock on some doors while we're here," he said. "People will be home from work by now."

They spoke to people who weren't home when they'd canvassed earlier. Nothing new came of it.

Back in the car Mark said, "I don't think Hogart's our guy, but I bet he's good for something else."

"Like maybe sexual assault. Condom. I nearly fell over," she said.

"They all think they're so smart," he said.

"We should let Davis know about this guy," she said.

"Yeah, tonight."

By the time they got back, Davis had left for the day. Syd left her a message and sent over their reports on their interactions with Hogart. Mark made arrangements for extra patrols in Hogart's neighbourhood. Having someone sit on the house wasn't feasible.

Mark asked Syd, "You want to go shopping at Urban Paradise? See what we can find out?"

Syd googled Urban Paradise. "Closed. Maybe tomorrow."

Mark obtained a garbage collection schedule and map. "It would be easier to let patrol run the garbage routes," he said.

"But then every cop and everyone in the legal community will know we're looking for that vacuum," she said.

"I know. I'm just sayin'."

They split up to cover more ground. They drove down all the streets where it was garbage night. No one had thrown out a vacuum on those routes. They both knew they would be driving the garbage routes every morning. It was a long shot, but they'd solved other crimes by being willing to work the long shots.

# Chapter Twenty

Syd picked up Radar and took him to the park in Mrs. Linton's neighbourhood. She didn't want to run by Liza's house, not ever. Her phone buzzed in her pocket. She looked at it. Two texts from Branson. The first, sent right after he'd seen her at the courthouse said, *"R u ok?"* The second said, *"Where r u?"* She slid the phone back into her pocket. She walked Radar back to her car parked outside Mrs. Linton's house in time to see Mark getting into his car with a pretty blonde woman, Amy. Syd loaded Radar into her car and drove home. Branson was sitting on her front porch waiting for her.

She brushed past him, taking Radar inside. Branson followed her.

"I heard," he said. "Do you have any leads?"

"I can't discuss that with you," she said.

"All right," he said, following her to the kitchen. "Are you okay?"

She grabbed the open bottle of wine from the fridge. She turned to face him. "Where were you last night?"

"Are you questioning me as a detective?"

"I'm questioning you as your girlfriend who is pissed off about being stood up."

She stood there, bottle in her hand, watching his face, waiting for an answer. Radar paced back and forth in the kitchen.

"Girlfriend? Is that what you think you are?"

She hadn't expected that response.

"We share a bed. I'd better be something to you," she said.

"You're more than a girlfriend, Sydney. You're my future."

"How's that going to work when we have to be so secretive we can't even go to a show?"

"We'll figure it out."

He reached for her. Radar leapt at him. Syd didn't try to stop or correct Radar. Branson stepped back, stunned.

"Answer the question, Branson."

"I had to work late," he said.

"You couldn't call or text?"

"I lost track of time," he said.

"Bull. But whatever." She turned away and poured wine into a glass. "Then what?"

"Then nothing. What is this?" His voice was raised.

Radar stood, eyeballing him.

"It's your future going up in smoke if you keep evading."

"This is unhinged, Syd. You're treating me worse than an accused criminal."

"How do you figure? Do I have you cuffed to the table?"

"You're standing in front of me angry with a vicious dog behind me," he said.

She rolled her eyes. "Oh, give me a break."

"What did *you* do last night, Sydney? You had plans to go to Liza's. You saw us out to lunch together. Maybe you were jealous and confronted her."

Syd felt the volcanic rise of fury in her.

"Get out!" she yelled.

Radar's pacing quickened.

"It doesn't feel very good, does it," he said.

"I'm not playin' games," she said. "You give me a straight answer now or get the hell out of my house."

"Can we just sit down and talk?"

"If you tell me the truth we can talk. Otherwise, fuck off. Mark will question you officially."

"Okay, fine. I worked late. I lost track of time and I fell asleep."

She threw her arms up. "Bull. Shit."

"It's not. Ask Michael. I slept on the couch in his office. He woke me up this morning."

"What time did you fall asleep?"

"I don't know."

"I called your private line," she said.

"I heard it."

"Fine," she said, walking to the couch, purposely not asking the next obvious question.

Radar loping behind him, Branson walked to the front door, put on his shoes, and walked out.

Thirty minutes later Mark showed up with wieners and marshmallows.

"Did you miss me?" he asked on his way to the kitchen.

She smiled but he saw through it.

"What's wrong?"

"Besides Liza? Branson, of course," she said.

He put the wieners and marshmallows on the counter, pushing them to the back to protect them from Radar's curious nose.

"Tell me," he said, opening a kitchen drawer.

She gave him a detailed account of their fight. He turned to face her, holding two long bbq forks in his hand.

"I'll question him. But you can't sit in," he said.

She nodded.

"But right now let's eat and relax by the fire pit. Tomorrow is going to be a long day."

"You're right. You can tell me all about you and Amy," she said.

Radar followed her out to the garage. Her bin of firewood sat near where she kept her gardening tools. She looked at them and thought of Liza happily planting petunias. She shook her head, loaded her arms with firewood, and took it to the fire pit.

They sat in front of the fire roasting wieners, slapping at mosquitos, and talking about Mark's blossoming relationship. It was good to see him happy.

Radar ran into the long weeds along the fence, the garden bed that was usually full of flowers. He leapt and snapped at fireflies. It reminded her of the night with Branson on her front porch, when they'd seen fireflies out there, when things between them were sunny and warm. *And now it is night*, she thought.

She left Mark fastidiously roasting a wiener. She went into the house and grabbed a mixing bowl. She filled it with ice. She used all the ice she had. She marched back to the fire pit and dumped the ice onto the fire. The ice cubes popped and steamed. The air filled with smoke, the fire's complaint.

"Hey!" Mark said, pulling his half-roasted dinner out of the plume. "What are you doing?"

"Testing a theory."

He looked up at her. She stood there staring at the mess, the bowl hanging from her hand.

"Could you have at least waited until I finished roasting my hot dog?"

"You've already had three. The fire is still hot. Have a marshmallow."

He looked at her with an expression of puzzlement and annoyance.

"What theory? You trying to solve a crime here?" he asked.

"The crime of my own stupidity," she said. "I made a mistake."

"What are you talking about?"

"Fire and ice cannot exist in the same space."

"Everyone knows that," he said. "So what were you trying to figure out?"

"I wanted to see if the ice would put out the fire, or if the fire would consume the ice, or if they would cancel each other out."

"And your conclusion?"

"I need more ice." She walked away.

He got up and followed her into the house. She tossed the empty bowl sending it clattering into the kitchen sink.

"Syd. Is this about Liza or about Branson?"

"I don't know."

"Do you think he could have done it?"

"No. I truly don't." She sighed.

"But you know you're biased."

"I know I'm not thinking clearly. I know my heart and head are tangled up with him and I don't know how to get out of it. I feel like a worm on a pin."

"I'm going to check, Syd. I'll find out where he was."

She nodded. "Fire's still hot and Radar is out there alone."

They went back outside and sat in front of the smouldering fire. Mark poked at it, causing it to glow brighter. She put a marshmallow on a bbq fork and handed it to him.

"I think I have to tell the chief about my relationship with Branson."

"You might not have to. Let me check his alibi first."

"I think I do. It feels dishonest not to tell him, considering the circumstances."

"Okay. You want me to go with you?"

"No. I have to face it alone." She stared at the dying fire. "One more thing."

She waited for him to make eye contact. He did.

"Go hard on Branson," she said. "Don't give him a pass on anything. I need facts, evidence. It's the evidence that will free me one way or the other."

\*\*\*

She paced outside the chief's door at the end of the hall, her heart pounding in her throat. She mentally ran through ways she could start the conversation but her brain felt muddled. Fireflies and petunias.

"Good morning, Sydney," the chief said with a smile.

He stepped past her and waved his key card over the sensor to unlock his door.

"Come on in."

He sat at his big old rosewood desk with its hand-carved side panels that had been polished and cared for as it had been passed down through generations of police chiefs. "What can I do for you?"

She sat in the roomy worn leather chair across from him. She felt small in that chair. She felt small in this room, in this moment. He looked at her over the rims of his glasses.

"What's troubling you?"

"I've messed up, sir."

"Okay." He leaned back. "Give me all the pertinent facts."

She blurted out the story. It came out in a rambling mess but he listened patiently and intently until she was done. He leaned far back in his chair, his hands clasped together resting on his belly. She felt like her heart might run out of beats as he looked at her for what felt like an eternity while she awaited judgment.

"Well," he said, "There's no policy against the two of you having a relationship." He paused. "It was prudent to keep it quiet. Is it your intention to continue the relationship?"

"It depends," she said.

"You don't trust him."

"I do. But the situation,"

He sat up. "This is what we're going to do. Lewis and Davis are going to interview Mr. Oleander. They'll check his alibi and his phone. You can't have any part in that process. I can't order you to stay away from him but I can re-assign you if you want to keep seeing him before he's eliminated."

"I can stay away from him," she said.

"Good. I hoped that would be your decision," he said. "Thank you for coming to me."

"That's it?" she said.

"That's it," he said. "Unless there's something you haven't told me."

"No. I've told you everything."

"Don't worry, Sydney. I know Branson. I can't imagine him hurting anyone, but we'll find out. Everything will work out."

She sat there dumbly.

He smiled at her and raised one eyebrow. "Unless you're looking for relationship advice, in which case my wife is better at that, I think we're done here, Detective." She stood. "Thank you, sir."

She walked back to her office letting drops of relief seep into the cracks of her humiliation.

# Chapter Twenty-One

"How did it go?" Mark asked.

She told him.

"See," he said. "Now we can focus on work. We have interviews with some of Liza's co-workers before nine, two over the lunch hour, and more this afternoon."

"Want to go shopping after the morning interviews?" she asked.

"Urban Paradise? Yeah."

After the fruitless morning interviews they drove out to Urban Paradise. Syd took the lanyard holding her I.D. off and shoved it in her pocket. Her gun was well-concealed by her suit jacket. She went into the garden centre alone. She would be a shopper and Mark would wait a couple of minutes before going in to ask questions.

She roamed the aisles. She watched the reactions of employees when Mark came in and started questioning the cashier. None of them acted nervous or tried to duck out. They all reacted with curiosity. In one of the aisles she found the same style of doormat Melissa had described as Liza having at her front door. She purchased the doormat. The cashier ringing her out commented that the doormat was very popular. Syd took her purchase to the car. She jotted down all the licence plate numbers in the lot and the makes and models of the vehicles. They would check them against the security footage from Liza's street.

Mark met her in the parking lot. "They all recognized her," he said. "Said she's here a lot. They were cooperative, all gave alibis. One guy offered his DNA. I got the info for the three employees who aren't here."

"Okay. We'll check it all after the lunch hour interviews."

\*\*\*

The interviews with Liza's co-workers were short. Nobody had anything to tell. They all said Liza was a good worker and a nice person. None of them knew about Liza's personal life, not because she was secretive, but because no one had ever asked. No one had seen her socializing with anyone.

Mark asked Syd, "What's Branson's personal cell number?"

She told him. He jotted it down. He scrolled through Liza's phone.

"There are no calls or text to or from that number," he said.

"Anything else that looks like a creeper or suitor?"

"Nope."

Before handing the phone over to the tech guys Mark wrote down the names and numbers of everyone in Liza's phone. He spoke to them all, including businesses. He found nothing unusual and no one could provide any useful information. Syd worked on checking alibis.

At three o'clock Mark said, "You have to be out of here for four-thirty."

"Why?"

"Branson is coming in for an interview."

"Oh, okay."

"There's a vigil tonight for Liza," he said.

"We should go," she said.

"Yeah, see who shows up."

"Where?"

"The park down the street from the courthouse. The court clerks organized it," he said.

"You're kidding." She shook her head.

"What do you mean?"

"All day long they've been telling us about how great Liza was. Poor Liza, such a lovely person, they're so sad, but while she was alive they treated her like crap. The care *now*? Bullshit. This vigil is about their guilt, not about her."

Mark listened, letting her blow off the steam.

"And it's the same with the guys here," she said. "Oh, they all care *now*, but they sat around joking about her tits. They acted like she was a *thing*, not a human being." She kicked her desk.

"You done?" he asked.

"Yes," she said, shaking her head.

She called Mrs. Linton to tell her she'd be late picking up Radar. She could hear him barking in the background.

"Okay, dear. When is Mark coming home?" Mrs. Linton asked. "Because there has been a strange man hanging around here for the last half an hour."

"Don't open the door. I'm on my way to see you," Syd said.

She told Mark about her concern and then left for Mrs. Linton's.

She parked down the street and watched for a few minutes. She saw no one suspicious. She got out of the car and walked to the front door.

Mrs. Linton made tea in a porcelain pot and set it on the green Formica topped chrome-legged kitchen table. While they drank tea together Mrs. Linton expressed optimism about Mark's new relationship.

"I hear you have someone, too, dear."

"Maybe not any more," Syd said.

Mrs. Linton put her hand on Syd's arm. "Oh do work it out if you can, dear. It's worth it. I was married to my Lyle for thirty-two years."

Radar barked at the front window. Syd got up to look. Across the street stood Brice Avery.

"Is this the man you saw before?" she asked.

Mrs. Linton shuffled to the window. "Yes. That's him. Radar tells me he is not a nice man."

"Stay here," Syd said.

She burst out the front door and strode across the street. Avery stood there smirking.

"What are you doing here, Avery?"

He held up a cigarette. "Looking for a light. I'm not allowed to carry a lighter."

"Go downtown then," she said.

He turned and started sauntering away.

"You didn't answer my question," she said. "What are you doing here?"

He turned to face her. "Just visiting a friend."

"What friend?"

"I'm not breaking the law, Detective. I don't have to answer your questions."

"Then get lost."

He smiled. "This is a public sidewalk."

"Don't loiter here."

He held his hands up, smirking. "Okay, I'll go. You don't have to get hot with me."

He walked away.

She shouted after him. "If there's so much as a rubbish fire in the neighbourhood I'm coming for you."

She watched him walk down the street and turn the corner. She went back into the house.

Mrs. Linton insisted on feeding her. They shared homemade soup and freshly baked bread and Mrs. Linton proudly showed her pictures of her children and grandchildren. Syd stayed until it was time to go to the vigil.

She met Mark there. They hung back, photographing the crowd, watching behaviour. Branson wasn't there. Syd's personal phone buzzed. It was him.

"Where r u?"

She slid the phone back into her pocket without responding. After the vigil she picked up Radar and went home. She dreamt she was in a wooden boat in a lake of fire while angels with blackened wings watched her boat burn.

# Chapter Twenty-Two

The trilling of her personal phone woke her just after three in the morning. Through the fog of sleep she answered as if she was at work.

"LaFleur."

"Syd, get over to the General. Mark's been hurt."

She sat up. "What? What happened?"

Adrenaline cleared the fog from her brain. She realized the voice on the other end of the phone belonged to a staff sergeant.

"There was a fire at his place. He flew out the second storey window. When they found him his legs were paralyzed but he was still trying to get back inside the house."

"Probably to save Mrs. Linton," she said.

"The old lady downstairs?"

"Yes. Is she okay?"

"She didn't get out."

The news hit her like a cinder block slamming against her chest.

"Brice Avery," she said. "He was hanging around there earlier."

"Okay. I'll put it out. We'll pick him up."

She threw on her work clothes and raced to the hospital. She ran into the E.R., then to where several offers were standing in a group.

"Where is he?" she asked.

"Back there," one of the guys said, indicating the doors to the E.R. examination area. "Three curtains down on the right."

Syd pulled the door open and went in. She found Mark in a bed, shirtless, still on a backboard, with a cervical collar holding his head and neck still. His hand with the I.V. in it rested on top of the clean white sheet. Soot and sweat and blood smeared his face.

"Hi," he said. "Did you miss me?"

"Yes. It's been so long since I've seen you," she said as she pulled the curtain closed.

"Check on Mrs. Linton for me. They won't tell me anything," he said.

The look on Syd's face told him what he didn't want to know. His tears came instantly. He tried to blink them away but those kind of tears don't go away by blinking; those tears demand to be cried. She held his hand and cried with him. She used the sheets to wipe the tears and soot from his face.

"I tried to get down there," he said. "The staircase was gone." His voice broke. "I tried to get back in. My legs wouldn't work. I tried, Syd."

"I know you did." She wiped her own tears away with her sleeve. "I know."

"I smelled gasoline," he said.

She nodded.

"Don't stay here," he said. "Go get the shit who did it."

"I will," she said. "Do you know the phone number for any of Mrs. Linton's sons?"

"In my apartment."

"Okay. What's Amy's number?"

"Don't call her."

"Why not?"

"Because it's the middle of the night and I can't feel my legs."

She shook her head. "Don't do that. If she's all you say she is, she will want a phone call."

Mark recited the phone number.

An orderly opened the curtain and said, "I have to take him to MRI."

Syd nodded. "See you later, brother."

On her way back to her car she called Amy and gave her what information she could. She drove to Mrs. Linton's house. The Duty Inspector saw her. He approached her.

"They picked up Brice Avery only three blocks from here," he said. "Witness saw him running away when the sirens got close."

"I saw him here earlier," she said.

He continued, "He had a lighter in his pocket. We arrested him for breach probation. Fire Captain says an accelerant was used but we'll know more after the Fire Marshal's investigation."

She nodded. "Has someone arranged the notification?"

"An officer is on his way with Victim Services now. I figured you'd be at the hospital for a bit."

"Okay."

"One more thing," he said. "There were shoeprints in the gardens around the house. The suppression efforts destroyed them but Dave thinks there's one he can get."

She glanced around. She saw Dave photographing something on the ground. She walked over to him.

"What have you got?"

"Partial shoeprint."

She leaned forward to look.

"See that? Where the ball of the foot sits?" He pointed.

"Yes. What am I looking at?"

"There's an odd almost triangular shaped gouge in the sole. Along with the other wear marks, that will be easy to match."

"We have a suspect," she said. "I'll check his shoes. Thanks."

She went back to the station to question Brice Avery. She had him put in interview one. She sat across from him.

"Have you cooled off yet?" he asked.

"It's you who will be cooling off," she said, "in a jail cell."

He shrugged.

"Relax," she said. "Put your feet up."

He looked at her with suspicion. She looked at his clothes, the same faded green t-shirt and blue jeans he'd been wearing when she's seen him earlier. No soot, no singe marks sullied his clothes.

"You're doin' that 'nice' thing you do but I know better than to talk to you," he said.

"Why? You got something to hide?"

He stared at her. Syd could smell smoke, but couldn't distinguish whether it was coming from her, him, or both of them. She noted the absence of the smell of gasoline.

"You were hanging around that house and, poof, it goes up in flames. What do you have to say about that?"

He smiled. "I have that effect on things."

She wanted to slap him. Instead, she leaned back and put her feet on the table.

"Relax, Avery. Chill, put your feet up."

"We played this game before," he said. "You act all nice and I get talking and I go to jail."

"You're already in jail," she said. "Why did you have a lighter?"

"I smoke. Imagine havin' to walk around begging every time you want a puff."

"Why were you hanging around that house? Not looking for a light then, were you," she said.

"There was a dog barking in the window. It was funny. I was just watchin' it."

"Where did you go after that?"

"My buddy's house."

"What's your buddy's name and phone number?"

245

Avery provided the name and number. Syd left him in the interview room and went to run the guy. He turned out to be a previous surety with no record who did live a few blocks from the Linton house. She made a note to speak to him as well. She returned to Avery.

"I checked. Your buddy does live there. But that still puts you in the vicinity of the fire and you were seen running away. You need to explain that."

"I was going home. It was already on fire, I swear."

Syd put her feet on the table. "Might as well relax, Avery. You're gonna be here a while."

"All I did was watch," he said. "That's all."

"You like fire."

His eyes lit up. "It's fascinating."

"Let's say all you did was watch. Tell me about the fire. What did you see?"

Quietly he sang a line from a Johnny Cash song, "*It burns, the ring of fire,*" He laughed.

"A woman died, Avery. Not funny."

"I saw a ring of fire. Around the whole house. He used gasoline."

"Who did?"

He shrugged.

"You did," she said.

"I don't use gasoline." He held up his arm showing his ugly burn scar. "I tried that once. Fire is beautiful but she'll bite you if you don't love her right, if you underestimate her. Bad lovers use gasoline."

"What do you use?" she asked.

246

"You're trying to trick me again."

"I'm really not. I really want to know who did this. If you didn't do it then help yourself out here."

He stared at her. She took her feet off the table and sat up.

"So you're walking home and you see the fire. What time was that?"

He held out both of his hands. "I don't wear a watch."

"Okay. So what did you see?"

"Her."

"The old lady?"

"No. Fire." He stared, not focussing on anything.

"Okay. What was she doing?"

"Circling the house. Inside she was gasping for air."

"How do you know what was going on inside?"

"Thick black smoke sneaking through the cracks around the door, then it disappears and comes back. Like it's breathing. Inhale, exhale. Then she claws for air around the door. Then *pow*. She kicks out the door and breathes. She rose up in all her glory." He lifted his arms to imitate rising flames.

"Then what?"

"Then the lights go on."

"What lights?"

"Neighbours. Then I hide in the hedge. I should leave but she's so beautiful I want to watch just a little longer."

"Did you see anyone else?"

"No."

"What about earlier?"

"No."

"Then what?"

"I hear sirens. Gotta run."

"Why did you have the lighter?"

"I told you. I smoke. I need to smoke," he said.

"You want a smoke now?" she asked.

"Yeah."

"Yeah, me, too. But we're here. Might as well put your feet up and chill."

"You're playing a game with me, Detective."

"Show me your shoes."

He looked down at his shoes, loose on his feet because custody had taken the laces.

"They're on my feet. You can see 'em."

"I want to see the soles."

"That's why you wanted me to put my feet up."

She smiled and shrugged.

"See. You tried to trick me."

"Yes, I did."

His expression of indignation melted away and his smirk reappeared. He kicked off his shoes.

"Go ahead. Look," he said.

She picked up both shoes and turned them over. They weren't even the same tread pattern as the print Dave had shown her.

Avery said, "And that's it. I'm not saying another word until I can speak to my lawyer."

She put his shoes down in front of him and stood up. "Okay. Thanks," she said.

"Don't I get a smoke?" he asked.

"What?"

"You promised me a smoke."

"I did not."

"Yes, if I showed you my shoes. You induced me. Everything is inadmissible now."

"I didn't and it's not."

The whole way back to the cells he hollered that she'd induced him and that everything was inadmissible and he was going to sue them all.

Syd went back to her office and put on a pot of coffee. There was no point in going home. She looked at what she and Mark had lined up for the day. They'd planned for a lot on Liza's case. She would have to do it alone. Now there was the fire to investigate and still plenty to do on Henson and Beaufort. She picked up the phone to ask Mrs. Linton to keep Radar, then remembered. The phone suddenly felt heavy. She put it down. Radar was at home and Mrs. Linton was gone.

She went home and brought Radar back to the office. Ecklund could go ahead and have his aneurysm. She settled down to work. One pot of coffee later, Pete stopped in.

"How's Mark?" he asked.

"Broken up over Mrs. Linton," she said. "And he can't feel his legs."

"Shit."

"I'll check up on him again later," she said.

"You know those shoeprints we found around your house?"

She looked at him.

"They match the partial we found at Mark's."

"Oh."

"Size nine Asics. I went ahead and checked. They haven't manufactured that tread pattern for two years," he said.

"Okay, thanks."

"You want me to send Liza's rape kit to CFS, see who the second DNA belongs to?"

"What? Is the autopsy done already and no one told me?"

"No. From the previous rape," he said.

"Are you telling me you never sent in the kit?"

"I thought you knew. Thought you would have pulled up the reports on that case."

"It's on my Mount Everest of things to do," she said. "Haven't got that far yet."

"Liza changed her mind, didn't want to proceed," he said.

"Not uncommon, but did she say why?"

"Yeah. Apparently she'd been with someone earlier and didn't want his name brought into it."

"Holy hot tamales," she said. "Yes, of course, send it."

"Okay." As he walked away he said, "You know, Mark would say 'hot damn' or 'we're hot'."

She nodded. "Yes, he would."

As Pete was leaving, Leena Davis from the Sex Assault Unit poked her head in. "LaFleur, you got a minute?"

"Come on in," Syd said.

Pete left and Davis came in.

"Branson Oleander checked out," she said.

"A hundred percent?" Syd asked.

"A hundred percent. I just finished talking with a woman on the cleaning crew who cleans at the courthouse. She said she went in to clean the Crown's offices at around midnight and saw Oleander sleeping on the couch in Cortez's office. Mr. Cortez already told me he found him there, still asleep, at eight in the morning. He was wearing the same clothes as the day before."

Syd said, "Depending on the time of death, he still could have had time to go to Liza's then go back to the office."

Davis shook her head. "Surveillance cameras in the parking lot show his car there from two in the afternoon until the next day at one in the afternoon. He never left the building. Mark asked to see his phone. He handed it over without hesitating, gave consent to search. Cellphone towers show his phone was in the neighbourhood of the courthouse all night. He's not your guy."

"Okay. Thanks. Did Liza not want you to proceed on the sex assault?"

"Yeah. At first she was eager to proceed, but then she changed her mind. Was adamant about it," Davis said.

"Did she say why?"

"She said something about having been with someone else earlier. I tried to reassure her about that, but then she said she was worried about having to go through a trial."

"She say who the someone else was?" Syd asked.

"No. And I didn't think it was relevant to press her on that."

"Do you think the guy who raped her is your serial?"

"I know it is," Davis said.

"I think your serial seems too disorganized for this one. What do you think?" Syd asked.

"I don't have the details on yours, but based on what I've seen and heard, I agree. Did your guy use a ligature?"

"Doesn't appear that way," Syd said.

"Our serial leaves plenty of forensic evidence behind. I'm hearing you guys got nothing," Davis said. "Our guy never moved a victim or tried staging, either."

"Okay. Thanks."

Syd felt horrible for having been suspicious of Branson. Of all the people who should have believed in him, she should have believed in him the most.

She texted him. *"I'm sorry."*

She dug into her work, stopping only to take Radar outside and to put on more coffee. The report from the coroner's office came in. She read it.

After dropping off Radar at home, she went to the hospital. She walked into Mark's semi-private room to find Amy sitting in the chair at his bedside.

"Hey," Mark said.

Syd took a step back. "I can come back later."

"No." Amy stood. "I need something to eat anyway." She kissed Mark. "See you later." She smiled at Syd and walked out.

Syd sat beside him. "Any news?"

"I think Branson is in the clear," he said. "I should have told you last night."

"I meant news about you."

"Look," he said, pointing at his toes wiggling under the sheet.

"That's great," she said. "Can you walk?"

"Not yet. Gotta do physio and stay on meds for swelling. They're getting me a wheelchair."

"That's good, right?"

"I guess. I'm getting sprung tomorrow. I'll be back at work by noon."

She tilted her head to one side and raised her brows. "No you won't. No way they'll let you."

"Then soon," he said.

"You can stay at my place until you're better," she said.

He grinned. "I'm moving in with Amy."

"Oh, wow." She smiled. "Good for you."

"Liza's death is confirmed a homicide."

"C.O.D.?" he asked.

"Asphyxia. Mechanism was pressure. Looks like he sat on her chest."

"Sexual assault?"

"No evidence of sexual activity at all," she said. "No hairs, fibres, skin cells, nothing."

"Damn," he said.

"And get this. There was damage to external tissue from freezing."

"External," he said, thinking. "So she wasn't totally frozen but partially frozen? Put in ice maybe?"

"That's what it looks like," she said.

"That would obscure the time of death," he said.

"Ambient temperature when she was found was twenty Celsius. Add cold water and ice. They still think it was between nine and three."

"So what did this guy do, bring in coolers full of ice?" he said.

"That's premeditation if he brought it with him," she said. "Makes it first degree."

"Her creeper neighbour seems too inept for that kind of planning," he said.

"I agree."

"Yeah, he's not our guy," Mark said.

When Amy returned, Syd said her goodbyes and went home. When she got there Branson was sitting on her front porch smoking.

"Hi," she said tentatively.

He looked at her, letting his silence speak, but she didn't know what it was saying. She sat beside him. His cigarettes and lighter were sitting on the top step between them. She picked up the package and took a cigarette. She noticed the lighter was a black Bic, not his usual pink.

"You switch to black?" she asked, holding up the lighter?

"I stole it from Michael," he said.

"Why?"

"Someone stole mine, or I lost it," he said.

"You coming in?" she asked.

"I left my grey suit in your closet. I'm just here to get that."

Her heart sunk. "Oh. Okay."

They went inside. She stayed in the living room with Radar while he went up to the bedroom and retrieved his suit.

When he returned she said, "Don't you want to talk about it?"

"No. I'm still thinking about things."

He left. She felt like her chest had been hollowed out. It felt charred and empty like a house gutted by fire.

She was so tired she felt dizzy. She realized she hadn't eaten all day. Too tired to eat, she fell into bed, sleeping in her clothes. She dreamt of giant flaming balls from outer space smashing into the earth and knocking it from its axis.

# Chapter Twenty-Three

It had been nearly a week since the fire. Every morning Radar sat at the front door with his car harness hanging out of his mouth, staring at Syd with sad imploring eyes, waiting for her to take him to Mrs. Linton's. When she'd take the harness from him he'd wag his tail in happy anticipation thinking they were finally going to see his beloved friend, and then as the realization hit him that he wasn't going, he'd retrieve the harness again and cry at the door. He cried loudly every day when Syd left for work. Her human hugs and compassionate words meant nothing to him. Every night when she came home Radar would still be lying at the front door, his harness on the floor, his food bowl in the kitchen untouched. He would eat in the evenings but then mope around, wandering slowly and aimlessly about the house, flopping onto the floor and exhaling in great sighs. He wouldn't play, wouldn't run with Syd.

One evening she put him in his harness to take him to the pet store and he came alive, so much so he could barely stay still enough for her to get the harness on him. He dragged her to the car and leapt into the back seat, tail wagging, tongue hanging out, so excited that his body trembled. When they got out of the car at the pet store parking lot his joy was suffocated by the black cloud of realization they were not at Mrs. Linton's. He looked around, barked, and then jumped back into the car. Radar loved the pet store but no amount of coaxing would make him get out of the car. He sat in the back seat barking and whining. She drove him home and it took a good half hour to get him out of the car. Once inside the house, she tried to pet him but he turned his head away and wouldn't look at her. That was four days ago. Today, once again, he sat at the door with his harness in his mouth. Today, Syd would take him to say goodbye to his friend.

Syd still hadn't heard from Branson. She didn't expect she would. She should have trusted him. Apollo would shine, but not on her. It was a grey day all around, fitting for a funeral.

In their greyness even the heavens mutedly bemoaned the loss of light, that light named Elsie Linton. Mrs. Linton's three sons were among the pallbearers. Mark would have been, too, if he wasn't injured. He and Radar were made honorary pallbearers. During the funeral procession under the grieving sky, Amy pushed Mark, jaw clenched and stoic in his wheelchair, behind the casket, Radar trotting beside him. The sight of that made Syd cry.

The guttural groans of grief from Mrs. Linton's family, the mournful sighs, the silent weeping, and the bewildered tear filled faces of grandchildren cried to a silent shrouded god in vain. Mrs. Linton's offspring and their offspring with her DNA and their memories would carry her with them through life but that's contrived consolation. Syd cried.

At the graveside, Radar lay down beside the casket and wouldn't move even as the miserable crying rain poured down upon him. Syd cried at that, too. Who did this evil thing?

Afterwards, Amy took Mark home. Regardless of the rain Syd had to go back to work after she dropped Radar off. As she pulled in her driveway she noticed an envelope stuck in her front door. She opened the door and looked at the envelope. "Sydney" was written across the front of it in Branson's handwriting. She and Radar went inside and she shut the door behind her. She stood in her foyer and opened the envelope. It was a handwritten letter.

"My Beloved;

It is not my intention to cause you consternation. If you throw this letter away without reading it, I will understand, but I'm pleading with you to hear me out. I have repeatedly turned things over in my mind, considering everything from every angle. I recognize I was unduly harsh with you and the failure in that respect was mine. I allowed temporary emotion to sully my response. When I saw the suspicion in your eyes it was untenable. I had believed that what we are to each other would supersede any external factor. My surprise and fear got the best of me. I've been searching my whole life for you and once I knew you actually existed, once I found you, the thought of losing you was, is, unbearable. You are the light in my eyes, the spring in my step, and without you everything is dark and devoid of life. I cannot live without you. You are my future. I cannot see a future without you. Can you see my future? Our future? Knowing that I will do whatever you need, will you look at the future? Will you be my Oracle? I am begging for a chance. You are my One.

Immortal love,
Branson

Her hands trembling, she folded the letter and returned it to the envelope. She could smell his cologne on the page. That smell stoked the fires of her memory, fire still there beneath the rain, beneath the failed attempt of ice at extinguishment, requiring a mere poke to wake it up and burn down the house. She put the letter on top of the bookcase, made sure Radar had plenty of food and water, then walked out, closing the door behind her. She went back to work.

\*\*\*

Having cleared away half of Mount Everest from her desk, and still getting nowhere on Liza's or Mark's cases, she decided to take a break. She'd intended to find a bite to eat but found herself driving past the courthouse. She pulled into the lot across the street and walked in through the back door. Eleanor buzzed her in to the Crown's office without asking what she was there for.

Syd walked down the hall and peeked into Branson's office. She was shocked. It was a mess. Files and papers littered the floor. She stepped inside. The garbage can sat in the middle of the room surrounded by balls of crumpled paper, empty chocolate bar wrappers, and paper coffee cups. A leaning tower of Pisa stack of files sat on the chair in front of Branson's desk. He looked up from his cluttered desk. Upon seeing her he straightened. He stared at her with those green eyes wide. He looked like a worried child.

"Hi," he whispered.

"You look busy," she said.

"No, no, come in." He stood and moved the pile of files from the chair, plopping them onto the floor.

She stepped forward toward the chair. He backed away like she was some animal about to devour him. She noticed his shirt was full of hard fold lines, like he'd put it on right from the package. He sat down, not removing his eyes from her. She sat in the chair across from him. Already primed with sorrow she felt sorry for him.

He waited, staring.

"I got your letter," she said.

He waited, hands in his lap, not his usual relaxed confident posture.

So laden with darkness, her life enveloped by it, her lungs breathing in the sordid soot of unrelenting evil, she desperately wanted to poke a hole in the suffocating shroud, to touch even a single ray of sweet sunshine.

"I'm sorry, too," she said.

"And what news from the gods have you? What do you foretell?" he asked.

She shrugged. "What do you want?"

"You," he said. "To move forward. With you."

"I don't want to hide," she said.

"Okay. But you do realize that comes with different problems."

"I do," she said. "I told the chief about us."

A mild look of alarm flashed over his face, then disappeared.

"And?"

"And there's no policy against it. I'm not saying we have to flaunt it. I just don't want to hide. I don't like it."

"Okay."

"And I want you to meet my Aunt Mary. And I want to meet your family."

"I would like to meet your Aunt Mary. I have no family for you to meet," he said.

"You have a brother."

"He's in B.C. I guess we could arrange a trip out."

"Okay," she said. "And what's with your desk?"

She picked up a cupcake wrapper and dropped it back down beside the candy wrappers and pistachio shells piled on the corner of his desk. He smiled and pulled open the top side drawer of his desk. She stood and looked. Cupcakes, candy, gum, and nuts filled the drawer.

"I haven't felt like going out for food." He grabbed a handful of nuts and a nutcracker. "Want a walnut?"

"Sure," she said.

261

They sat at his desk eating nuts while he cracked jokes about Riker, cinders falling onto the grey shroud, burning tiny holes through it as they talked about a lot of nothing. It was as if nothing had gone wrong between them.

# Chapter Twenty-Four

Syd heard voices in the hall outside her office. She heard Mark's voice. She walked out into the hallway. Two officers stood in front of Mark in his wheelchair.

Trying to hide her smile she said, "Hey, Lewis. You gonna sit around socializing all day or are you gonna get some work done here?"

He looked at her and grinned. The two officers carried on down the hall. Mark wheeled himself to the office door.

She said, "Did you miss me?"

He smiled. "Only when I was bored."

"I'm wounded," she said, smiling.

She hurried to his desk before he could get there and moved his chair away.

"Why you takin' my chair?" he asked.

"To make room for your wheelchair."

"You think I want to sit in this thing all day? Put it back."

She put the chair back. He stood from the wheelchair, pushed it into the corner and walked to his chair. With one hand on his desk for support he pulled out the chair and sat. She stood near him ready to help if he needed it.

"Stop it," he said.

"What?"

"Hovering. Don't go soft on me, LaFleur. And don't think I've gone soft."

She walked around to her desk and sat down. "Well, if you need anything,"

"I know. It's good for me to walk. I'm supposed to be walking," he said.

"So why the wheels?"

"They got a letter from my doctor saying I could walk but they insisted that I use the chair. Liability worries I guess. Stupid, but they weren't going to let me come back if I didn't agree. Now I gotta take that stinky elevator."

She rested her chin on her hand, staring at him.

"What's that look for?" He screwed up his forehead and his eyes shot her a defensive empty accusation. He sounded annoyed but she knew he was just feeling vulnerable and he didn't like it.

"There's something you're not telling me," she said.

"I have to be careful, is all," he said. "Light duties only. I'm stuck in the office. Can't even go to court."

"Careful how?"

"No high impact anything. No running, can't lift anything over thirty pounds. The doc said re-injury might be permanent. If I avoid that and do what the physio says, I'll be good as new in a couple of months."

She didn't hide the concern on her face.

"Don't look at me like that," he said. "And don't mother me."

"Okay. No mothering," she said.

"Can you get me a cup of coffee?" he asked.

She jumped up from her chair. She saw him smirk. She went to the coffee pot and used two hands to pick it up.

"Ooh, the coffee pot is so heavy. It must weigh more than thirty pounds," she said.

He laughed.

"Let's go over the Liza McNeil file again," she said. "I'm sure there was a guy, but it's like he's a ghost."

"Maybe the sister is wrong. Maybe there really is no guy," he said.

"She made a credit card purchase at that lingerie shop on Vine less than a week before she died," Syd said as she put his coffee in front of him.

"Maybe she bought it for herself," he said.

She shook her head. "I'd believe it if we found more than the one garment or if what we found was comfortable. You ever try to sleep wearing that crap?"

"Can't say I have," he said. "Slept beside it, though. That's nice." He grinned.

She threw a pen at him.

"Assault with a weapon, LaFleur." He tossed it back. "Let's say there was a guy. They would have to communicate somehow."

"I thought about that, too. We got nothing from her phone or computer."

"If he was married maybe they used a burner phone."

"But she wouldn't have to do that. Only the guy would have to," she said.

"Then they talked in person."

"Which brings us back to someone at work," she said.

"Or a neighbour, or somewhere she frequented. Didn't she take her niece to dance class every weekend? Maybe she met a married guy there. Maybe they made arrangements for their dates when they were there," he said.

"I interviewed everyone there."

"Well somebody's lying," he said. "I think we've already crossed paths with whoever he is."

"I think so, too. Everybody's alibied."

"Then we dig deeper into the alibis, see which ones break. Maybe someone's covering for him."

Leena Davis stuck her head in the door. "Welcome back, Lewis."

"Thanks."

"We got the serial rapist. One for the dumb criminal books," Leena said.

"Oh?" Syd smiled.

"He got into the victim's house while she was at work. He goes and hides in the closet of her spare room and waits for her to go to sleep. Except she doesn't just go to bed early and alone like always. She brings home a guy. They stay up late." Leena grinned. "So buddy's sittin' in the closet waitin' for the dude to leave, but he doesn't. He stays the whole night. In the morning, new boyfriend goes to get a towel out of the closet next to the spare room. He hears snoring. Buddy fell asleep in the closet waiting. They call 9-1-1 and uniforms go wake him up." She laughed.

"Beautiful," Syd said. "Who is he?"

"That's the other thing," Leena said. "He lives just down the street from one of our victims, your victim."

Syd and Mark looked at each other, sure they knew who it was.

"What's his name?" Mark asked.

"Hal Hogart."

"We talked to him," Mark said.

"We did, too. But we didn't have cause to search his place, nothing to tie him to any of the crimes. He's toast now, though."

"Good," Syd said.

"Gotta go," Leena said. She left.

***

Branson's car was in the driveway. He'd asked Syd for a house key and she'd given it. Radar didn't greet her when she walked in. She looked through the window to the back yard. He was out there on his tie-out playing with a ball by himself. She found Branson upstairs watching television.

She stood in the doorway of the room. "Hi."

"I cooked," he said, not taking his eyes off the television.

She felt that now familiar twist in her gut. Guilt. She leaned against the door frame.

"I'm sorry."

He looked at her. "I know."

She went and sat beside him. "I don't forget you, you know."

He gave her a look that told her he didn't believe her. Then he turned his eyes back toward the television.

"When I work late I feel bad for not being with you and Radar. But if I had come home on time I'd be sitting here thinking about work," she said.

He picked up the remote and pressed 'mute'. "Did you get anything new on Liza?"

"No. But they caught that serial rapist. They're sure he's the guy who raped Liza. He lived close to her."

Branson turned and looked at her, his glumness replaced by a spark of interest.

"He has to be the one who killed her," he said.

She shook her head. "Of course we looked at that but we're sure he isn't."

Branson's eyes were on her, but not focussed. It was that look he got when he was thinking.

"I don't understand," he said. "It's the obvious answer."

"It's not like you to jump to conclusions without knowing the facts," she said.

"It would be nice if you would give me facts," he said. "I'm going to be prosecuting these cases. It's not like I'm not going to be privy to everything anyway."

"You know there's always a hold back," she said.

"From the Crown?"

"Hold back is hold back until the case is done. I know she was a colleague and everyone wants this solved. I get it."

"How are they connecting this guy to her? I mean, the rape, not the homicide?"

She sat there considering whether or not to answer.

He said, "Is there enough similar fact? I can get a conviction on that even without the rape kit."

She caught her own reaction in time to keep a straight face. "What do you mean without a kit?"

"There's no kit. Pete told me," he said.

"What? When?"

"Around the time it happened. Liza told me, too," he said.

"When were you talking with Liza about that?" she asked, studying his face.

"Around the same time. She came to my office. She'd seen enough sexual assault trials. She was worried about proceeding," he said.

"What else did she say?"

"She didn't give me details, if that's what you mean. She just said she was worried about proceeding. I didn't have to tell her much. She already knew how victims get treated in court. She left my office in tears."

Syd remembered the day she'd seen Liza running from his office crying. So that's what it was about.

"Is this another interrogation, Syd?"

269

"No." She knew not to push it further right this minute. "Hey, let's have Mark and Amy here for supper some night soon."

"I can't get *you* here for supper," he said.

"If not supper, then let's go out somewhere," she said.

"Can't you be without Mark for a night?" he said.

"There are lots of nights I don't see Mark," she said. "What's going on?"

He shook his head and picked up the remote. He unmuted the t.v. and turned the volume up loud. She knew that was the end of the conversation. She went downstairs to let Radar in. In the short time it took her to do that, Branson walked out the front door.

# Chapter Twenty-Five

Ecklund stood in the doorway of the Major Crime office. Mark wasn't there yet.

"LaFleur. Gather what you have on Hogart and go to bail court."

"Davis has everything," she said.

"The Crown's office called. They want you over there."

"Why?"

"It's a bail opp. Hogart is a suspect in the McNeil homicide. They're saying they want you there."

"He's not a suspect," she said. "And he's not charged with murder. And since when are they dragging detectives over for bail? Is Davis going over?"

"They called me and asked for you."

"You don't find that strange?"

"It's a high profile case. Are you arguing with me, LaFleur?"

"No, sir."

"Good." He left.

She called Leena Davis' office. She wasn't in. She called the Crown's office and spoke to Eleanor.

"I didn't call Ecklund," Eleanor said. "I would have called you."

"Do you know what it is they need from me?"

"Sorry. I don't."

"Who's in bail?"

"Mr. Oleander."

*This is some sort of game on Branson's part,* Syd thought. But he had the power and she didn't.

"Can you ask him what he needs from me?" she asked.

"Just a minute."

Syd waited on hold until Eleanor came back.

"He says to just bring the entire McNeil file," Eleanor said.

This was Branson's way to get the information on Liza that Syd had denied him, the information she and Mark needed to hold back. She grit her teeth. She was furious and wanted to vent, but Eleanor wasn't the person to do that with. Eleanor adored Branson.

"Okay, thanks, Eleanor."

"And he wants you to come now," Eleanor said.

"Thanks."

She hung up the phone as Mark rolled in.

"What are you miffed about so early?" he asked.

She told him.

"That's bullshit," he said.

Ecklund walked past the office. Seeing her, he stopped. "Why are you still here, LaFleur?"

"I'm going," she said.

She took Liza's file, minus the coroner's report. She wanted the mechanism of death held back. She took her notebook from her suit jacket pocket, put it in the bottom drawer of her desk and locked it. She put the key in her pants pocket. 'Forgetting' her notebook was an utterly unbelievable thing for a detective to do, but that notebook was a treasure trove of information, including information that didn't make its way into reports. In it she had written about the vacuum. That was not in any report yet. Notebook pages were always photocopied and provided to the Crown, and subject to disclosure, but not until it was time to hand everything over to the Crown.

She drove to court and went in through the back door. She stashed two cigarettes on the doorframe before walking to the police room. She hoped to find Leena Davis. Maybe Leena could offer an understandable explanation for the premature demand for the McNeil file and Syd's attendance. No one was in the police room. She walked down the hall to the public waiting area. At eight-thirty it was quiet. The front doors were unlocked, but most people didn't show up this early for court. Not seeing Davis, she went up to the Crown's office. Eleanor buzzed her in.

"Branson's waiting for you," Eleanor said.

Syd walked to Branson's office. He'd cleaned it up. It was immaculate again. He, or maybe Eleanor, had finally hung his degrees on the wall.

"Come in," he said, without looking up, without a hint of warmth or even familiarity.

Taking the seat across from him she asked, "What did you need from me?"

He looked at her. Those eyes looked into hers for several seconds, assessing her. He finally answered, his words and tone businesslike.

"I understand you questioned Hal Hogart in relation to the McNeil murder."

"I did."

"He's in bail this morning. I need whatever you have on him," he said.

"Davis got a copy. Is it not in the bail brief?"

"No."

Syd thought this incredible. Davis was thorough and organized.

"I can give it to you, but my interaction with Hogart was in relation to the homicide, not the sexual assault."

"We will be proceeding with the sexual assault on similar fact. Forensics found Hogart's prints at her house."

"Yes, but not at the time of the sexual assault and only in the veranda and he has an explanation for that."

"Are you arguing the defence case for him?" He stared coldly at her.

Holding Liza's file in her lap she pulled out the section on their interactions with Hogart. She held it out to him.

"I want the whole file," he said.

"There's no reason for me to give you the whole file," she said.

"When I spoke with your inspector he indicated you would provide the entire file. Shall I call him again?"

She pressed her lips together lest her anger move them to say the wrong thing. She put the pages in her hand back into the file. She gave him the file. He opened it and began reading. Her stomach knotted and her head pounded until she let her glacier of defence flow over her.

He looked up from his reading. "This file is incomplete."

"The investigation is not complete." She moved forward to the edge of the seat.

"Where is the coroner's report?" he asked, leafing through the file.

"It's not in there."

"Don't play games with me, Detective. I know it's back. Where is it?"

"How do you know that?"

"Do you think I don't talk to people?" he said. "What was the cause of death?"

She stared at him.

"Detective LaFleur, you are interfering with a case currently before the court. You do understand the potential consequences."

"The McNeil homicide is not before the court," she said. "You have Hogart."

"And I'm trying to determine whether Hogart killed McNeil, whether we can charge him with murder."

"The investigation is not complete."

"Obstruction, Sydney. Cause of death."

She frowned, trying to hold in her irritation. "It's not obstruction."

He shrugged. "Maybe I wouldn't win in court on it, but you would lose."

She stared at him. "Asphyxiation."

"By what means?"

"I can't say." She felt every muscle in her body tense.

"Can't or won't?"

"The investigation is not complete."

"You do know I can get that report without you."

He stared at her with those eyes, but it was the ice queen, not Sydney, sitting in the chair across from him now. He turned his attention back to the file.

"Fine. You can wait downstairs for me."

The icy dismissal felt like a hot spear in her chest.

"I have to stay with the file," she said.

"The file is safe. It will be returned to you."

"I stay with the file," she said.

"Shall I call Ecklund?"

"If you wish."

He picked up the phone. Her heart jumped into her throat.

"Eleanor," he said, "Will you please come in and make a photocopy of the McNeil file?"

He put down the phone. He looked at Syd. She saw the corner of his lips turn up slightly. She wanted to scream at him, throw her fury at him. At the same time she wanted to say something to make the sun shine, to fall into

Apollo's arms and have everything go back to normal, for them to be that dynamite team again.

Eleanor cheerily walked into Branson's office and took the file. Syd sat there waiting.

Branson said, "I thought you had to stay with the file."

Syd stood up and walked out of his office. She waited at the front of the Crown's office where Eleanor was copying the file. Branson walked into the front of the office just as Eleanor gave the original file back to Syd.

Syd asked Branson, "So you don't need me for anything else?"

She wanted to get back to the office and work.

"Stay for bail," he said. "I might need you."

He walked out of the office. She looked at the wall clock above the photocopier. Quarter to nine. Bail court didn't start until ten. Wilkie might be in the police room. She could have a smoke and then maybe she could vent to him. She walked down the back stairs expecting Branson to be leaning out the back door for his smoke. He wasn't there. She stuck her head in the police room. Wilkinson's court bag sat behind his chair, but he wasn't there. She retrieved a cigarette from the doorframe, stepped outside and smoked it. It didn't help.

She heard Wilkinson barking at someone. She stepped into the police room as he hung up the phone.

"Politics," he said to her. "What do I care? I've got two-hundred-twenty-three days and seven hours until I retire. Hi, Syd."

"What's going on?" she asked.

He waved his hand like he was batting away a fly. "Doesn't matter. I'm fire proof now."

"Fire proof?"

"Yeah. What they'd have to pay me if they fire me now is more than what they'll have to pay if I work my time. Fire proof."

"Hey, have you seen Davis this morning?"

"No, why?"

"Her serial rapist is in bail today."

"Yeah, so?"

"I thought she might be here for it."

He looked at her like she had three heads. He shook his head. "What are you doing here?"

"Ecklund sent me over to bail court."

"Ecklund did? And it's nine o'clock."

"Politics, I think," she said.

"Then I don't want to know."

She sat down and picked up the dockets from his desk.

"Hey," he said, "Don't walk off with my dockets."

"I never do," she said, leaning back, leafing through the pages.

He made a show of staring at her like she was going to abscond with his dockets. She read through the names. Brice Avery's name was on the docket for bail. She sat up straight.

"Hey, why is Avery in bail?" she asked.

Wilkinson shrugged. "He never had a hearing. Just got remanded."

"Is he having a hearing today?"

"They're all supposedly having hearings, but you know how it goes. Ask Duty Counsel."

"Thanks, Wilkie." She stood up, still holding the docket.

"My docket," he said.

She smiled and placed it on his desk. Now she wanted to stay for bail court.

\*\*\*

Ten minutes before ten she caught Duty Counsel on his way out of the interview area in the cells.

"Are you doing Hogart?" she asked him.

"He leafed through the papers in his hand. "No. He has out of town counsel. Renfrew."

He went on his way before she had a chance to ask anything else.

Syd walked into a packed bail court. The woman from Victim Witness sat at the table beside Branson. Syd found a seat in the peanut gallery, ensuring she sat at the end of a row. The court constable stood leaning on the door that led to the cells, awake, and scanning the room. He spotted Syd and nodded at her. She nodded back. The drone of voices. The smell of old sweat and stale smoke clinging to the guy next to her. The flickering fluorescent light on the ceiling above defence counsel table. The court clerk stood up.

"Remove your hat," she squawked to a guy walking in wearing a Blue Jay's cap. "No food or drink in the courtroom. All cellphones off."

A dozing defence lawyer lifted his head at the noise of her voice, then let it drop again.

Syd heard Branson laugh. That laugh she loved so much. She looked in his direction. He and the woman from Victim Witness had their heads together, laughing about something. Something that wasn't quite jealousy grabbed at Syd's gut. She didn't mind that Branson was warm and sharing his laughter with another woman. Syd felt no need to possess him. But this display of warmth and sharing and togetherness with someone else was like a stinging slap in the face driving home the distance between them and the high stony wall blocking the sun, locking her out to flail alone in the barren cold of winter while he stood on his castle's turrets publicly firing stinging arrows of rejection that hit their mark with rebuking humiliation. She pulled herself from her miserable rumination and looked around the miserable courtroom packed with miserable people about to see their own miserable lives on display.

Eternally harried, Duty Counsel fell into his seat, exhausted even before court began.

"Are we ready yet?" the clerk asked at quarter after ten.

Branson looked around. "Yes, we're ready."

"Who's first?" the clerk asked.

Branson said, "We have out of town counsel."

Syd thought that meant Renfrew for Hogart, but no.

280

"Fuller," Branson said to the court constable. "Then Avery."

The constable spoke into his shoulder, telling custody the line-up. The clerk left the room.

Behind the witness stand the door to the room opened. The clerk walked in saying, "All rise." Everyone rose as the clerk announced court in session. When the Justice of the Peace was seated, the clerk said, "You may be seated." Everyone sat down, the drone of voices replaced by sounds of shuffling and the occasional cough.

Syd let her brain meander through its file on Liza while court dealt with Fuller. She paid attention when they brought Avery in. He looked around the courtroom as they put him in the box. He spotted Syd. He smirked at her. Branson stood and addressed the court.

"This is a consent release, Your Worship."

Syd couldn't believe her ears.

Branson continued. "Mr. Avery is charged with breaching his probation by being in possession of an incendiary device, to wit a cigarette lighter. Mr. Avery is a smoker. He said he got a light from a friend and, like many smokers do, absent-mindedly slipped the lighter into his pocket."

The J.P. interrupted him. "Which means he was in possession of the lighter at the time he lit his cigarette."

"Yes, Your Worship, technically a breach. In any case, Mr. Avery has spent time in pre-trial custody and has a date for a guilty plea next week. As the Crown is seeking time served on a plea, with credit, his continued detention is contrary to the principles of justice. He has never failed to appear, so the primary ground is not at issue. The Crown is suggesting bail on a recognizance without a surety. Conditions to keep the peace, attend court, and notify the court of any change in address."

The J.P. agreed and made the order. The constable led smiling Avery back to the cells. He would be out of court before Syd was. She waited as they brought up one accused after another, but not Hogart. She felt increasingly annoyed at the waste of her time. She could be working on Liza's case, or talking to the Fire Marshal's office, or any number of other things instead of being held hostage beside some guy who was oblivious to the merits of soap and water.

At lunch she went to the back door for a smoke. She would ask Branson what time he thought Hogart would be up. Branson didn't come back there for his smoke. She ran up to the Crown's office where Eleanor informed her that Branson had gone for lunch. She left and walked the two blocks to an all-day breakfast place the lawyers never went to. She noticed Branson with the woman from Victim Witness across the street in the park. Syd stood frozen as she watched Branson put his arm around the woman and lead her to a bench where they sat together. Syd stepped into the restaurant and chose a table in the corner where she could see the door but not the park.

Hogart's hearing happened right after lunch. The clerk read the charges. Sexual assault bodily harm, break and enter, choking, all times three, so only in relation to three of the victims. Liza was not one of them. Syd knew there were many more charges coming in relation to other victims. He'd not yet been charged for any crime against Liza. Syd listened to Branson read the facts into the record and present the Crown's case against bail. He never once mentioned Liza. He used nothing from the file he'd fought so hard to get.

Renfrew presented the defense case for bail and proposed a residential surety. The surety was a sketchy looking guy with scraggly grey hair that fell over the shoulders of his holey black AC/DC tee-shirt. The questions posed to the surety were the usual. Syd thought the surety was weak, that Branson would easily have him disqualified. But he didn't push the guy at all. It might not have been so bad in front of a J.P. with a tendency to detain, but this J.P. regularly twisted himself into a pretzel finding ways to release even on a reverse onus.

Hogart was released on the residential surety with a curfew and a no-contact with the victims. *This J.P. has just made an accomplice out of this surety,* she thought. She left court disgusted, disheartened, and confused.

She told Mark about the whole thing when she got back to the office. His only words about it were, "It's all bullshit."

\*\*\*

She drove by Hogart's house on her way home. She saw him and his surety sitting in lawn chairs on the front porch drinking beer and laughing. The victims of Hogart's crimes wouldn't be laughing or relaxing tonight. By now the victims named on the no-contact order would have been notified of his release and conditions. Hogart had his liberty; It would be a long time, if ever, before his victims had theirs. Syd stopped at the stop sign at the end of the street. Liza's house sat directly in front of her. A 'for sale' sign stood in the middle of the overgrown lawn. The petunias were gone, choked to death by the dominating weeds. Syd swallowed back tears and drove home.

# Chapter Twenty-Six

She took Radar for a run. Radar and her runs were like re-
set buttons. Afterwards, she played with him in the
backyard for a bit before going upstairs for a shower. As
usual, while she showered, Radar stuck his head around
the shower curtain and bit at the stream of water. It was
odd when he turned and left the bathroom. She turned off
the water and listened. She didn't hear anything unusual,
didn't hear Radar bark. She turned the water back on and
lingered in the soap and steam. There were some days
when she took too long in the shower, as if that would
wash away the grime of the world. It never worked. This
was one of those days.

She wrapped herself in a towel, scooped her dirty
clothes off the floor, and padded to her bedroom. The door
was closed. She didn't remember doing that.

"Radar," she called.

Nothing.

She quietly turned the door knob. She pushed open the
door. A black dress that didn't belong to her lay neatly atop
her blue comforter. At the foot of the bed, placed in
alignment, stood a pair of high-heeled shoes. She *never*
wore high heels. Her heart raced, her breathing sped up

trying to keep pace. She stepped back. With her back to the hallway wall she hurriedly threw on her dirty clothes her hands shaky from adrenaline. Where the hell was Radar and why hadn't he barked? Where was her phone? Downstairs.

She crept down the stairs, skipping the third one from the top that creaked. At the bottom of the stairs she stopped and took a breath. The door to outside was right in front of her. She could simply walk out. That's what she would advise someone else to do. But where was Radar? She heard noise in the kitchen. She stepped around the corner into the living room and looked through the dining room to the kitchen.

"Oh," she said.

Branson turned around, knife in one hand, a tomato in the other.

"I knew you had a frustrating day. I thought I'd cook for you, he said. "Did you see your present?"

Reminding herself that her pounding heart and the feeling of electricity through her major muscles were merely a result of epinephrine in her system, fight or flight, and no longer useful, she tried to level her response.

"Yes," was all she could manage in the moment.

"Sheila from Victim Witness actually helped me get it."

"Oh?" She stepped closer to the kitchen.

"She didn't pick it out. I did. But she went and got it for me. I had lunch with her in the park today."

"Oh?" She could smell onions. She glanced at the counter. He was chopping onions and tomato. "I suppose lunch is a good price for a personal shopper."

He smiled. "Maybe that's true. I had to go to the bank machine anyway and it was just better to bring her along. That way I could give her the cash there, not in front of everyone at court."

Too many details, Syd thought. He's lying. But his bank is over there. I'm overreacting, misreading. I'm being stupid again.

"Oh," she said. "Is Radar out back?"

"Yes," he said. "I hope you feel like bruschetta. I'm not sure what goes with the wine in the fridge."

"I thought you were mad at me," she said.

He brushed the ciabatta with the olive oil. "Why?"

"We had words last night and you left."

"Words? I left because I needed a good sleep. I knew I had an intense day today."

She stood in doubt of her perceptions.

"We could have gone to bed early," she said.

He turned to face her. "Sydney, you know that a good sleep in this house is not guaranteed. I'm still not use to having a one-hundred-twenty pound dog jumping on the bed at three in the morning."

"Oh."

He turned back to his food prep. She stepped an inch closer.

"So what was all this today with the file? And calling Ecklund?"

"I thought if I called Ecklund and he ordered you to provide the file, then it would take you off the hook."

"You demanded the file and then you didn't even use it."

He put the knife and cutting board in the sink. "You were in there. You saw there was no opening for me to use what was in that file."

"I told you that from the beginning," she said.

He turned to face her. "Sydney, *you* told me that. I didn't know what was in that file. The police are a great help but it's my responsibility as Crown to look and make those determinations myself. You know this." His tone was paternalistically scolding.

He turned away and turned on the tap to wash his hands. The tension in his back and the tone of his voice told her he was getting frustrated. All of his explanations were plausible, but she still didn't feel good about it all. Maybe that was more annoyance at herself for having misread so many things so badly. She decided not to push it. She walked past him and peeked out the back window to check on Radar. He had dug three holes in the back lawn and was happily working on a fourth.

"Don't you want to know what the dress is for, why I went to all the trouble?" he asked.

"Oh. Sorry. Yes," she said.

"I have theatre tickets for the two of us." He smiled. "I know you've been wanting to go out."

"Wonderful." She smiled, relaxed a little. "When?"

"Wednesday night. Sorry it's not a Friday. It was the best I could do."

"Wednesday is great."

"Go try on the dress and make sure it fits. I'll pour you a glass of wine."

She did. They drank wine and ate bruschetta. They walked through the neighbourhood holding hands. They kissed while fireflies danced around them. It was sunny again. But there was something heavy in her. It was like one of those sunny days when the sky is blue and cloudless, yet the wind silently sweeps through the treetops turning the leaves so they look silvery.

# Chapter Twenty-Seven

"We're missing something," Syd said. "I was hoping you'd see something I haven't, come up with a question I didn't ask."

Mark sipped his coffee and shook his head. "I don't see it. Maybe we're at that point."

"You mean waiting."

"Yeah. CFS is always backlogged. How was your night?" he asked.

"Good. We're actually going out to the theatre." She checked to see if anything had come in from the Office of the Fire Marshal.

"About time. What are you seeing?"

She stopped and thought. "You know, I didn't even ask. I think I was just happy he actually wants to do something."

"When's the show?"

"Wednesday."

"Who goes to the theatre on a Wednesday?" he asked.

"Me, I guess," she said. "Will you take another look at Liza's file? I want to pull up the stuff on the fire."

Mark started going through Liza's file from the beginning. Syd pulled up everything they had so far on the fire. She saw the report from the arresting office on Brice Avery's breach, the one that hadn't been done yet the last time she looked. She read through it. It said everything she'd already been told, except for one detail. That detail froze her. Avery had a cigarette lighter in his possession, specifically a pink Bic lighter.

"Shit," she said.

Mark glanced at her, then went back to what he was reading.

"Avery had a pink lighter," she said.

"So?"

"How many guys choose to buy a pink lighter?" she asked.

"Some guys like pink. Besides, Avery will take whatever he can get his hands on," he said.

"In court they said Avery got a light from a friend and slipped the lighter into his pocket. I know the friend he saw that night was a guy."

"So maybe he saw another friend earlier, a woman, and got it then." Mark returned his attention to Liza's file.

Syd stood up and walked toward the door.

"Where are you going?"

"To find Brice Avery." She turned to face Mark. "You know who always buys pink lighters?"

Mark shook his head.

"Branson," she said.

"Oh, come on, Syd. You don't think Branson set my place on fire. Why would he do that?"

291

"Maybe he's jealous of you. Maybe he's jealous of Radar and thought he'd be with Mrs. Linton."

"You've left the ballpark," Mark said.

"I'm following up on details."

"So what's your theory? Branson hired Avery to set the fire and gave him his pink lighter to do it?"

She felt her shoulders sink a little. "That does sound ridiculous," she admitted.

"Right. If he was going to hire someone to off me then he would hire a professional. Avery is a freak but he's not a hitman."

"After the fire Branson had a different lighter. He said he lost his."

"People lose lighters all the time," he said.

"What do we say about coincidences?"

"That there aren't any, but we both know there are. Next you're going to say 'where's there's smoke there's fire'," he said.

"Look, I don't know what it means. I do know it's a detail that's bugging me. I don't know why. I just want to dot our i's and…"

He finished her sentence, "And cross our t's. Okay. Go. But I'm going to bring this up forever." He grinned. "Hey, Syd, remember that time you thought a Crown Attorney hired a low level criminal to burn my house down?"

"Hey, Mark, remember that time when Jolene beat you up with her purse and you still wanted another date?"

"That's not the same."

"Remember Amber?"

"Oh, no. We don't talk about Amber."

She laughed. He grinned and shook his head. She left. She went to Avery's address. He wasn't there. She drove around downtown. She spotted him loitering. She parked the car and got out. He hadn't noticed her. He pulled a lighter from his jeans pocket and lit a smoke. He saw her. He chucked the lighter into the busy road and ran. She chased him. He weaved through people on the sidewalk, then ran between two parked cars. She veered toward the road to cut him off. He had a good head start but she knew she would catch up to him eventually, that he would peter out before she did. There was too much traffic for him to get across the road quickly. He ran alongside the parked cars.

She yelled, "I just want to talk to you."

He kept running. He darted left toward the park. A woman with two small kids grabbed them and held them close.

"Stop running," Syd yelled.

He glanced back at her. He stumbled. He fell and didn't get up. She caught up and stood beside him, her hands on her knees. Still face down on the grass and coughing, he put his hands behind his back.

"For pete's sake, Avery, get up."

He rolled over and sat up. "I'm not breaching. You can search me. I don't have a lighter. I'm not in breach."

"I should arrest you for making me run," she said. "Get up. Let's go sit on a bench."

293

He looked at her with both surprise and suspicion. He stood up.

"Over there," she said, pointing to a park bench.

He squinted at the park bench, thinking.

"Oh come one. What are you afraid of?" she said.

He looked at her. "Every time I talk to you I go to jail," he said.

"Because the only times I talk to you is when you've committed a crime. I'm not here for that today."

"Oh, you wanna be friends?"

"No."

He smiled. "Okay."

As they walked toward the bench she said, "I believe you that you didn't set that fire."

"Which one?"

"The one where the lady died."

"Good, because I didn't."

They stood in front of the bench. He pulled a crushed pack of Export A's from his pocket. They sat down.

"You are a witness, though," she said.

He pulled a cigarette from the package. Filterless. *A filterless cigarette burns completely in a fire,* she thought.

"You got a light?" he asked, smirking.

She reached into her jacket pocket and pulled out a lighter. He held out his hand for it.

"Don't try," she said.

He stuck the cigarette in his mouth and leaned forward. She lit the end of it.

"The night of the fire," she said.

"Which one?"

"You know which one. Is there another one you want to tell me about?"

"No." His left knee bounced up and down.

"Why you so nervous?"

"Talk to Detective LaFleur and go to jail."

"It's different this time," she said.

"Oh yeah?" He took a quick nervous puff on his smoke.

"You've always been the suspect, the accused. Now you're a witness, my witness."

"Do I get a reward?"

"No."

He took another two puffs of his smoke.

"You've never killed anyone," she said.

"No. I always make sure nobody's home," he said.

"Why is that?"

"I don't want to kill anyone. I like the fire."

"You know some people set fires because they're angry," she said.

"I know that." He held the tiny bit of remaining cigarette between his ridged yellow nails, taking a final puff before dropping it into the grass.

Syd put her toe on the butt and ground it out.

"I wanted to watch it go out," he said. "It would have gone out."

"Do you ever set fires out of anger?"

He shook his head, pulling out another cigarette.

"Angry ones make mistakes," he said, putting the cigarette to his lips.

Syd lit the end for him.

"I think whoever started that fire was angry," she said.

He leaned back on the bench and took a long slow drag, nodding his head.

"Are you *sure* you didn't see anyone else around that house?"

"I'm sure."

"Where did you get that that pink lighter?"

He sat up straight. "Oh, no. You're doing it again."

"Doing what?"

"Playing tricks."

"You're my witness, remember?"

He turned his eyes to look at her. "I found it."

"When?"

"That night."

"Before or after the fire started?"

"After."

"Okay. Where?"

He turned his face away and puffed hard on his cigarette. The lighter still in her hand, she held it close to her lap and flicked it. He turned back to glance at it.

"Where?" she asked again.

He dropped the tiny butt on the ground. It went out on its own. He took another cigarette from his pack. His knee started bouncing again.

"Why are you afraid to tell me? I don't care if you stole it."

He held his fresh cigarette up, waiting for her to give him a light. She flicked the lighter in her lap.

"I know someone who uses a pink lighter," she said.

The bench vibrated from the accelerated bouncing of his knee.

"No matter who did it, I'm going to get him. No matter who it is."

The vibrating stopped as he froze. He looked at her, eyes wide. He turned away.

"Gimme a light," he said.

"Tell me where you got that lighter."

"That's inducement."

She flicked the lighter again.

"Inducement," he said.

"You're a witness."

"On the street."

"Which street?"

"In front of the old lady's house. Right in front of the house in the middle of the street."

She held up the lighter to the tip of his cigarette. He took a big drag and coughed.

"Who owns that lighter you found?"

"I don't know. It was just there," he said.

She stood up. "Thank you. Next time don't run from me."

"You're not going to arrest me for the breach?"

"Did you breach?"

"No."

"Then I can't arrest you."

"I like being a witness better," he said.

"Then don't do anything that makes you a suspect."

He laughed.

"I mean it, Avery. Don't breach or you'll go back in."

"Do I get a reward?"

"No." She walked away.

On her way back to the car she looked for the lighter Avery had tossed into the road. She saw it in pieces, the lunch hour traffic continuing to pulverize it. Feeling her blouse sticking to her back, she took off her suit jacket and tossed it onto the passenger seat. She sat in the car and turned the air conditioning on full blast.

As she stepped into the office Mark asked, "So did you eliminate the diabolical Crown?"

"No." She checked the coffee pot, saw the dregs, and changed her mind about coffee. "But Avery found that lighter in the street right in front of your place."

"Oh."

She sat down. "When I left with Radar that night there was no pink lighter in the road. I'd have noticed that."

"Still might be nothing," he said.

"Uh-huh." She had started writing the report on today's interaction with Avery. Mark left her to it. When she was done she shared the information with The Office of the Fire Marshal.

She didn't run that night. She decided to tackle the garden and fill the holes Radar had dug in the lawn. Radar helped with the weeding by digging furiously in the garden bed, disturbing the roots of the invasive plants. Syd heard a clattering sound on the patio next to the garden bed where Radar was digging. She looked for the source of the sound. It didn't sound like a stone. It had bounced under the barbeque. A dirt caked pink lighter. Branson must have dropped it and it bounced into the weedy garden bed. She felt stupid and embarrassed and guilty once again.

She took a picture of it with her phone. She texted the picture to Mark with the message, *"Look what I found in my yard."*

He texted back with. *"Lmao. Forever."*

She responded, *"Jolene."*

Before she put her phone down on the patio table it buzzed again.

Branson. "Going to hockey. Miss u already."

She texted back a heart and a smiley face. Covered in dirt, but not minding it, she sat in her lounge chair. She watched a squirrel bury something in the grass. She thought about the squirrel in Liza's garden the day they found her. It had taken a pistachio. Pistachios. Pistachio shells on Branson's desk.

She phoned Mark and told him.

"Stop it, Syd. He was cleared," Mark said. "Stop this."

# Chapter Twenty-Eight

She stood just outside the office door watching Mark as he walked slowly from the coffee pot to his desk. It seemed to her that he was thinking about each step, trying to trek the eight feet without spilling his coffee or taking a spill himself. She waited until he put his mug down before she made her presence known.

"Hey," she said.

"Hey. I might have found a small crack we can pry open, check out."

"Oh?" She sat down.

"Before we get going, Branson called to talk to me."

"You? For what?" she asked.

"He asked if I could do anything to make sure you get out of here so you wouldn't be late for your theatre date."

"Oh."

"He asked me something else I thought was kind of weird."

She looked at him, waiting.

"He asked me if I had a key to your place."

"I wonder if he wanted you to take Radar."

"Maybe. But that's not what he asked me."

She shrugged. "So when you told him you had a key what did he say?"

"I lied to him," he said. "I told him I didn't have a key."

She leaned back. "Why?"

"I'm not even sure why. I just did."

"You're both weird," she said. "Tell me about the possible crack."

"I promised him I'd make you leave here by three," he said.

"Okay. Tell me what you found."

"Yeah. You interviewed the Milfords," he said.

She put her feet on the desk. "Yes. From the niece's dance school."

"I thought they gave too many details," he said.

"I thought that, too but then I chalked it up to nervousness about being asked for an alibi."

"They both say they heard teenagers outside at twenty after ten. They both gave you a rundown of what they watched on t.v. and what time they turned it off."

"You think the statements are too much the same," she said.

"Yeah. I could see one of them looking at the clock when they heard the teenagers outside, but both of them? And why do they both give a rundown of what programs they watched? Why not just say they were watching t.v.?"

"Yes, that was odd," she said.

"One more thing." He sipped his coffee. "They said they were watching Dracula on CBC Live at one in the

301

morning. I checked. That's what the program guide says, but it was an error. What actually aired was a re-run of a nature program."

She let her feet fall from the desk. "See. This is why I miss you when you're not here."

"Oh, and here I thought it was because of my lovely personality," he said.

"You take the husband, I'll take the wife?" she asked.

"Yeah. Let's call them before they leave for work," he said as he picked up the phone.

***

Mrs. Milford sat in the chair in interview one and smoothed out her blue and white floral print dress over her knees. She had her salon highlighted blonde hair pulled up in a breezy summer do that showed off her pearl earrings. She crossed her legs. Syd noticed the designer logo on her blue sandals. The dress was good quality material. Mrs. Milford placed her professionally manicured hands in her lap, her left hand wearing an ostentatious oval cut solitaire diamond ring with her wedding band.

After the usual spiel and an offer of water which Mrs. Milford declined, Syd began the interview.

"Thank you for coming in on such short notice. We're just going over everyone's statements and making sure we understand everything correctly."

"Okay."

"You said that on that night you heard teenagers outside your home."

"Yes."

"What were they doing?"

"Laughing and hollering. Walking in the middle of the street."

"Do they live in your neighbourhood?"

Mrs. Milford paused, then said, "I don't know where they live."

"Had you had problems with them before?"

"No."

Syd wrote down the question and answer while Mrs. Milford watched.

"I don't want them to be in trouble," Mrs. Milford said. "They didn't come back."

"So you'd never had any problems or issues with them before."

"None. I don't want anything done about them."

"Did they worry you?" Syd asked, pretending to be focussed on her open binder.

"No."

Syd looked up from her binder. "So why did you make note of the time?"

Mrs. Milford blinked. "I don't know." She blinked again. "My husband looked."

"Was he worried about them?"

"Maybe they were going to break into cars," Mrs. Milford said.

"Oh, well if that's the case, we should find them."

"I didn't say they did that. There's no need to find them."

Syd made eye contact. Holding it, she said, "I see."

Mrs. Milford squeezed her hands together in her lap. Syd waited a few seconds, letting her be nervous.

"You said you and your husband were watching Dracula at one in the morning."

"Yes."

"What channel was that on?"

"CBC Live."

"CBC Live Toronto?"

"Yes."

"Was it a good movie?"

"Yes."

Syd nodded. "I've seen that one. Pretty suspenseful."

"Yes."

"And you both went to sleep after that."

"Yes."

"You sleep in the same bed?"

"Yes."

"If you were asleep how can you be sure your husband was there all night?"

Mrs. Milford blinked and squeezed her hands. "I got up for a glass of water at three."

"How do you know it was three?" Syd had stopped pretending to look at her binder and kept her eyes on Mrs. Milford.

"Because I looked at the clock."

"The clock in the bedroom? Kitchen?"

"The clock on the microwave." Mrs. Milford took a deep breath.

"So you went to the kitchen for your water."

"Yes."

"Exactly three o'clock? Exactly?" Syd asked.

"It was a few minutes after three."

"You said you looked at the clock. So what did the clock say?"

"Five after three."

Syd looked her in the eyes. "Mrs. Milford, why would you lie to me about a glass of water?"

Mrs. Milford's cheeks and chest flushed. "I'm not lying."

Syd looked at her, waiting. Mrs. Milford sat unnaturally still, composed except for her eyes that betrayed her by being unable to look at Syd's without darting away.

"Let's go back to watching t.v. At one you were watching the movie."

"Yes."

"Are you *certain* it was live television?"

"Yes. I'm certain."

"Mrs. Milford, we checked and the CBC's program guide contained an error that night. The program guide said the movie was airing at one but what actually aired was something else. So I'm trying to understand why you would lie about what television show you were watching."

Tears welled up in Mrs. Milford's blue eyes.

"And why you would lie about a glass of water."

The tears spilled out.

"And it makes me ask myself what else you might be lying about. Like maybe your husband wasn't home."

Tears. Silence.

"If your husband wasn't home that's not illegal. But now I'm asking myself if he wasn't doing anything illegal, why lie about it?"

Mrs. Milford pressed her lips together tightly and shook her head, her pink face reddening. "You can't pin this on him," she said jutting her chin up. "He didn't strangle that woman!"

"What woman?"

"That Liza woman."

"How do you know she was strangled?"

Mrs. Milford blinked. She blinked again. Her mouth hung open. Syd waited for a few seconds.

"So were you an accomplice or just an accessory after the fact?"

Wide eyes.

"I'll lose everything," Mrs. Milford blurted out. "The house, the cars, the cottage."

Syd was unmoved. "Who is going to take care of your daughter while you're in jail for covering for him?"

Mrs. Milford put her face in her hands and shook her head. "Oh my god. Oh my god."

Syd waited. Mrs. Milford lifted her face and wiped her mascara stained tears away with her fingertips while she calmed her breathing and straightened.

"I'm going to try to help you," Syd said. "I'm going to give you a chance to get out of this."

Mrs. Milford stared at her, grey-faced and trembling.

"But only one chance. If you tell me the truth you might stay out of jail, stay home with your little girl. But lie to me even once and your one chance with me goes up in smoke."

Mrs. Milford nodded.

"Let's start over," Syd said. "Tell me about that night."

"I was home with my daughter. She was in bed."

"And where was your husband?"

A new wave of tears brimmed in her eyes. "I don't know."

"What time did he leave the house?"

"He never came home from work."

"Where was he?"

"I don't know. I think he was having an affair. He came home at around five in the morning stinking of sweat and perfume."

"Did you confront him?"

"No. I never do. I don't work. He gives me a good life. When he has his affairs, I pretend I don't know. But I know."

"Who was he having the affair with at that time?"

"I don't know. I don't ask questions."

"Doesn't it bother you that he does that?"

307

"Of course it bothers me. But he has disgusting needs and if he gets them filled elsewhere he doesn't bother me with them."

"What kind of disgusting needs?"

"Do I have to answer that?"

Syd waited, not answering her.

"He likes to," she looked down. "He likes to, to choke, during, you know."

"I need you to tell me."

"He likes to choke me during intercourse. There. I said it."

"I'm sorry to have to ask you this, but does he use his hands or some other tool?"

"His belt. That's why I said 'strangled'."

"I understand."

She looked Syd in the eyes. "It scared me, you know."

Syd nodded. "It's a dangerous practice. Did he ever do that without your agreement?"

"No. He never forced anything like that."

"Whose idea was it to come up with a false alibi?"

"Mine."

"What was his reaction to that?"

"He just went along with it. I think he was just glad I wasn't asking questions."

"Why did you think you needed an alibi? Why not just tell us he was having an affair?"

"Because I saw Liza's picture in the news and I knew everyone who knew her would be questioned. He would be a suspect."

Syd leaned back in her chair. "Why would he be a suspect?"

"Because he was out all night."

"Do you think he was having an affair with Liza?"

"I don't know."

"How did he react to the news that she'd been killed?"

"He thought it was awful."

"Do you think he killed her?"

"No."

"Okay. Thank you for coming in." Syd stood up.

"Am I going to be arrested?"

"I'm not arresting you today. We'll check to see if you've been truthful here and you haven't left anything out. Wait here a few minutes. We'll get you on your way soon."

Syd listened at the door of interview two where Mark was still with Mr. Milford. She stuck her head in. Mark picked up his binder and stepped out into the hall.

"He was out all night," Syd whispered. "He's into choking."

"He's involved with a married woman. Said he was with her all night," Mark said.

"Got a name? I'll check," she said.

Mark gave her the name of Shelly Shaw and a phone number. Syd went to their office and made the call. Mrs. Shaw sounded alarmed at hearing from the police. She agreed to come into the station for an interview with Mark as long as she didn't have to tell her husband about it. Syd arranged for Mrs. Shaw to come in at three o'clock.

# Chapter Twenty-Nine

## Mark and Pete

Syd had happily gone home just before three to get ready for her theatre date. Mark conducted the interview with Mrs. Shaw who corroborated Mr. Milford's statement that he'd been with her all night. Mark poured himself a coffee then carefully made his way toward his desk with it. The message light on the phone blinked at him. He turned his attention to his computer. He noticed he had email notifications. He ignored that and the phone, pulling up the forms he needed.

Just after four, Pete barged in. "Don't you answer your phone or pick up messages?"

"Who put ants in *your* pants," Mark said.

"Branson Oleander was at your house," Pete said.

"What are you talking about?"

Pete sat at Syd's desk. "You remember the shoeprints we found around Syd's house?"

"Yeah."

"And then we found the same one at your place the night of the fire?"

"Yeah."

"They're Branson's."

"How do you know that?"

"I had lunch with him today on the patio at Papa's Bistro. It was freakin' weird. He wasn't dressed for court. He's wearing track pants and running shoes. All through lunch he was pumping me for information on cases we're working. He's done that before but he's always casual about it, like just talk, but it's sometimes just a little too much. So we're done lunch and he sits back with his coffee and crosses his legs. I can see the bottoms of his running shoes. Asics."

Mark raised his eyebrows, listening attentively. Pete continued.

"So I can see the tread on his shoes. It's the same as the prints at your place and at Syd's and I'm trying to see if that unique triangular gouge is in the sole but I can't. So I drop a spoon so I can bend down to pick it up, get a closer look at the sole of his shoe and it's there. The gouge."

Mark stared at him. "Are you *sure* it's the same?"

"No. It's not like I do forensics for a living. Of course I'm sure."

"Why didn't you tell me right away?" Mark asked.

"I had a B&E. And I did call you, like five times. Are you hearing me?"

Mark rubbed his temples. "There's an explanation for his shoeprints to be at Syd's."

"Facing the windows? Is he creepin' her?"

"No. There still could be an explanation," Mark said.

"What about your place, then?" Pete asked.

"I don't know."

Mark picked up the phone and called Syd. No answer. He sent a text telling her to call him a.s.a.p. He decided he'd email her as well. He opened his email and saw the notification from the Centre of Forensic Sciences.

"CFS report is in, probably on the McNeil kit. I'm going to shoot Syd an email. Maybe she's upstairs and not hearing her phone," Mark said.

"Look at the report," Pete said.

"One sec," Mark said as he typed an email.

"Look at the report now. Maybe Syd wasn't out of the ballpark after all," Pete said.

Mark opened the secure portal for the forensics report.

"There's a familial match on one of the DNA profiles from Liza's kit," Mark said.

Pete stood and came around the desk to read over Mark's shoulder. "Match to who?"

"Unknown. It's a paternal match to a fetus found in a murdered prostitute in Timmins, Ontario," Mark said.

"Branson is from Timmins," Pete said.

Mark called Syd again. No answer. He pulled up the number for the Timmins Police Service. He called and got the name of the detective who worked the unsolved homicide, Detective MacAdam. Once connected to MacAdam, Mark put the phone on speaker so Pete could hear.

"Yeah, I remember that case," MacAdam said. "She was found in the water. Strangulation. No forensics except the fetus. Frustrating case. You know how those go."

"By any chance was a Branson Oleander involved in any way, even peripherally, on that case?" Mark asked.

"No. Branson was a Crown here. The case is unsolved, never made it as far as the Crown's office."

"So his name didn't come up as knowing her or ever having met her?" Mark asked.

"Actually, he was interested in that case. He was Crown on another one where our victim was accused of utter forged document. He agreed to a conditional discharge for her. Said he felt sorry for her. When she turned up dead six months later he remembered her, wanted to be kept apprised of our progress."

"So he was calling you about it, in an official capacity?" Mark asked.

"No. Not like that. There's a bar we all hang out at. He was there a lot, playing pool with the boys. Sometimes the guys talk."

"Do you happen to know if Branson has a brother who lives in Timmins?" Mark asked.

"I think he has a brother, but he doesn't live in Timmins. Somewhere in the GTA, maybe Toronto. What's all this about?"

Mark explained briefly.

"You know who would know," MacAdam said, "Weaver, our forensics guy. Branson and him were fishing buddies."

"Like he cozied up to me," Pete said. "He pressed me to lose or destroy the McNeil rape kit. Said he was trying to protect her, that she didn't want to proceed. Now we know why."

MacAdam said, "You think he was responsible for our homicide."

"At the very least he got her pregnant and didn't want to be tied to her," Pete said.

"Or maybe she threatened to expose him, sue him for child support," MacAdam said.

Mark thanked MacAdam and told them they'd be in touch again. He called Syd again. No answer. He called the Crown's office and asked for Branson.

"I'm sorry, Mr. Oleander left for the day just before lunch," Eleanor told him.

Mark looked at Pete and said, "We've got to go to Syd's right now."

# Chapter Thirty

After a good play in the yard with Radar, Syd sat in front of the computer in her home office. The image of the words, 'poison flower' written in Liza's hand on the front of her gardening magazine had popped into Syd's head. She knew it would keep popping up until she appeased her constantly craving curiosity. She googled it. Finding too many results she switched to an image search and scrolled through them. When she spotted an image that looked like the flowering shrub in her front yard, she clicked on it. The name of the shrub was 'oleander'. She sat back, staring at the computer screen. Did Liza write down 'poison flower' because she'd found the coincidence with Branson's last name interesting, or was it more than that? Syd felt her brain chugging away like trains in a busy station going off in different directions, destinations unknown. She put on the brakes. Branson had been cleared and her mind was behaving like a nagging mosquito that you slap at and miss, only slapping yourself in the end. She turned off the computer and stood up, mosquito be damned. She was happy and determined to keep it that way, to bask in the sunshine while she had it.

She took a long shower. Radar pulled the bath towel from the rack and ran off with it. She laughed at that. Nothing could annoy her today. She was focussed on all the good things in her life, right down to her gratitude for the luxury of a hot shower. She had everything a person could ask for and now things with Branson had turned around for the better. Life was wonderful.

She threw on her bathrobe and ambled down the hall to her room. She was surprised to see Branson sitting on the foot of the bed. Not yet dressed for the theatre, he wore track pants and a t-shirt, and running shoes. He never wore shoes in the house. His gorgeous green eyes looked her way. She smiled brightly at him.

"Well, hello. I didn't expect you so early," she said.

He smiled back at her. That perfect smile, that perfect face.

"I thought we could spend some time alone together," he said.

"Sure. Where's Radar?"

"Outside." He nodded toward the dresser where a bottle of Syrah sat beside a full wine glass. "I poured you some wine."

"Oh, it's too early," she said. "I don't want to be sleepy for the show."

"Don't worry. Just one glass won't matter. And I'm driving."

"Why not," she said.

She took the glass from the dresser and sat beside him on the bed. She sipped the wine feeling warm and relaxed.

"Are you wearing one of the suits you have here?" she asked.

"Yes. I'm looking forward to tonight's events."

She walked to the closet, placing the wine glass on the dresser on her way past.

"What are you doing?" he asked.

"Getting my dress."

"Sit with me a while. Finish your wine at least," he said.

"Okay." She retrieved the glass and sat beside him. He smelled good.

"How was your day?" he asked.

She smiled. He had stopped asking her how day was, so it was nice he was interested again.

"Good." She took a sip of wine. "The report on Liza's kit will be back any day now. We're sure it will lead us to her mystery boyfriend."

"You know, I tried to protect you," he said. "You wouldn't let me."

"What?" She took another sip of wine.

"I tried to protect Liza, too. You know, she was just as stubborn as you are. She was more emotional in her stubbornness. You can't reason with emotion."

Syd drank her wine, looking at him, trying to process what exactly he was saying to her.

"I thought I'd be able to reason with you, Sydney, but you have endless questions. Every puzzle piece has to fit perfectly or you aren't satisfied. Sometimes in life you have to let things be."

The fireflies dancing in her head scattered as the cold wind and clouds rolled in. She heard her phone ringing in the distance.

"Everything would have been fine if Liza had just taken a minute to think and if you didn't have this need to think too much."

*Change in behaviour*, she thought. Pre-incident indicator. The change in his behaviour had been a positive one. It was a change she'd wanted to see, so she'd missed it as an indicator.

The realization hit her harder than the Rohypnol in her wine. The room spun around. She grabbed at the edge of the bed for support as the empty wine glass tumbled from her hand. She steadied herself and looked at him, his face telling her she was not mistaken. She hadn't misread. All of her self-doubt had been misdirected.

"You," she said. "You were the boyfriend." Tears like acid filled her eyes.

He nodded, his face solemn.

"Did you...." She didn't finish the sentence, didn't want to say those words.

In spite of knowing better, like everyone else she wanted to believe in fairy tales, to believe in gods and monsters. She wanted to believe in gods close by and monsters who lived under bridges and in caves and dark alleys, not in her house, not sharing her bad and giving her wine and dresses and theatre tickets. Do monsters kiss you in a garden full of fireflies? Yes. Yes, they do. The love of a god was an illusion, an insidious trick of the monster with which she'd been complicit by her yearning for the sunshine, by her failure to see her own, her denial of her own spark, the fire that burned within her, fire and ice co-existing in one soul, her own. And so she'd fallen into the arms of a god when there was no such thing and the god was a monster who had her firmly in his clutches and the monster was a man. The wound of her self-betrayal ached profoundly, the weight of her stinging shame burned like a lake of fire.

"I had to," he said.

"No. No, you didn't have to." Tears ran down her cheeks. Her limbs felt rubbery and weak. She looked at the wine glass at her feet. "What did you put in it?"

"Don't worry," he said. "It was a small dose. You'll metabolize it quickly."

She stood up and stumbled toward the door. He stood and pulled a pair of blue nitrile gloves from his waistband. Calmly, he put them on. She staggered along the hallway, putting her hands on the wall to steady herself. A foggy thought of Pete finding her handprints there after she was dead floated through her mind. A thought of what she could do to help herself floated by just beyond her reach. Then it was gone, dissipating into the mist. She heard her phone ringing. Downstairs. Get downstairs.

"Radar," she called out weakly.

Branson caught her by the arm. She looked down at his gloved hand gripping her.

"Come on, Sydney." He pulled her toward the bedroom.

"You'll never get away with it." Her words spilled out slurred and quiet.

She stumbled as he pulled her along.

"You think I'm going to kill you?" he asked. "You're over-reacting again."

He pushed her onto the bed then helped her sit up. He sat beside her. The aroma of his cologne filled her breath. The aroma of a flower, a poison flower. She could smell his sweat, faintly. The faint smell of sweat in Liza's bedroom. Stench. The sooty breath of a dragon here in her room, a dragon who burns his victim on the inside, incapacitating and devouring her inside before his work of final destruction of the body.

"My beloved Sydney, I'm not going to kill you. You are going to kill yourself once we're done talking."

That thought again, floating through the fog. Where did it go? *Evidence. Leave evidence. Fingernail scrapings.* She swung at him, trying to scratch him. He saw it coming and moved away.

"That wasn't wise, Sydney."

With two fingers he pushed her backward. She fell on her back on the bed.

"Mark." She struggled to form her words. "He'll get the report. Can't hide."

He stood. He paced at the foot of the bed as he spoke.

"My twin brother in Toronto came to stay with me in Timmins. I know I told you he lived in B.C. but I couldn't have you pestering to meet him. Anyway, he had an interlude with a local prostitute. When he found out she was pregnant he came back and killed her. I know nothing about that, of course. As an officer of the court I would have had to turn him in. And if I'd known his dark secret I never would have introduced him to poor Liza. She was smitten. I was happy for them. When he came back into town to see her, I had no idea. And I had no idea he sat on her chest, stopping the poor girl's breath. And he'd heard me talk about enough cases that he knew to clean up, to keep her Dyson, to put her on ice and use the shower to wash away evidence. When they find that vacuum and doormat at his house, he'll lie and claim I gifted it to him. We never liked each other much. Well, I never liked him much. He was always competing with me. They'll think it was me, of course, but the DNA of identical twins is, well, identical. I'm a respected Crown Attorney. He's an engineer who drinks too much and got divorced because he slapped his wife around. I'm alibied. He isn't."

She knew his explanations would make for a good defence. He was going to get away with everything. The fog in her mind was slowly clearing, the drug wearing off. She could see the look on Brice Avery's face when she'd told him she knew someone with a pink lighter. Brice had seen Branson at the scene of the fire at Mark's and recognized him. She was sure now. Branson had set the fire to get rid of Mark. As long as Syd had a close friend Branson would have less control over her. Brice Avery was the key to convicting Branson, the only key. She remained still, debating whether to make a move now or to wait for the effects of the drug to lessen further. Branson sat on the bed beside her.

"Is it wearing off yet?" he asked.

She felt a prick in her thigh, then cold filling her leg. She pulled her leg away, but it was too late.

"Where's Radar?" she asked, pulling herself up.

Branson sat there, watching her, waiting for the injection to take effect. She grabbed at his hair.

He laughed. "My hairs are expected to be here."

He pushed her onto her back. She tried to get up again but couldn't move. She tried to lift her arm, but it wouldn't obey. She tried to speak, but couldn't move her lips. A squeak came out of her mouth without form. It was like a night terror, that state in which you're awake but your body is still paralyzed and you feel a sense of terrible danger yet can't move or yell.

He laid beside her. He took off a glove and stroked her cheek with the back of his hand. His touch that she once longed for, that touch that set her on fire, now sent a cold sick though her.

"You're so beautiful," he said. "I wish it had worked between us. I wish you could have understood the meaning of devotion." He put the glove back on. "Radar is probably in the neighbour's garden. Or maybe he ran to the woods. I took his collar off. He likes chasing cars. Is that what you're worried about? Maybe he tried chasing a car and got hit. Poor Radar. Hope he doesn't suffer too much before he dies."

Tears flooded her eyes, spilled from the corners and streamed down her temples making pools in her ears. Her heart screamed in terror and agony for Radar. She tried to scream but for all her effort only made a squeak.

He walked to the closet and pushed the clothes on the rod aside. He went back to her and lifted her from the bed. He carried her and put her down so her head was inside the closet.

"Poor Syd failed to solve the case, then she lost her dog and got ditched by her lover." He knelt beside her. "I stood you up. My car is still in the parking lot across from the courthouse, being filmed by surveillance there. I was not here today. I took Anna, the court clerk, to the theatre. Everybody saw us. You've been so confused for a while now. You stopped going to hockey, stopped socializing, made mistakes on the case. You've been depressed, Syd. They'll find three different suicide notes that you wrote on different dates. You deleted them but they'll find them on your hard drive. They'll show your descent, how unhinged you've become. The newspaper will say, 'promising young detective takes her own life after spiral into conspiracy theories'. No one will defend you. In a couple of days Mark will find you hanging in your closet. The ligature marks and the lividity will be right. The evidence will show a suicide. The coroner will rubber stamp it. Mark will have to let it go and he will."

Branson leaned forward and retrieved the shoebox from the closet, the one that held the high heels he'd bought for her for tonight. He opened the box and reached inside. He pulled out Radar's long nylon leash. She hadn't put it there. Branson must have done it ahead of time, just like he'd put fake suicide notes on her computer. He wrapped the leash around her throat and pulled it tight. He knotted it and checked the knot.

Syd heard yelling, someone calling her name. She heard the pounding of feet coming up the stairs. Branson stood and picked up the wine bottle from the dresser. She heard the creak of the third stair from the top. Pete's voice called for her. Then a thud. The smell of wine. Silence.

Branson returned to her. He threw the end of the leash over the rod in the closet. He pulled. Her head screamed and the rod creaked with the pressure. Pain and fear and fog. Radar barked somewhere in the distance. A trick of an oxygen deprived mind? A burst of lights in her brain. Fireflies exploding and disappearing into dark death.

# Chapter Thirty-One

Mark had given Pete the key to Syd's house and sent him in. Mark heard Radar barking a strange hoarse kind of bark out back. Thinking Syd might be back there, he followed the sound of the barking. He found Radar barking and clawing frenetically at the locked back door. Blood streaked the length of the door. Radar's paws bled as he continued his destruction of the door.

Mark yelled at him, "Radar, front yard."

Radar bolted toward the front, Mark lagging behind. Radar ran through the open front door and tore up the stairs, ears back. Mark struggled up the stairs, hauling himself up with the railing. Radar sped into the bedroom. He leapt onto Branson's back causing him to lose his grip on Syd. She crumpled to the closet floor as Branson tried to turn around. Radar was too quick. Like a lighting strike he bit into Branson's calf and yanked back. Branson fell forward over Syd. He writhed and kicked but Radar kept his jaw clamped on his leg. Mark stumbled over Pete's body in the bedroom doorway. He scrambled over broken glass toward Branson. Between Mark and Radar, they successfully subdued Branson enough for Mark to cuff him.

***

Two days later:

Pete was still in the hospital recovering from surgery on his eye to remove glass from the wine bottle. Mark had gone to visit him. Syd sat alone at her desk doing the paperwork on Branson, Liza, and the Linton fire. There was one more piece, a necessary piece. Brice Avery. He'd seen Branson leaving the fire, seen him drop his pink lighter in the road, and knew who he was. With Branson in custody Avery was finally willing to come in for a videotaped statement. He was scheduled for four o'clock.

Mark walked into the office carrying a red gift bag. He dropped it onto Syd's desk. She smiled and looked in the bag. She pulled out the paperback.

"Not a textbook," he said. "I figured you wouldn't like a romance or a detective novel so I got you a historical fiction."

"Thanks." She flipped through the pages.

"There's something else in the bag," he said.

At the bottom of the bag she found a key.

"Amy's parents have a cottage up in Southampton. It's yours for the weekend."

"Wow. Radar will love it," she said.

"And I'll do the interview with Avery," he said. "You go pack."

"Make sure you don't use inducements," she joked.

He laughed. "Go now. And turn off your cellphone. No work this weekend. They won't die without you."

\*\*\*

Later, as she drove through downtown to get to the highway, with Radar happily sticking his nose out the window, she noticed two cruisers parked on the sidewalk and a crowd of spectators gathering around. She kept driving. She'd turned her cellphone off as Mark suggested. She didn't know that Brice Avery never showed for his interview. She didn't get the call that he'd been shot dead in a downtown alley.

The End

4

Printed in the USA
CPSIA information can be obtained
at www.ICGtesting.com
LVHW041033271024
794926LV00007B/191